MORTAL
INTENT

▼▼▼▼▼▼▼ A NOVEL ▼▼▼▼▼▼▼

Gripping suspense from *Mortal Intent* ...

Evelyn's threat reverberated powerfully. Wednesday morning dawned on a bedraggled Franklin Justice.

On one hand, Evelyn had always been an irresolute and compliant wife during their many years of marriage. They had their disagreements, and she had gotten her way most of the time. But that was only because the issues were minor.

Until now.

Last night she'd been angrier than he'd ever seen her. She might just do it. She might just tell some crazy story to the press. Or she might just find Annie and confront her. She'd taken the knife from the kitchen and she must still have the handgun he'd insisted she carry. She might use them on Annie.

Or on herself.

Anyway he looked at it, things were becoming unraveled. Fast.

TO MY DIANNA:
I love you more today than yesterday,
but not as much as tomorrow.

ACKNOWLEDGMENTS

My Most Sincere Thanks:

- To Mary Katherine, Matt, and Emily for the gift of steadfast love to a distracting and distracted dad;

- To Dale and Eunice Massie for the gift of confidence;

- To Les Stobbe for the gift of a chance;

- To Dan Benson for the gift of patience;

- To Ruth Macchia for the gift of insight from a keen eye;

- To Steve and Buck for the gift of an occasional swift kick;

- To the staffs of Here's Life Publishers and Thomas Nelson Publishers for the gift of your dedication;

- To Henry and Marilyn Date for the gift of use of the Date Oasis while working on this manuscript.

- And to the Father, for His breath of life in our world.

MORTAL INTENT

INTENT

▼▼▼▼▼▼▼ A NOVEL ▼▼▼▼▼▼▼

BOB MASSIE

THOMAS NELSON PUBLISHERS

NASHVILLE

Published in Nashville, Tennessee, by Thomas Nelson, Inc.

Library of Congress Cataloging-in Publication Data

Massie, Bob.
    Mortal intent: a novel / Bob Massie.
       p.   cm.
    ISBN 0-8407-4545-1
    I. Title.
PS3563.A7997M67   1992
813'.54—dc20   92-18336
                                                CIP

Printed in the United States of America
1 2 3 4 5 6 7 - 97 96 95 94 93

▼ ▼ ▼ 1 ▼ ▼ ▼

Annie Minnis sat in a dark corner of The 15th Street Pub as if she were the guest of honor at a reception in the State House six blocks away. A model's deportment and the confidence of a sophisticated woman made her presence as palpable as the smoke that hung in the air.

She relished the distance she put between herself and the kind of people who chose to come to a place like this. The Pub's regulars noticed the difference with long, hungry looks and nods of approval as they passed by on the way to favorite spots. She generated more than the usual boy talk among the brothers nursing beers at the bar.

Annie had held court in the booth no more than five minutes when one of the pub clowns pushed away from the bar. After some braggadocio and prodding, he sauntered over to Annie's table, buried his thigh in its edge and leaned over her with a swagger. He looked her up and down very slowly with only the movement of his eyes, and said in a voice that he apparently considered sexy, "Mmm, what fine black legs you have, mama."

Annie smiled fire and ice as she leaned forward, provocatively, to meet him. She pursed her lips once, wetted them as if longing for a kiss, then spoke as she stared defiantly into his eyes: "One touch and you're a dead man."

She held those eyes with her insolent gaze while the clown froze, rethinking the situation.

He backed off.

Her message sunk into the other jerks lined up at the bar, sucking lite beer and peanuts, their right feet raised to the rail. They made Annie think of elephants raising up one leg and putting on a show for some stupid treat. Elephants and clowns. This Pub was a circus, all right.

A circus of fools.

In any case, no one else had the audacity to put a move on her. It was far too early in the evening. Here was a woman drinking by herself in The 15th Street who definitely was not looking to be picked up.

Annie resumed her almost regal bearing, sipping a vodka martini—the bartender didn't know how to make a real one—letting her cigarette burn slowly, and savoring the chasm between her and the regular clientele. Between her and her people. Between her and her past.

Governor Franklin Justice's paramour *was* on a different level. She was especially appreciative of this "otherness" on these occasions when she had to meet her courier. She needed the distance.

And she made sure to increase the distance on the occasions of her visits to The 15th Street with a carefully chosen series of disguises. A wig here, a different hairstyle and outfit there, all designed to allow her to be a different person on each visit.

It wasn't that she was afraid of her courier knowing her true identity. He spent his days as a private investigator and he was careful never to step over the boundaries that hemmed in that occupation. No blackmail, no extortion, no hanky panky. But he did supplement his legit income with a trade in flake by acting as a courier for a top corporate client. His client load for the company included elite customers in the black community, of which Annie Minnis was one. He and his clients had an understanding. Neither rocked the boat.

But Annie was careful to conceal her identity, not from her courier, but from the low-lifes that slithered in and out of The 15th Street Pub. She didn't need complications from them.

Though she took pains to disguise herself, her courier held no such compunctions. Inevitably he would come dressed like the cover of *GQ*, but this guy was as much at home in a dive like The 15th Street as she was out of place. When she looked at him, she always felt that whoever dubbed him the Black Frog had never spoken truer words—a black frog dressed up like a man in expensive clothes.

Annie was as careful in maintaining an unruffled exterior at these meetings as she was in applying whatever outside physical changes she wanted. She never allowed herself to be shaken on the outside.

But this man disturbed her profoundly, deep down in her secret heart.

She had worked hard to mold herself into her image of the complete black woman—educated, independent, aggressive, and yes, beautiful! The thing that bothered her—at least the part she was willing to admit to herself— was that these contacts were the last remaining strings attached to the old Annie, the Annie who had grown up in the streets and yet had stood up in society on her own two feet.

Between the cultural distance she felt so keenly and the flinty exterior she cultivated so assiduously, she had a wall she could relax behind.

Annie Minnis was not like the others.

"Yo, mama," the courier said as he slipped into the booth beside her. He motioned for the bartender to bring him one of what she was drinking.

Annie was so deep in thought about his repulsiveness and her dread of these meetings, she hadn't noticed him entering the bar. Without an outward flinch, Annie pulled as far behind her inner wall as she could and shook off any sense of relaxation. He was the worst of what she had worked so hard to leave behind. His presence made her skin crawl.

Only her wall made these meetings bearable.

Her wall and the Colombian snow.

"What's a sister like you doin' in a place like this?" He didn't look at her as he intoned the same idiotic words with which he always greeted her. Instead, he had leaned over the table and spoken the phrase to a conspicuously expensive leather clutch which he turned in slow circles on the table top with the first finger of each hand.

Annie felt a chill as she watched him manipulate the clutch. That clutch was really her. She was the one being turned in pointless revolutions. He was the one drawing ever-shrinking circles around her, like the street hoods of her childhood who slowly closed around their victim, relishing the fear before they flashed knives and drew blood.

She could feel him coming.

But her wall and the snow wouldn't fail her.

Without a word, she reached for the clutch.

In a heartbeat the man turned, thrust his right hand under her left arm, all the way up under her armpit, grabbed her left wrist with his other hand, and lifted her roughly off her seat as he twisted. A sharp pain shot through her shoulder. "Let's do it slow this time," he said threateningly, looking into her eyes for the first time. "I haven't had my drink yet."

He had shoved his face so close she could smell his vile breath mixing with designer cologne.

Annie Minnis bit down on her pain as if it were an anesthetic. Without dismantling the protective expression on her face, she caught and held his stare. She had learned young to stare danger in the face, that scavengers are only frenzied by the weakness of a deferred gaze.

Then her hand darted for the martini, guided by her instinct rather than her eyes. She slipped the stem between her first two fingers, tilted the glass enough to get her thumb under it, and in one sweeping movement broke off the base of the glass on the edge of the table and brought the jagged shard to rest on the Frog's throat.

"I've finished mine."

The man slowly, defiantly, released the pressure on Annie's arm and inched backwards as she moved toward him, prodding him with the glass as she slid her hips across the cracked naugahyde.

By the time she reached the edge, the Frog was out of the booth and had retreated to a safe distance, re-aranging his Brooks Brothers shirt inside his Armani suit with more than a little embarrassed awareness that the brothers were watching the show.

"One day," he said, rebuttoning his jacket. "One day you'll make a wrong move—just one—and then you're mine."

Annie stood erect, as poised as if this creature were the final guest in the receiving line. She placed what was left of the martini glass back on the table and gracefully lifted the Frog's leather clutch to her breast.

Her rage and fear boiled inside, steaming to escape in some vindictive release.

But she was different. She would not allow herself to indulge her impulse. She raised her chin and said in a cold but polite tone, "Send the bill to me. Make it out for two cases of champagne."

Then she walked away.

The bar erupted in obscene cheers for the beautiful David's defiance of the black Goliath.

But Annie just turned from the courier and from the suffocating reality of The 15th Street Pub and from her past and walked away.

The wall was a little thicker.

And the cocaine hadn't failed her.

"Umm, uh! What a woman!" the Frog croaked as he found his way to the bar and a second round of bawdy insults. "I love these deliveries."

▼ ▼ ▼ ▼

Across the room, tucked away in the darkest recess of The 15th Street Pub, another man muttered the same words as he rewound his film, unobtrusively removed the long lens from his camera, and made his way to the exit.

▼ ▼ ▼ 2 ▼ ▼ ▼

"Governor! Governor Justice!" Lindy Blakely's shouts were almost swallowed in the din of voices and movement that arose from the floor of the crowded news conference as reporters vied for Franklin Justice's attention.

He had just completed an announcement concerning implementation of a ground-breaking drug policy, his third major policy initiative in as many years in office, and was fielding questions from the group.

Lindy knew that his M.O. for his Tuesday news conferences never varied: simple, direct announcement, brief and hardhitting Q & A, abrupt termination. She was afraid that if she didn't get his attention soon, her shouts would bounce off the back of his head as he marched out the door.

She waved her left hand as she shouted, pencil flailing. He pointed to someone else.

Lindy jotted notes on his response, poised to spring into her journalistic gymnastics as soon as he wound down.

" . . . volunteer drug testing among state employees *will* work, certainly not as a panacea, but as one small step forward among many that must be taken, one small step in a far-reaching plan."

His tone in the last few words sounded final, so she shot up her arm before he was finished, raising and lowering her notepad above her head like a sailor with a

pale green semaphore signaling a sinking ship. As soon
as he stopped to take a breath, she began shouting.

He looked her way and raised his chin, pointing.
"Lindy."

The clamor instantly ebbed to its normal rumble.

Finally, she thought as she recomposed her posture to
speak. "Governor Justice, a question and a follow-up. Sir,
no doubt you realize that any program of drug testing for
state employees will be met with stiff opposition by
various groups around the state, not to mention the
factions in the government itself. What hope do you have
of seeing such a policy survive?"

The Governor pulled his head back, as if the question
had slapped him in the face. He scowled disapprovingly
at Lindy, then with a silence out of place in what is usually
bedlam, he slowly ogled the gathered reporters. Gradually, the noise of private conversations and the shuffling
of paper died to nothing. It was only a few seconds, but
it seemed much longer as the quiet filled with the bustle
of expectancy—just as the Governor wanted it.

When his eyes returned from their trip around the
room to refocus on Lindy, he spoke slowly and with deep
conviction, "My dear young lady."

Lindy bristled at his patronizing tone.

"Minutes after I entered my first office on my first day
in the law firm in which I would spend my entire professional life, one of the janitors strolled into the room to set
up a lamp on a credenza. I didn't know him from Adam
and had no more use for the lamp or the credenza than
he did. I was a poor rookie who needed only about one
square foot: a place to hang my diploma.

"I busied myself as if I had something to do while he
fooled with the lamp, plugged it in, and tested it. As he
puttered at the chore, he asked, 'First day on the job?' I
nodded yes but he didn't see me. He wasn't looking my

way. 'You'll like workin' here,' he said to the bulb as he screwed it back in. 'I do.'

"Then he did something I've never forgotten. He dusted the lamp off with a little flourish of pride, turned to me with a smile and said, 'It's amazing what can be done when nobody's out to get the credit.' And he walked out of my office.

"To this day I don't know if he was telling me what made him happy as a janitor or if he was giving a green-horn lawyer a piece of advice. It doesn't matter. It stuck.

"Throughout my career as an attorney and my career as a public servant, I've believed that what that humble man said to me is the essence of leadership.

"Now I've taken time to tell you that story so that I could make this point." The Governor had been meeting eyes all around the room as he was talking, but he found Lindy again and looked directly at her. "Politicians very often make decisions based on whether they will get credit for a certain program or action, and whether the credit they receive will be good for them or bad for them.

"As far as I'm concerned, worrying about whether an initiative survives implementation is strictly in the category of worrying about good credit or bad credit.

"My dear young lady, that is not leadership. That is politics. Leadership is doing the right thing for the right reason and dealing with the consequences as they arise."

He really believed that. Franklin Justice had pulled out of his law practice like a train pulling out of a station, pointed in the right direction and building up a head of steam. In campaigning, first for mayor of the state's largest city and then for Governor, he had been just like he was now—straight up with people, boldly laying out initiatives and pledging to remember his promises when he got into office.

And remember those promises he did! As mayor, he'd tackled the problem of unequal access to city services by decentralizing those services into local hubs and appointing neighborhood associations as boards of directors for each hub. When success came, he gave all the credit to the volunteer leadership and to the city employees who worked the centers.

As Governor, he had tackled the budget his first year in office in a way that both cornered his opponents and gave them a way to get the credit for his reform if they played along. He issued executive orders cutting personnel and non-vital programming in his administration by 10 percent *before* the end of his first year, explaining to the press that he was sure the legislature would require cuts of him, and that end-of-year was the best time for such cuts.

At the same time he privately sent his version of a budget with a tax cut and further reduction measures to General Assembly leadership, timed to arrive well before the session began in late January. Both sides of the aisle were miffed at his maneuvering, for different reasons, but both sides saw an opportunity for the legislature to make a swift and very popular move.

They moved.

In his second year, he took another bold action in education policy. He mandated that every company doing more than $100,000 worth of business with the state be required to provide a volunteer business consultant to their local school district. The administrative advice proved invaluable to school boards and the business community acquired a pipeline to effect positive change in schools. Many business leaders were angry, but some lauded the move as the first chance they had ever had to do something about the problem of declining education which affected their businesses so much.

The mandate proved so popular that by the end of the year, legislators were posturing to get a piece of the action.

But this year was different. The drug problem was a thousand-legged creature. He realized that when he decided to wrestle it, he would be out-sized, out-manned, and all by himself. No one wanted the responsibility for tough, controversial measures against drugs.

But then, nobody wanted to tackle budget deficits or education problems either.

Franklin Justice thrived on purposeful, forward movement. He yearned to be leading and blew off the notion that he should play the reelection game. He believed with every fiber of his being that all or part of his initiatives *would* succeed, that society *would* be better as a result, and that he *would* keep moving forward.

In a sense, he was addicted.

Now he grew more animated as he spoke. "Drugs are a cancer eating away at our nation, but most people in leadership positions are afraid to do anything. They're afraid the ACLU will take them to court. They're afraid some special interest group will withhold their money. They're afraid of what you people in the press will say or print. So they end up talking about problems and never doing anything about them.

"I've outlined for you a multifaceted plan for *doing* something, for advancing the fight against drugs in our state. If one or more of the elements fails, or is overturned in court, or proves to be unfair, then we'll abandon it and try something new. But if we on a state level refuse, by our lack of initiative, to protect our own citizens, especially the economically disadvantaged ones, then we are absolutely unfit for the offices those same citizens elect us to!

"Is that clear enough for the press?" He held Lindy's eyes as the quiet dispersed throughout the room like a clap of thunder dissipated by the rain and wind.

She was profoundly uncomfortable under his gaze, especially since all the reporters, photographers, and sound engineers in the room had stopped their noisy shuffling and turned their full attention to the scenario in which she was now the co-star. The video cameramen had even looked up from the monitors in their eye pieces and were watching the show live.

Uncomfortable or not, Lindy knew that if she was going to get her follow-up question in, she'd better swallow her self-consciousness and speak up. Justice had just gotten a zinger of a last word in and would be out of there the instant the dramatic pause took full effect.

"Yes, sir," she said respectfully, her unexpected answer hooking him just as it became obvious that he was ready to turn and march out. "Very clear."

He hadn't expected a response. He had broken eye contact with Lindy and was looking downward, moving to gather his notes. When her words caught him, he looked up to nod a polite acknowledgment of her remark before he lunged for the door.

"And my follow-up, sir, as a final question. . . . " She had set the hook and was reeling him in. "I think I speak on behalf of the press corps when I say that we all have been concerned about Mrs. Justice in her recent illness. Can you tell us something about her illness and how she's doing?"

Justice again was a bit taken aback, this time not as a part of his routine. He hadn't expected this kind of question. "Satisfactory, Lindy. Satisfactory. As you may remember, Mrs. Justice contracted pneumonia during my gubernatorial campaign. Her doctor thinks that she hadn't really recovered from the pneumonia when she accelerated her already rigorous volunteer schedule after I took office. She's simply exhausted. I plan on enforcing a rest schedule for her that is as rigorous as her previous activity schedule was.

"Thank you for asking, and thanks to those of you here who sent cards to Evelyn. We both appreciate your kindness."

With that, he scooped up his notes, leaned toward the microphone with a concluding "Thank you," and strode out of the room, his entourage in tow.

"I'm sure he appreciated you blowing his big dramatic close with that question," said one of Lindy's co-workers from the *News* as they leaned over to pick up briefcases and purses.

"That's a cynical remark," Lindy said through a smile as she stood the briefcase on her knees and let her arms drape across it, pausing to reflect before she stood up. "Besides, I really was interested." She tilted her head and looked forward, focusing on dead air just above the platform the Governor had just vacated. "His drug policies are news, but once in a while I get tired of grinding hamburger. I really wanted to know."

By now, the other woman had stood up and was edging her way out of the narrow aisle. "Yeah, yeah, yeah."

"It's true," she continued, talking to the air just below the ceiling. "There's always more to someone than comes across in public. Did you notice that he wasn't really happy with the question? I'd bet there's more to this than meets the eye."

Lindy turned to her left to finish her statement, only to find that her friend had stepped out into the main aisle and was headed for the door of the conference room. She raised her chin, turned her head back to the podium and said, "And what's more, I'll do a story on it someday."

Then she turned and said over her shoulder, "One that you'll wish you had written."

▼ ▼ ▼ ▼

Franklin Justice *was* a bit taken aback by Lindy Blakely's final question. He was neither used to nor comfortable with any public discussion of his private affairs. Because during his campaigns he had been so completely forthcoming about his beliefs and his finances, and because his public agenda was so controversial, his private life had remained almost untouched by the media.

And this question! Why would some nosy reporter ask about Evelyn unless she suspected? Infernal snoops.

"Great job, Frank!" the chief of staff said as the door closed behind them and he put his hand on the Governor's shoulder.

"Great."

"On target."

"Super job."

Justice's aides echoed their superior's sentiments enthusiastically as they barrelled down the hall at a fast walk in order to keep up with the Governor.

"We'll see in the next few months," Justice said angrily, still irritated by the question about Evelyn. He took two more steps, then spun to face his aides. "One thing's for sure," he threatened, a dark tone shadowing his otherwise businesslike voice. "Every member of my entire staff *will* volunteer for testing during the first phase of this program, and every one of them *will* pass—legitimately—or it will be you"—he jabbed his finger in their direction—"who get thrown off this wagon!" He punctuated his threat by landing a glowering look on each one of them. "I'll not stick my head in a public noose over the drug problem and have anyone, *anyone*, who is close to me using."

Then he turned and strode off.

His aides were accustomed to this schizoid behavior. They all knew that the Governor had a dark, angry side—a Mr. Hyde—but they wrote it off to eccentricity and stress. Over late afternoon beers, a couple of them even joked about hidden personalities in a Frank Justice whose existence was hypothetical, like quarks or a black hole. They (or maybe it was the beer) loved to banter about what might be tucked away in the depths of their boss.

But it was the Dr. Jekyll in Franklin Justice that they loved and respected, the man of strength and vision and leadership, the man who hired them and inspired them. They were willing to put up with Mr. Hyde.

"Frank," a voice called from the opposite end of the hall as the Governor approached the door to his private office. "Frank, a minute please. This is important." It was the voice of George Barnett, Justice's longtime friend, campaign treasurer, and chief financial advisor. Barnett was moving at a brisk pace to catch the Governor before he disappeared from the hall.

Justice looked up at his friend as his hand found the long brass handle. He paused until Barnett was within six feet and closing fast, then shoved the door open.

"We got trouble!" Barnett whispered the warning as he scurried past Justice and through the opening.

The private office swallowed both men as the oak mouth closed heavily.

▼ ▼ ▼ 3 ▼ ▼ ▼

Evelyn Justice once had been the "right" political wife—born to a prominent eastern family, educated at Wellesley, genuinely interested in and committed to social issues, perfectly comfortable with the movers and shakers of society whether entertaining or being entertained—quite simply an elegant, gracious woman.

And she had enjoyed the role of political wife for most of the more than two decades she and Franklin had been together. She loved the action, the intrigue, and even the sometimes bitter politics so characteristic of the large law firm Franklin had joined fresh out of law school; she loved being involved in business and government events, both in behind-the-scenes roles and especially in the role of hostess; and she especially loved being First Lady of the capital city, and then the entire state.

Until recently.

When she was honest with herself, she knew that the roots of her problem went back years, maybe even to the beginning of her relationship with Franklin. They had married because each of the pair met the other's criteria for the "right" mate. There had been a physical relationship, and they enjoyed each other's company, but when it came right down to it, both she and Franklin had chosen marriage the way they had chosen a college: How far will this take me and how fast will it get me there?

That was a long time ago, when she was just a girl. Since then, she had grown to love Franklin—a benefit that was nice, but one she had been prepared to do without if necessary.

But Franklin never had grown to love her.

She knew it and had accepted it for years, believing that over time, he too would find love the way she had.

But he hadn't. At least not with her.

She knew that, too.

The whole situation was tolerable as long as the facade of happiness in their marriage was intact, as long as the basics of their unspoken, unwritten nuptial agreement were in place.

But a crack had appeared in the facade, more like a chasm opening between them: first the signs, finally unignorable, of Franklin's infidelity; then the growing loneliness of life as First Lady; finally the black hole of depression. That, in turn, had led to the suicide attempt, the hospitalization, and in her own effort to regain her sanity and her dignity, the hiring of a private investigator to find out exactly what she was up against.

But as she stood in the kitchen of the Governor's mansion listening to the coarse voice of the hireling detective droning the details she both wanted and hated, she realized that she wasn't ready to hear it all. Evelyn could feel her grip on reality slipping.

▼ ▼ ▼ ▼

Franklin Justice's gubernatorial lair was an office befitting a man of his accomplishment. The rich oak panels imbued his corner chambers with warmth, especially when the afternoon sun streamed through the giant windows in the southern and western walls. With expensive appointments, it had become his place of sanctuary.

No staff meetings here. No receiving of guests, no private meetings with legislators, no tours by visitors or constituents. He had made sure that other places were furnished for such activity.

This office was his. Only his closest friends and associates were allowed to enter it with him. Here, among those he trusted, he could relax and be himself.

George Barnett was one of those old and close friends. He had been the comptroller for Baker and Lewis (now Baker, Lewis, Justice & Pence, the law firm in which Franklin had gotten his start) when Franklin entered the firm.

Barnett served as campaign treasurer when Justice ran for mayor. Then Franklin persuaded him to leave the firm and become city comptroller after the mayoral victory. Five years later, one year into the mayor's second term, he became treasurer for the Justice for Governor campaign. Once more, when Justice moved up the political ladder, he brought his trusted ally with him. Justice reasoned that there were two people in the world in whom a man had to have absolute and total confidence: his mistress and his money manager.

And Barnett was one of the two people who had been pulled up the ladder of success with Justice.

The other was Annie Minnis.

Franklin had met Annie the same place he met Barnett, at Baker and Lewis. The day he was inducted as a full partner into the firm, Annie Minnis began her job as a paralegal, assigned to Franklin Justice.

Over the months that followed, they worked together on many cases. They researched, planned, tried, and celebrated victories on those cases together, sometimes well into the night. The close contact, the intimate late dinners, the rush of success at a common task—their relationship simply happened.

And it had worked for almost a decade.

Franklin Justice was a white attorney, full partner in the most influential law firm in the state, a man of wealth and stature. Annie Minnis was a strikingly beautiful black woman, very bright, a true equal to Justice in mental capabilities, and a woman who made things happen.

When Justice was elected mayor at age forty-two, his first round of appointments included the placement of Annie Minnis at the head of special event planning for the city—a significant increase in responsibility and salary as well as a perfect excuse for the two to continue working together and seeing each other, especially in private conferences. Annie was twenty-four at the time.

The Justice for Governor campaign hired Annie away from the city five years later so she could coordinate special fund-raisers for the campaign. Following Franklin's victory, Annie naturally enjoyed appointment to a similar, better-paying, state-level position.

As far as Franklin and Annie were concerned, their ten-year relationship was perfect: no one ever suspected a salt-and-pepper affair, they had plenty of time together to enjoy the fire, and they had plenty of time apart to keep the fire hot.

He did trust his mistress and his money manager completely. They were the only two people besides his chief of staff who had free access to his private lair. And Barnett had exercised that right as he followed Justice into his office after the press conference.

"Frank, I know how you feel about Annie and I know the latitude you've given her. But I'm worried."

"Why don't you just get straight to the point, Barney?" Justice smiled at his friend's directness. "No one could ever accuse you of beating around the bush or of not worrying enough. I've never seen a bean counter yet who didn't end up with ulcers or prison stripes. What's the problem?"

"I *am* worried, Frank. Annie's spending large sums of money—*your* campaign money—on items that may be questionable, especially if the Federal Election Commission was ever called in to investigate a complaint."

"What kind of questionable items?" By now Justice was beginning to give Barnett a bit more serious attention.

"I have a list here." Barnett stood up and walked around the huge desk, laid it out in front of Justice, and leaned over it as if he were about to check a column of figures. "For example, three times this year she has requisitioned payment for cases of expensive champagne."

"What kind?"

Barnett picked the list up and drew it to his face as he lowered his chin so he could see the paper over the half-glasses perched precariously on the end of his nose. *"Moët & Chandon."*

"That's my girl."

"Frank, I'm serious. Two cases of *Moët* bills at over a thousand dollars. What has she done with three thousand dollars of French champagne in only four months? Are you raising money from the Rockefellers?"

"Barney—"

"There's more. Look. Here's a case of perfume. Perfume, Frank! Twelve one-ounce bottles for twelve hundred dollars—that's a hundred dollars an ounce! Are you drinking French perfume after the French wine runs out?"

"These must be gifts for our major donors. A hundred-dollar bottle of perfume or a seventy-five-dollar bottle of champagne is nothing compared to the amount of money some of my best supporters are giving."

"Absolutely. It's just a token. But Frank, the people who give you that money want just one of two things: They are either altruistic citizens who want their thank-yous to come in the form of your effective leadership of our state, or they are shrewd businesspeople who want you to be in office so that government contracts flow their way. In either case, they aren't interested in prissy French gratuities."

"All right, Barney. I see your point."

"But there's more. In every instance of what I consider a frivolous expense there are two commonalities: the vendor and the amount. All of the invoices are approximately a thousand dollars and all of them come from Bruhof Distributors International."

"Doesn't Bruhof deal in gems and gold?"

"Yes, gems from the Orient and gold from South America. As far as I know, they do no business in France or any other place in Europe and they have no contracts with the state. Something doesn't smell right to me." Barnett apparently fancied that this little pun was quite clever in a discussion about perfume, but Frank wasn't taking. He never laughed at a bean counter's jokes.

"Barney, are you telling me they do not distribute French goods?"

Barnett looked over his half-glasses at his friend and shook his head. There was no smile on his face. He knew how Frank felt about Annie.

Justice knew that Bruhof didn't do business with the government. They'd never tried to get close and as far as he knew, they'd never given a dollar to his campaign fund. They certainly weren't high-profile in the political arena. With no French connection and no stake in government contracts, it just didn't make sense.

"Okay, what do you think the deal is? Are you saying Annie is buying jewels on the side and having Bruhof bill us with bogus invoices?"

"Could be," Barnett said as he walked back around to the front of the desk and sank into the leather wingback. "Or it could be that they have their claws in her some other way."

Justice frowned.

"Don't ask me how," Barney continued hurriedly, preventing his strong-willed friend from taking the floor. "That may be nothing but a figment of my imagination. Maybe *all* of this is a figment of my imagination. But Frank, you and Annie have been together for years. Someone is bound to have found out by now. Maybe Annie's being blackmailed."

Justice sat quietly, taking in the implications.

"And Frank, that would be disastrous," Barnett kept talking as his words sank in. "But my main concern is for you. One thing's for sure: If I can pick up questionable patterns in your campaign spending, so can the FEC, if they ever decide to take a closer look."

"Okay, Barney. You've made your point. At the very least, Bruhof won't get another dime from us. I'll speak to Annie about this and see that she finds another source for liquor and gifts. In the meantime, suspend all payments to Bruhof. Whatever bills are outstanding, we'll consider them in-kind contributions to the Reelect Justice campaign in lieu of the cash contributions I'm sure they just forgot to make." Justice loved payback.

"One more thing," Barnett said. "Tell Annie to cut back on the gift-giving, too, will you?"

"Done. Now, will you leave me alone? I've got to make a drug policy fly."

"Yes, sir!" Barnett said with a smile as he turned to leave.

"And, Barney . . . "

Barnett turned to face his friend.

"Thanks."

Barney just smiled broader as he leaned into the massive oak doors.

Bean counters, Justice said to himself as he swiveled to face his in-basket. What would this world be without 'em? He picked up a stack of papers and spread them out front of him. But then, what would the world be without lovers who spend your money on French champagne? What a woman!

▼ ▼ ▼ ▼

Evelyn Justice stood beside the sink in the cavernous kitchen at the back of the Governor's mansion, dazed as she hung up the phone.

Dazed and alone . . . enraged . . . broken.

It was Tuesday, the only day possible to be alone in this house because it was the only day Franklin chose to be surrounded by the crowds in the press briefing room. That made the news from the caller even worse.

Franklin was superstitious. Stupid-stitious, as far as Evelyn was concerned. He had some childish reason to believe that Tuesday was the only day he should meet the press, so from the beginning of his public career as mayor seven years earlier, he had institutionalized this nonsense. Everyone knew that if there would be a press conference during the week, Tuesday was the day. It was also the weekday he insisted on dismissing the help. "My dear, they work weekends, and you know that when I go before the press during the day, I must work late to ensure the proper spin is placed on my announcements. One simply must follow up on such events. So there's no reason for these good people to be working."

Every Tuesday was a sentence of solitary confinement for the entire day and much of the night in this giant dungeon. Every Tuesday (like every other day except multiplied by loneliness), she had stood in the calm of a deserted, lifeless mansion while a storm raged inside her. Every Tuesday *he* calmly stood in the eye of a raging storm of press and public response and media hype without so much as a hair blowing out of place.

But her storm had no eye. There was no relief for her.

Except when the storm jockeys who cared for her in their bleached white smocks and their god-among-men smirks seeded her storm with their chemicals. Or when she found someone like Maria among the hired help to sit and talk and spend time with her.

Oh, how she hated them. The doctors. Franklin. The voters. Tuesdays. Life.

This Tuesday, Evelyn stood by the sink in the cavernous kitchen and felt alone, really alone, abandoned.

She picked up a knife, her favorite, and stared into its shiny surface as if she could see more than just her reflection in the cold steel. This knife was her favorite because it was the one that was so sharp she could use it to peel an apple in a way that the peeling came off in one long, continuous strip.

She liked to do that. She was right-handed, but she liked to take the apple in her right hand and the knife in her left because when she switched like that, she really had to think about peeling the apple without cutting deep into the flesh of the fruit or slicing its tender skin into pieces.

If she'd just put the knife in her right hand and the apple in her left, the normal way, she could peel the apple with her eyes closed. But this way, her favorite way, she had to concentrate.

And when the job was done, when she had skinned the apple successfully, she would throw away the flesh. She didn't like apples anyway. She would throw away the flesh and hold the long corkscrew peel so that it stretched out in front of her, then let it slowly coil in her hand and become an apple again, an empty shell of an apple that she had sliced on and scarred.

Just like her. An empty shell of a woman she had sliced on and scarred.

Evelyn let her gaze fall from the knife, her favorite, to her wrists and the scars where the smirk-faces had brought her peel back together. The peeling had just lay in their hands in the shape of Evelyn Justice. If the idiots had looked closely, they could see through it, they could see their own hands through it if they'd just look. She was empty, a shell of sliced skin that some condescending doctors had held up in front of their lights and allowed to fall back together so that it looked like a person.

She looked up from her wrists and again at the knife. It was her favorite. It was sharp and shiny. She pulled it closer to her face so she could see her reflection. She stood dead still, gazing into its depths as if it were a crystal ball and its scenes the portents of the future.

Evelyn turned to the far counter, holding the knife, her favorite, in front of her as if she were an acolyte carrying a sacred candle down the aisle of a shrine to participate in a holy ritual.

She wrapped it lovingly in a cotton handkerchief, placed it gently in the cradle of her purse, and closed it in.

She called a cab, then walked to the security shed at the end of the drive and stood quietly. As she bent to enter the cab, she spoke one phrase to the driver—an address, *the* address that had been spoken to her before she hung up the kitchen phone. She arranged herself in the back seat of the cab and then sat, unmoving, until they reached her destination.

She got out, paid the driver, then stood in front of the building and looked up. This was her shrine. This was where she would redeem herself.

Without a word, Evelyn slowly lifted her purse to the face of the building as if she were a priestess offering an oblation to the face of a dreadful idol.

Then she stepped inside and found her way to the elevator corridor where one of the doors stood open, waiting for her, waiting as if it were there to carry her on her sacred mission.

She pressed no button, but the door closed and the carriage climbed skyward.

It stopped on the eighteenth floor and opened. She stepped out purposefully, turned slowly to her left, and proceeded down the hallway to the door marked *1845*.

She knocked and waited, unmoving, holding her purse at waist level with both hands, as noise emerged from the front of the altar.

Again she knocked. Again she waited. Again the noise.

This time she discerned one muffled statement: "Your wife!"

She didn't knock again. She just stood.

Finally the door opened to reveal Franklin, anger flaming from his eyes. They stood silent for a moment.

"Evelyn, go home."

Evelyn raised the purse till her hands rested just beneath her breasts, and she walked past her husband into the room.

Annie Minnis stood behind Franklin the way you would stand behind a wall when danger threatens. She was wearing an expensive silk robe, obviously pulled hastily over street clothes that were in some stage of removal.

Franklin was disheveled, at least compared to his normally fastidious appearance.

"Evelyn, go home."

Evelyn ignored Franklin. Her eyes focused on the gorgeous black woman like the eyes of an Amazon priestess concentrating on an animal sacrifice tied to the altar in an utterly helpless position and writhing in fear.

She could see inside Annie. She *was* a lamb, a worthy sacrificial lamb tied by invisible cords to the horns of this altar. And she *was* helpless, writhing inside from fear. Waiting, as ignorant as a lamb, for whatever it was that she feared would come.

"Evelyn . . . go . . . home." His words were more insistent.

Evelyn continued toward Annie as intently as if she were that priestess, approaching the sacrifice as solemnly as the occasion demanded. The sacrifice had backed up until the wall interrupted her retreat. Evelyn stopped, her face only inches from her lamb.

Evelyn now stood between Annie and Franklin.

Franklin turned, his eyes following Evelyn as she moved toward Annie. "Evelyn," he said to her back, his voice resounding with the authority of a leader of men, "for the last time, go home."

Without looking from Annie's eyes, Evelyn opened her purse and drew the knife, her favorite, from its cotton sheath and thrust its steel point deep into the throat of the waiting lamb. Amen.

"Evelyn, no! Are you mad?" Franklin rushed toward Annie as she slumped to the floor. "Annie!" he screamed. "Evelyn, what have you done?"

Evelyn was impervious to Franklin's howling. She was utterly disaffected by the spasms twisting Annie's body. She saw Franklin watching in horror as she took the knife, her favorite, in her left hand and concentrated hard as she began to slice into the peeling of her own already scarred wrist, releasing the emptiness that filled her.

Then she dropped the knife and stood, wrists upturned, in a final defiant pose.

As she stood over Franklin and Annie, much the wounded martyr, a light swelled from the walls and ceiling of apartment 1845 and enveloped her.

It was warm, inviting.

Blinding.

The glare gradually softened to reveal the shape of a tunnel, a hollow shaft of light, opening before her and stretching out for what appeared to be a very long distance. Franklin and Annie and the apartment and the noise of life were washed away in the warm glow as the tunnel lured her with a seductive power.

She moved toward it. Not walking, really. She just felt herself moving toward it.

She heard sounds from somewhere deep inside the tunnel, sounds of many people cheering or shouting, maybe even celebrating.

No, it wasn't from inside the tunnel. It was like the tunnel was a conduit bringing just a feeble hint of riotous clamor taking place in some enormous vaulted chamber that lay at the end of the shaft, at the end of the world.

Fascinated, she allowed herself to move more swiftly toward the commotion and the warm womb of light. She didn't make a move, didn't hurry along as she would in her body. She just allowed herself to be engulfed more rapidly.

Dreamily, she moved toward the light and the sound.

Somewhere in what seemed to be the mid-section of the shaft, Evelyn felt a change in the direction of her movement, and the warm, inviting light grew warmer. She was moving downward now—ever so slightly, but downward nonetheless. And the noise was different. It *was* the sound of many people, but not a celebration. There was pain, or maybe fear, in the roar. She could sense that she was drawing relentlessly nearer the end of the tunnel and the threshold of the luminous cavern that now was her apparent destination.

She could sense that it must be immense. The tunnel gave it away. In her life, walking down the halls of the capitol building, she always could tell when she was nearing the towering, cavernous rotunda. The noise in the hall would change as she moved in its direction. It wasn't just the sound of feet and voices bouncing around twelve-foot ceilings anymore. It was as if the sound of feet and voices was being enveloped in a tentacle that wriggled its way down the various halls from the center to draw its quarry into the heart of the lurking octopus rotunda. She loved the feeling.

But now, the serenity Evelyn felt in the first glare of the light was abating. The warmth was turning into heat. The comforting noise of a large group of people was turning into the wretched cries of a multitude. The tentacles of the grotto were now dragging her inward, sucking at her being. The light before her was blackening with an inky cloud spurting from somewhere within a fathomless depth.

She was falling now, a terrifying plunge toward black light and fearful heat.

With a suddenness that made her gasp, a suddenness that felt as if someone had reached within and snapped breath and spirit out of her, Evelyn tumbled out of the tunnel's gullet and into a vast, gaping, sulphurous, bottomless pit.

Her mad screams were lost among the wails of fear and pain rising from the canyons of the damned as the ebony tentacles of the grotto drew her into its darkness forever.

▼ ▼ ▼ ▼

"Evelyn! Darling!" Franklin had torn the long paring knife from Evelyn's hand to keep her from hurting herself and was shaking her to bring her to her senses.

He had come home from the office early, to spend a few minutes with her before he left for Annie's apartment and his evening "business." He found her standing alone by the sink in the kitchen, screaming as she stared blindly into the blade of a knife.

"Not again, Evelyn!" he shouted.

It was no use. Some paranoid or depressive illusion had her in its grips and would not let go.

He couldn't get her to stop, so he scooped her into his arms to take her to a soft couch where she'd be safer. As he lifted her, her feet left the ground and flailed wildly, searching for something firm as one long, terrified shriek arose from somewhere deep inside her and filled the room.

Then she fainted. The fight and the fear and the screams left her and she fell into unconsciousness.

Relieved by the calm but burdened by the recurrence of her delusions and the sudden deadness of her weight, Franklin carried her to the main hallway. He had intended to lay her on one of the sofas in the receiving room so he could call her doctor. Instead, he entered the caged door of the antique open elevator and let it lift them to the second floor. He carried Evelyn to her bedroom and gently arranged her limp body on her bed.

Her bed. Not their bed. It had been a very long time since he had sat next to her while she was in bed. Something had happened to her as they passed into middle age. She had become ... well, different. The fun-loving woman he married had moved on and a person he didn't know had moved in, a person who had become depressive, who had attempted suicide, and who now constituted an embarrassing bloody nuisance. Oh, to be relieved of the nuisance.

But the shell was still the Evelyn he married. Out of pity he leaned down and kissed her forehead. Oh, Evelyn. Something happened to you. Or maybe something happened to me. Or maybe something happened to both of us.

He turned, picked up the phone on Evelyn's night table and made two calls. The first was to Evelyn's doctor. He'd be there in ten minutes.

The second was to apartment 1845. "Annie, I'm going to be late tonight . . . . "

▼ ▼ ▼ 4 ▼ ▼ ▼

Lindy Blakely's cubicle in the newsroom was, well, different from the others. At least that's how the kinder members of the newsroom described it for visitors, mainly to avoid embarrassment that always comes with eccentric co-workers. The truth was, most everyone, including the custodial staff, steered a wide berth around her space.

It *was* different.

Her little office had three distinct levels, horizontal planes divided from one another by their marked contrast—almost like the different levels of a landscape formed by grasses, shrubs, and tall trees.

From desktop-level upwards, a cacophony of paper splashed across the carpeted wall dividers. Lindy had hung self-made posters with pushpins. She swore she read them every day. They were heavy sheets of cold-pressed watercolor paper turned so the rectangular surface was tilted, like cockeyed diamonds.

On them she had made bold, expressive strokes of primary colors with various-sized brushes as background, then lettered sayings by her favorite philosophers, one per poster.

Problem was, she had tacked so many other bits and pieces of paper with sayings jotted on them that the statements on all but one of the handmade posters were obscured. There were at least a hundred of the little intruders, but the bright colors from the cockeyed diamonds still leapt out at passers-by.

You could still read her Camus: *If you don't die today, you'll die tomorrow or the next day.*

Desktop down to ankle-level was completely different. Absolute order reigned. Even the paper clips in the little well at the front of the wide main drawer were lined up like hollow soldiers ready for inspection.

She cleaned and dusted her computer terminal every morning, and the old electric typewriter stood at attention, a piece of clean white paper rolled in at the proper setting, at the ready.

Drawers were neatly organized, files on current stories were arranged in a special standup rack on her desktop so that the edges all aligned, and the flexible-arm fluorescent lamp was centered exactly over the blotter.

Visual harmony.

But from ankles down, the visual noise surged again with an affront to the eyes. The floor was blanketed with papers from one corner of the cubicle to the other—newspapers, magazines, letters, spent typing paper, photocopies—a full two inches deep that extended even under the desk.

The only clearing was the short path from door to desk, shaped like a mushroom, narrow up to her swivel chair, then widening so the chair's wheels could turn unimpeded.

She cleared the floor once a quarter—New Year's Day, Easter Sunday, Father's Day (in memory of her dad), and Labor Day (in honor of her boss). The only time the custodial staff did anything but empty the diminutive trash can was on the workday following her four cleaning days each year.

When she first began collaborating on stories with Dan Li-pong, her next-cubicle neighbor, he once plopped himself down sideways in the only other chair in her office in a way that allowed his feet to remain in the narrow part of the mushroom. He had to ask his new partner why the "different" way of organizing. "Lindy, your cubicle looks like a sandwich with a slice of kempt between two slices of unkempt. What's the deal?"

"Simple," she said, her back still turned to Dan. She raised her right arm and with her first finger, pointed to the floor with jabbing motions, "This is yesterday. It's the debris of passing time, like the strata of dirt and artifacts in an ancient city." She swung her chair to the side, bent over and sent her hand deep into the mound of papers covering the floor, wiggling her hand right and left to get through the mess. When she reached the bare floor she snatched up the bottom sheet.

"Here. January sixth. The fourth page of that follow-up article on the little girl who turned up missing on Christmas Day."

Dan's eyebrows raised. "That was one of the first stories we worked on together," he said.

"That was yesterday, Dan. Yesterday! Like everything else built up layer upon layer on this floor." She held up the sheet in front of her face and let it drop. "Part of the debris of time," she said as it fluttered to the floor.

"This!" she said as she swung around and opened her arms as if to embrace the air above the desk. "This is today. This is what's happening now. Yesterday's minutes have ticked off and lie strewn on the floor. Today's minutes line up neatly on the clock's face, each one in its place waiting for the inexorable pass of the hand to sweep it into yesterday."

As she spoke, she moved her arm across the top of the desk in a jerking motion, like the movement of a hand across the clock face. As she came to the recent issue of *Time*, squared neatly in its place on top of the periodicals, she scooped it up and dropped it on top of the "yesterday" pile that was the floor.

"Our 'todays' must be kept in order!"

"Lindy, you're quite the philosopher," Dan said with a smile.

"Philosophy!" she squealed as she swiveled the chair 180 degrees to face Dan. "That's the future! That's why I keep these jewels of wisdom pinned to my walls.

"Dan, you look at my office and see neatness or messiness. I look at it and see my life. It's an allegory. What I put on my walls, what I see when I lift my eyes above today," she dramatized her point by dipping her head and slowly raising her chin to look up again, "is philosophy. It's the meaning of life. It's the future."

With that, Lindy stood up and turned around. "The future," she pointed to the wall of philosophy. "The present," she said as she pointed to the orderly desk. "And the past," her arm dropped toward the ruinous floor. "Opportunity. Order. Oblivion. That is my office and that is my life!"

She dramatically dropped back into her chair, her hands gripping its arms. "Any questions?"

"My Chinese grandmother might have had a few, but I don't. She used to say, 'The source for dealing with things belongs to the mind.' It appears, partner, that you should be able to deal with most anything."

That was very early in their relationship and he had wanted to score a few points.

But while Dan thought her a bit eccentric in the beginning, he had come to appreciate Lindy's attitude, her talent, her instincts for news, and her terrific cooperation as a collaborator.

In fact, he did finally get around to asking her why she was so keen on the past, present, and future bit. "I guess it's from my dad. He and Mom named me Elliot Linda Blakely. One day as a teenager, when no matter what your name is you're ashamed of it, I asked him in anger why he'd given me such a stupid name.

" 'Sweetheart,' he said. ' "Elliot" ' has a dignified aura about it and that's your future. "Linda" is a strong woman's name. That's how you are today. And "Blakely," well, that's your heritage. It's what the past has given you, like it or not.' "

Dan *had* come to appreciate her as a partner over the months they had worked together. He also had come to appreciate her as a woman, quite apart from her professionalism.

It was well past five o'clock. He didn't wear a watch but he knew even in a windowless room when the time came that real people got to go home. When he could distinguish the individual stubs in his five o'clock shadow as he raked his hand across his cheek, he knew it was rush hour. A heavy black beard was one of the genetic endowments he had received from the Caucasian half of his parental duo.

As usual, he walked into Lindy's cubicle and sank into the extra chair. As usual, she was sitting with the back of her chair facing the door, staring at her philosophical wall or into the future or something. "How was the press conference?"

"There's something there," she said. "I can feel it."

"What do you mean?"

"There's a story there, just begging to be uncovered and written."

Dan stood up and pushed the top of her chair to the left so she would turn and face him. "What story?" he said, with almost a doubt or a dare in his voice.

She was looking off into the future again.

"Lindy." He was growing more stern. "Come on. What?"

"I don't know." She still wasn't looking at him. "Governor Justice has been so effective with his programs in the past. Even when he was mayor. But he's never tackled anything as evil and immense as the drug problem." She looked at him now. "That's what the news conference was all about—'A bold new initiative.' "

"So what's the story?"

"I told you, Dan, I don't know. There wasn't anything, really. It's just a feeling, mind you. Part of his drug initiative . . . . " She stopped and smiled. "I love that phrase. They use it for their programs but every time I hear it or say it I think of a nervous kid trying grass for the first time."

Dan's eyes opened wide into a full-faced glare. "Get back to it."

"Sorry. Anyway, part of his drug initiative—" she grinned and said the words slowly with a twist of tease, "—involves volunteer drug testing among state employees. I don't believe that aspect will ever make it out of the hangar, let alone off the ground. When I asked him about it he turned very dramatic and, it seemed to me at least, more than a little offended. It was like I had brought up the transparency of the Emperor's new clothes. He answered something like 'Some parts of the plan will work, some won't.' "

She looked away again, thinking. "It seems to me that his answer was irrelevant, even though it was a good one. I think the story will be in the reaction of those government employees to this proposal. I think the failure itself is the story I'm looking for."

"What's the big deal?" Dan asked. "You and I both know what's going to happen. Tomorrow or the next day the ACLU or someone will howl about how unconstitutional volunteer drug testing is. They'll stir up dust and keep it stirred up till Justice cries 'Uncle!' And every newspaper in the state will run the same story.

"Forget it. Strike one for your intuition."

Lindy waited until Dan had disappeared into the hall in the direction of his office before she responded. "That's not the story!" She loved getting the last word.

No response.

Lindy waited patiently, watching the hall.

A full sixty seconds had passed when Dan appeared in the doorway.

Lindy continued, "Everyone knows the state workers will never sit still for this. The question is, who will *have* to sit still for it and 'volunteer,' whether they like it or not?"

Dan's frown deepened. "Justice's staff, of course."

"Exactly! And how many would you say are on his staff?"

"Oh, I don't know. A dozen. Two dozen. I don't know."

"Out of a dozen or two dozen top-level staffers who live in the fast lane and love to rock and roll, how many would you say might test positive in a 'volunteer' drug test?"

With that, the light dawned on Dan. "Lindy, you're brilliant!"

Dan turned and headed for the chair. He dropped into it and leaned over, resting his elbows on his knees, hands outstretched and punctuating his remarks. "All we have to do is to get inside the Governor's staff and sniff out our story before the wind carries it to our competitors. Who do you know?"

"A couple of the lower-level staffers. Nobody that's likely to tell us too much unless we luck out."

"I know a couple of them, too. I went to school with the assistant press secretary. I occasionally have a brew with another guy."

"That's a start," Lindy said.

"Look, we can also fence these guys in a bit, too."

Now Lindy was smiling. They were a great team—she had intuition and persistence, he had a keen ability to exploit possibilities. It was her turn to be puzzled. "What do you mean?"

"I mean get out there and lay down little trip wires all around the staff so that if any of them stray from the flock—*ding-a-ling-a-ling*—they set off the alarm."

"Now *you're* beating around the bush."

"No, I'm not, it's simple. Let's make casual contacts *around* the staff, among people who are in a position to know if someone's upset about having to be tested."

Now the light was coming on for Lindy. "I see!" she said slowly, appreciating the idea. "I know several of the aspiring politicos in the statehouse. Some of them would love to see a staffer hung out to dry."

"I do too. And I have a contact or two at the state police and the metro police. There might be scuttle there." Dan was standing again, hand on the doorway-without-a-door, ready to leave. "Lindy, you contact your people, I'll contact mine. Let's touch base in the morning."

He disappeared down the hall.

Lindy raised her chin in the direction he'd gone with a discreet smile of satisfaction. She then turned slowly to her immaculate desktop, her "today," and reached for her Rolodex.

▼ ▼ ▼ ▼

Evelyn Justice could feel herself rising out of the blackness of the pit into which she'd fallen. It had seemed as if she had been swallowed whole and enfolded in thick billows from which all traces of light and consciousness had fled, so dense she couldn't even move.

She had no idea how long she had been unconscious, but the feeling of upward movement was waking her, bringing her back.

She still couldn't move her limbs, but she was definitely rising. The darkness was growing less suffocating as she rose. However, it was churning underneath her, clearly the agitated force that was driving her upward.

It's vomiting me, she thought with a rising sense of alarm. She struggled to move her limbs, to fight against the force, but could not move. In a moment of panic she opened her mouth to scream, but the putrid thick darkness rushed in, filled her whole being and seized her with absolute despair, choking off her cry.

At that instant, she hit the light and her eyes bolted open to drink in the brilliance, desperate to void herself of the blackness that had filled her.

She lay deadly still, eyes opened wide, unable to move.

At first she didn't recognize the surroundings, but slowly she realized that she was looking at a ceiling, a plain ceiling in a real room. As the darkness faded and her peripheral vision returned—she still couldn't move even her eyes—more of the room filled her field of vision. It was her room and she was on her bed.

She focused all her energy on her hands in an attempt to move her fingers. Just barely at first, her fingers did move. She felt the edge of the thick comforter that covered the bed, then with all her might she clutched at the down-filled spread, fearful that she would begin falling again.

As she lay secured to the comforter, other senses began to return. She actually felt the softness of the cotton and was reassured. She smelled the fragrance of the room.

She heard Franklin's voice.

" . . . to bother you at this hour, John, but Evelyn's had a recurrence of her problem." A pause. "That's right, but this time I found her in the kitchen, knife in hand, so fixated that she didn't even know I was there. When I picked her up, she kicked and flailed violently, then fainted."

I'm here, Frank. I'm okay. The words formed in Evelyn's mouth, but the darkness choked them off. She still couldn't move.

"Thanks. I'll meet you in ten minutes at the front door. All the help is gone for the day."

Evelyn struggled, wanting to cry for Frank to take her in his arms again and hold her so she could let go of the comforter and not fear falling back into the pit.

She tried calling out again, but no sound came. She tried to move herself, to jog the bed so he'd turn and see her eyes open, but she couldn't. She again concentrated on her hands and let go of the comforter with her left hand, but it would move no further. When the hand refused to be raised to Franklin's back, she groped again for the comforter and held on, hoping he'd turn to her on his own.

Instead, he dialed another number. The silence was as suffocating as the darkness had been.

"Annie, I'm going to be late tonight . . . . "

Inside, Evelyn exploded. She felt all the hatred and animosity of a lifetime come together in critical mass and erupt, rage filling her body with animation and fury.

She came up off the comforter with her claws flying. Before Franklin had finished his sentence, she had torn at his shirt, scratched his face and neck, pummelled her fists against the back of his head, and was screaming at the top of her lungs, "How dare you call that whore on *my* phone from *my* room!"

Franklin dropped the phone and spun around to protect himself, rising to his feet and backing away as he grabbed her wrists and held on. "Evelyn! Stop it! Evelyn!" He shook her as he shouted.

His shouts made Evelyn even more furious. With a burst of energy, she broke free her right hand and brought it smashing against his cheek.

Franklin dropped her other hand and with a lightning movement, slapped her back.

Evelyn froze in astonishment, the left side of her face stinging from the blow.

There was a long, terrible moment of deadly quiet. Waves of anger and shock and guilt and disbelief broke across her heart, and she collapsed back onto the bed into a whimpering mass. "How could you? How could you?" she sobbed.

Franklin picked up the phone and laid it back in its cradle. "Evelyn, what came over you?" He used his most innocent and befuddled tone of voice.

"You!" she sobbed, not lifting her face from her hands and the softness of the comforter. "You and that whore. And now you've struck me."

"Evelyn, that was Annie Minnis." He was pleading now. "She's on my staff. She works for me. I have a meeting scheduled tonight and just wanted her to let the group know I'd be late."

With that, Evelyn lifted her red, wet eyes in a look of defiance. "Don't insult me by lying, too," she said. "I hired a private investigator who reported to me today. I know all about your Tuesday 'meetings.' " She said the word "meetings" as if she were spitting, trying to rid her mouth of a nasty taste.

"I've known for a long time that something's been wrong but wouldn't let myself admit it," she continued. "I do have my pride! I hired the investigator just to find out if my worst fears were true."

She rose a little higher on the bed. "You're a liar, a two-timer, and a cheat. If you don't cut off your relationship with this whore and fire her from your staff tomorrow, and I mean *tomorrow*, the rest of the world will know it too—from my lips."

As Evelyn lowered her head to her hands, there were no more tears. The anger and pain had drained them from her body.

"Evelyn." Franklin began to insist that she let him explain.

But the doorbell interrupted him.

"That'll be Dr. Bates. I called him to come check on you and give you something to relax."

Evelyn didn't move.

The doorbell rang again.

This time, Franklin didn't speak. He simply backed away from the bed and his broken wife, and turned to go to the front door to greet their physician and friend.

▼ ▼ ▼ ▼

Evelyn waited motionless on the bed, listening to hear the sound of Franklin's receding footsteps on the stairs. When she finally heard the front door open, she jumped out of the bed and scurried quietly down the hall—in the opposite direction.

Relax me, indeed! She hurried down the back stairs and into the kitchen where her purse lay on the counter. She opened a storage closet and lifted out an old jacket, draping it over her arm. She scooped up her purse from the butcher-block counter and opened it.

Quickly she ran through her purse ritual, a three-point check: the main compartment for the wallet with her driver's license; the pocket of the main compartment for a compact; and the side pocket for the small handgun Franklin had given her to carry for her protection. Satisfied that she had what she needed, she headed for the door.

When her hand touched the doorknob, Evelyn paused and turned, looking back over her kitchen. *One last thing,* she thought as she turned decisively and crossed to the other side of the kitchen island. She stopped, opened her purse, and picked up the knife, her favorite, which she had held only minutes (or was it eons?) earlier. She dropped it into the open jaws of her waiting purse.

Evelyn dashed back across the kitchen and out the rear door, stealing away to the nearby garage and the promise of escape it held.

▼ ▼ ▼ ▼

"John, so good of you to come." Franklin shook his friend's hand. "I'm sorry to bother you at dinnertime."

"Comes with the territory," Dr. Bates responded. "Frank, you look like an accident ready to happen. Did I come to see Evelyn or you?"

"Evelyn, I assure you." Franklin closed the door, but did not usher the doctor to the bedroom. Instead, he drew a little closer, bent his head slightly toward him, and spoke in a subdued voice. "John, this ordeal is taking its toll on me. This is the worst I've ever seen her."

"Did she cut herself again?"

"No, she just stood there with a look of terror in her eyes. I called her name several times and even shook her, but she didn't respond."

"Is she conscious now?"

"Yes, very."

"Then I should see her." John leaned in the direction of the hall as if starting in that direction.

"One more minute." Franklin grasped John's elbow and held him. He was unsure how much to tell his friend. He knew Evelyn would embarrass him, so should he warn John of her "delusions" or tell him the truth?

John Bates was no fool. Franklin would risk it. "I think I know why Evelyn had this relapse."

"Why?"

"I've been seeing another woman for some time now."

The doctor's eyes widened.

"It's nothing serious, but Evelyn found out today. It was the first thing she mentioned on regaining consciousness. She's bitterly angry with me right now. I'm afraid that's what precipitated this incident."

John Bates just stared at the Governor, unbelieving.

"John—" The doctor's silence was disquieting to Franklin.

"Frank, of all the stupid tricks you could pull, how could you pull this one? Evelyn has been depressive and suicidal—suicidal!" Franklin shushed him with his hands, but John continued in a rough whisper, "And you're out fooling around?"

With that, John waited no longer. He headed for the stairs with the Governor in tow.

"Which room?"

"Her room."

"Her room?" John turned as he hurried up the stairs. "You mean you're not even sleeping together? No wonder she's depressive! You give yourself to everybody in the state but her."

Franklin said nothing except "Second door on the right."

John paused at the door long enough to tap a couple of times to announce his presence, then pushed it open and entered.

No Evelyn.

Franklin crossed to the bathroom and called her name. When no one answered, he opened the door to find a darkened room. "I don't know where she is."

"She must have gone to get something to drink," John said. "You look around up here and I'll check downstairs."

John headed down the front stairs when Franklin stopped him. "Go down the back stairs. They lead directly into the kitchen." Franklin crossed the hall and peeked into the darkened guest room. "Evelyn?"

No answer.

He moved down the hall to his room, the one adjoining hers on the right. He entered the room and headed back toward the bathroom. In his mind he could see her lying across the edge of the bathtub, wrists slit and submerged in a tub of warm water to hasten her own death. It would be just like her to kill herself in my bathroom, he thought.

But as he passed the window that opened onto the backyard, a movement of light caught his eye. He stepped to the window and saw Evelyn's car backing out of the garage. She was driving.

"John!" he shouted. "John, she's pulling out of the driveway. See if you can stop her."

With that, Franklin dashed down the back stairs to find John standing just outside the back door, waving his arms and shouting to get Evelyn's attention.

"I know she saw me," John said, lowering his arms as the car pulled away. "She looked right at me."

Franklin just stood there, fuming.

"This is at least partly your doing, Frank."

"Don't lecture me now, doctor. I don't need it." Franklin headed for the phone on the far side of the kitchen island. As he passed the edge of the island he stopped. "It's gone!"

"What?"

"The knife she was holding when I found her this evening. It's gone. I put it right here when I took it out of her hand."

"Frank, this is a critical situation," the doctor said as he moved to meet Franklin at the phone. "This could be very dangerous."

Yeah, dangerous for me, thought Franklin. "If you'd excuse me," he said in a sarcastic tone as he reached for the phone. "I was just going to call the State Police."

The doctor gave Franklin a sour look. "I'll try to follow her," he said as he left the kitchen for the front door and his car.

"This is Governor Justice," Franklin said as the dispatcher came on the line. "I have an emergency. I need to speak with Chief Brown immediately."

"I'm sorry, Governor. Chief Brown is in Washington for a seminar. May I route your call to the senior duty officer, Captain Gonzalez?"

"Do it now."

Franklin waited for only a few seconds.

"Yes, sir. This is Captain Gonzalez. How can I help?"

"Gonzalez, this is Governor Justice. I have an emergency, but it must be handled in the most discreet possible manner."

"Yes, sir. I'll do my best."

"Your best won't be good enough if you screw this up," the Governor ordered. "Listen. My wife has suffered from severe emotional problems in the last several months." He paused, then added awkwardly, "the stresses of public office, you know."

Gonzalez grunted an affirmation.

"She suffered another incident this evening, but while her doctor was en route, she got in her car and left. She headed south on Meridian Street, toward downtown, but I have no idea where she was going."

"Yes, sir. We'll put out an APB and find her."

"Gonzalez. Two things you must know and they must go no further than your ears or I'll have your head on a platter."

"Yes, sir." Gonzalez was dead serious.

"First, my wife has been suicidal in the recent past. Only months ago she made a very real suicide attempt. She may have a small caliber pistol in her possession."

"May have?"

"*May* have!" Justice answered emphatically, not liking a question from a subordinate. "She just walked out the back door and I have not yet had time to inventory all of her personal belongings to ascertain whether or not the pistol is in her possession!"

"Yes, sir." Gonzalez's response was feeble. "I just meant to—"

"Finding her," Justice interrupted, "and finding her now is of the utmost urgency."

"Yes, sir."

"You are to broadcast none of that. When she is located, you are to give information to the officers involved on an as-needed basis. Is that clear?"

"Yes, sir."

"Second, I have reason to believe that one of my staff might also be in danger. You are to assign an unmarked car to the high-rise at 1277 North Capitol."

"Yes, sir. What are the men to be watching for?"

"Mrs. Justice, you fool!"

"Yes, sir. What car is she driving?"

"*Her* car, idiot. A new Lincoln Town Car. Navy blue. Any other questions?"

"No, sir. I'm on this personally. I'll be in regular contact with you. Are you home?"

"Yes."

"I'll report to you every thirty minutes till we find her."

Justice realized he'd better soften his approach somewhat to keep from offending the officer. He was feeling very vulnerable. "Thank you, Captain. I know I can depend on both your professionalism *and* your discretion."

"Yes, sir. I'll report back soon."

Justice pressed the disconnect lever in the phone's cradle and got another dial tone. He dialed Annie's number.

"Annie, I'm sorry. All hell broke loose here. I've got trouble . . . . No, I won't be there tonight, but I must see you tomorrow, late morning . . . . No, it's Evelyn. Listen, she *could* show up at your door tonight. She's distraught.

Don't leave your apartment until I get there. Don't open your door to anybody." He paused, then added, "And don't worry. I've got the State Police on this!"

▼ ▼ ▼ ▼

The flush of relief Evelyn felt as she pulled out of the driveway of the Governor's mansion was ebbing rapidly. She realized that as long as she was in her own car, she could be found easily by the police.

Meridian was the main north-south street in the capitol city and the Governor's mansion was in the 2800 block, just a few minutes from the heart of the city in the old near-northside. Evelyn was heading south toward downtown, driving the speed limit. Don't call attention to yourself, old girl, she coaxed. This Lincoln is already like a neon sign.

By the time she had reached the edge of downtown proper, she realized she'd have to get out of the car. But go where? How?

She had fled the house on impulse, perhaps even because of a rekindled survival instinct. She knew that if she got back into the cycle of drugs and shrinks and hospitals, she would lose her mind—or her life.

Again on instinct, she wheeled the big Lincoln to the right, entering Michigan Street's westbound one-way traffic at about the 1100 block north. Two blocks later she turned right again, this time onto Capitol, then made another immediate right into the parking garage that occupied the second through ninth floors of 1111 North Capitol, one of three garages that serviced the posh condos and offices of this exclusive district. If she had to set out on foot or hail a cab, she preferred to be in this part of town.

She piloted the Lincoln through the monotonous spiral that led to the top floor. Just like my apple peeling, she thought as she turned onto the fifth floor, with someone holding onto the top. *Just like me.* Then she sighed one other thought as if she were praying; *I hope there's someone up there holding on.*

When she reached the top floor, she found the darkest open slot and pulled in. She pushed the buttons that lowered the driver's window and unlocked the doors, picked up her purse and jacket, and got out of the car. She left the keys in the ignition and laid the parking stub on the dash in plain view.

A little smoke where there is no fire, she said to herself, as the hope of police being led on a merry chase by a hapless car thief made her smile as she headed for the elevator.

On the street she hailed the first cab that passed and slid into the back seat. A fiftyish man wearing a weathered cabbie hat sat behind the wheel.

"Where to?"

"Drive!"

The cab headed north on Capitol as Evelyn sank down in the back seat with her head nestled in what she imagined to be the most ensconced position.

Think, Evelyn. Think! She commanded herself to combat the rising anxiety.

After several minutes of silence, the cabbie looked questioningly at Evelyn in the rear-view mirror. She spoke. "Do you know the McDonald's at 29th and Capitol?"

"The one near the Governor's mansion?"

"Yes."

"We're there. That's it just ahead."

"Pull into the lot and park the cab." Evelyn heard her words but didn't recognize the authority with which she spoke.

The cabbie pulled into an open slot, put the car in *park* and turned, elbow slung over the back of the seat, to look at his fare.

Evelyn Justice didn't hesitate. With some pointedness in her voice, she said, "I need to be alone for a few minutes. Leave the meter running and go into the restaurant." She opened her purse and fished out a ten-dollar bill. "Here, get yourself something," she said in a tone meant to dismiss him. "And there'll be a nice tip in this for you."

The cabbie plucked the bill from her fingers and shrugged his shoulders as he turned off the engine, removed the keys from the ignition—he wasn't going to trust his cab to anyone—and opened his door. "How long do you need?"

"Just get something to eat and I'll be ready then."

Time to think. What to do? Evelyn Justice slid her hand back into the purse and wrapped her fingers around the smooth wooden handle of the kitchen knife, her favorite, as she sank into the seat . . . and into her thoughts.

▼ ▼ ▼ 5 ▼ ▼ ▼

Wednesday morning dawned on a bedraggled Franklin Justice. He had passed an almost sleepless night and it showed on his face as he made his way toward his office, intending to call Annie first thing. He was worried about her, about the situation, but didn't want to phone from the mansion. Too difficult to explain if something had happened.

Evelyn's threat had reverberated powerfully when Gonzales called at 11 p.m. Troopers had picked up the subject's car in the possession of a petty thief. They traced it back to a parking garage in the 1100 block of North Capitol and confirmed that a woman of the subject's description had driven it in sometime earlier, and that the suspect had driven it out less than two hours before the troopers interviewed the attendant.

Eleven Hundred North Capitol was less than two blocks from Annie's apartment and only five blocks from the office of the *News!* The awful problem of which path to take to save his neck had stolen the sleep from his eyes. On the one hand, Evelyn had always been an irresolute and compliant wife during their many years of marriage. They had their disagreements, and she had gotten her way most of the time. But that was only because the issues were minor and Franklin really gave up nothing when he acquiesced. He believed that in life there were elephants and there were peanuts. Obdurate and unyielding as he was, he was still willing to give away all his peanuts in

53

order to retain all his elephants. And Evelyn only fussed about peanuts.

Until now.

Now her demand struck at the core of more than one elephant for Franklin. Last night she'd been angrier than he'd ever seen her. And her drastic step of leaving him and not returning all night was completely un-characteristic.

She might just do it. She might just tell some crazy story to the press. Or she might just find Annie and confront her. She'd taken the knife from the kitchen and she must still have the handgun he'd insisted she carry. She might use them on Annie.

Or on herself!

Any way he looked at it, things were coming unrav-eled. Fast.

And any way he looked at it, unless he found his wife—fast—he'd have a public relations problem the size of the national debt!

How could he cut Annie off as Evelyn had demanded? Ten years they had been together. He had grown to appreciate her, maybe even love her. Certainly he had grown to need her.

When he first met Annie, he was a man on the rise. A liaison with a beautiful woman seemed to him a part of a man's trip to the top. The fact that she was both beautiful and of different color made the affair more exotic, more thrilling.

At each succeeding peak along the way to his personal summit, he felt that he was becoming more powerful, more virulent. His relationship with Annie reinforced his feelings.

Evelyn did not.

He needed Annie's youth, fire, and willfulness to sat-isfy the needs of his growing prowess.

But now, for the first time in ten years, her fire and willfulness might be a real problem. If he did what Evelyn demanded and cut Annie off, God only knew what Annie might do in response.

After a fitful night, he had decided what to do. The only path was to take Annie into his confidence and conspire against Evelyn.

Not to do his wife any harm. Only to assuage her anger until after the election. Until, through treatment, Evelyn could become her old compliant self again.

Franklin Justice wouldn't have to give up any elephants. It just had to appear that way. Then he and Annie could resume their relationship without fear.

His determination shone on his brow as clearly as his sleeplessness showed in his eyes as he entered his office just after eight-thirty.

Rosemary Kleindorf, his longtime secretary, stood up to greet him, one hand full of pink message slips as she stepped from behind her desk. "Gonzalez from State Police is in your office, been here since just before eight. Mr. Barnett has been in twice already. He insists that he must see you this morning as soon as possible."

She moved to a coffee pot and drew off enough to fill a large, unadorned mug with the steaming liquid as she continued rapid-fire, "I cancelled your morning appointments as you requested. Lunch is still on with Senator Mills. Your two o'clock cancelled and re-scheduled for next week. There are two calls requesting you to speak, a personal call from Governor Simmons of Ohio, a call from a reporter at the *News,* and several calls from within the administration, mostly department heads who are taking flack from employees following your news conference yesterday."

Justice basically tuned out Rosemary's recitation until he heard, "reporter from the *News.*" That hit him like a bolt out of the blue. In as nonchalant a manner as his alarm would allow, he asked, "What did the reporter want?"

"An interview to follow up yesterday's news conference."

"Of course," Justice muttered as he turned to the entrance to his private office and continued talking to himself. Of course. Calm down. You're tired and edgy. Calm
down.

As the Governor came through his door, Gonzalez,
who had been lounging in one of the comfortable chairs,
stuffed the magazine he was reading back into the rack
and jumped to attention.

"Gonzalez," Justice acknowledged without looking at
the officer. He passed behind his desk, set his briefcase
on the floor, and thumbed through the pink message
slips. "Thank you for being prompt."

The second of the five slips from some of his department heads stopped him short: *From A. Minnis. She has an
important meeting at noon, needs your input.*

He was so tired, so stressed, so worried about what
Evelyn might do that the private meaning of this message
caught him off guard for a moment. But then the message
sank in and brought a little grin to his otherwise haggard
face. It was their code for "Let's meet at my place for some
noontime delight."

She must be all right. He'd save a call and see her at
noon. That would be one less thing to worry about right
now.

The grin disappeared as he looked back to the messages in his hand. He was satisfied that there was nothing
that would distract him. He walked around to the front
of the desk, seated himself opposite the state police captain and acting commander, and requested, "Update,
please. And do sit down."

Gonzalez thanked the Governor and timidly sat down
as instructed. "Sir, I'm afraid I have nothing new to report
to you this morning except the extent of our operation.
After finding the car, we sent teams of men to interview

restaurant managers, shop keepers, cabbies and bus drivers who have some contact with the area within a mile radius of the parking garage."

"And?" The Governor's tone made it clear that he wanted Gonzalez to get straight to the bottom line.

"And nothing, sir. No trace of Mrs. Justice. It's like she just disappeared."

"How do you explain that?"

"Our best guesses are that she either had made a previous arrangement for someone to pick her up or that she met someone she knew by chance and left the area with him or her."

"Gonzalez, let me make something perfectly clear. This is my wife, the First Lady, we're talking about. You are to stop guessing, get back on the street, and stay there until you find her—"

A loud knock at the hall entrance to his private office interrupted him. "Come," Franklin called out as the door began to swing open. He knew who it was. Only two people were allowed to make an entrance that way and he knew that one of them was in her apartment this morning.

When George Barnett realized he had interrupted a meeting, he apologized and began to back out the still-open door.

"No, come in, Barney." Franklin waved him in as he turned back to the captain. *"And,"* he said to Gonzalez with a rough edge in his voice to emphasize his displeasure, "get Brown back here on the next plane. I want this matter handled by him if it goes any further than today."

Gonzalez was now standing, almost at attention. "Sir, I informed Chief Brown late last night. He was to be on the first plane out of Washington this morning and should be in the office by noon."

"Thank you. Keep me posted."

With that, the captain turned briskly and disappeared through the office door and past Ms. Kleindorf.

Justice rose and moved wearily to the back side of his desk, easing himself down into his chair as if straining against the unseen weight on his shoulders. George Barnett took a seat and pulled it close to the huge desk so that his knees almost touched the glossy wood.

"You look like a freight train hit you," Barnett said.

"You're the second person in twenty-four hours who's complimented me that way. I'd prefer that you keep it to yourself."

"Did you have a bad night or something?"

"That's not the word for it," Justice said. In a few short minutes he briefed his friend on the events of the previous evening.

"Geez. What are you going to do?" Barnett's face showed his empathy for his friend's terrible predicament.

"The only thing I can do and still save this office. I'm going to bring Annie into it fully to get her cooperation. I think if I explain the whole situation she'll play along until the whole thing blows over.

"Then, when Evelyn is finally found, I can tell her that I called off the whole affair with Annie. That should calm her down enough to keep her from doing something stupid with the press and should allow time for me to get her back in treatment. I just don't know what else to do."

Barnett could hear the frustration and even a little pleading in his friend's voice. "I'm really sorry for you."

"Thanks, buddy."

"Look, I don't want to make things worse, but before you do anything with Annie, I think you should hear why I've insisted on seeing you this morning."

"Okay, talk."

"Well, after our little session yesterday afternoon, I got to feeling guilty. After all, I know how you feel about

Annie. I like her, too. I thought maybe I'd been a little rash and that maybe I'd spoken out of turn."

"Barney, you know I trust you more than any other person on earth. It is always appropriate for you to raise issues that affect me. Who else would?"

"Well, I felt guilty anyway and decided to do a little checking to see whether or not my concerns had any basis. So I followed the Bruhof paper trail to see where it led. The bottom line is that it leads nowhere."

"What do you mean?"

"I mean that I have invoices that are in order, but nothing else on file. The bills are all drawn against your war chest with Annie's authorization, but I have no purchase orders, no bills of lading, nothing to substantiate the transactions. For all I know, Bruhof is receiving checks for nothing."

"How could this happen? This is irresponsible!"

"You ordered me to give Annie free reign. She didn't like all the paperwork, so you suspended the rules for her."

"Barney!" Justice looked at his friend with a sneer of frustration. "Why'd you let me do such a thing?"

"If you'll remember, I protested fairly vigorously."

Justice grimaced as he closed his eyes and buried his face in his hand.

"I think this whole thing could be the tip of an iceberg—the very unusual pattern of regular invoices in similar amounts, the European goods from a distributor that doesn't do business in Europe, the lack of documentation. It's all starting to worry me. This *is* donated money."

Justice looked up and boomed, "Now's a fine time to be worried about it. This should have been found and resolved long ago." It was a rage born of fear.

"I'm your friend, your political ally, and your financial watchdog. But I'm not your whipping boy. If there really is a problem, it's because of your decision, and it's up to you to get to the heart of it so we can find a solution."

The Governor was silent for a moment, then heaved a ponderous sigh. "You're right, Barney," he admitted, the ire drained from his voice. "I'm sorry. You've done all I've ever asked and more. I'll talk to Annie today and see what I can find out."

"One more thing."

Justice looked at his friend.

"I'm the campaign's treasurer. I have as much culpability in issues related to this money as you."

"Your point?"

"Don't let your passion blind you. There might be a lot riding on your next conversation with Annie."

"A word to the wise, Barney," Justice said as he leaned forward to hunch himself over the work on his desk.

Barney got up and headed out the hall door. "Call me," he said as he entered the huge open hallway in the heart of the Capitol building.

▼ ▼ ▼ ▼

On her bus ride to work that morning, Maria, the maid responsible for all the upstairs rooms in the Governor's mansion, decided that the right time to do what she had to do would be immediately upon arrival at work.

She greeted the other staff, spoke to a few of them, then headed straight for Mrs. Justice's bedroom. She didn't close the door, but pushed it until it was nearly closed, then walked directly to the First Lady's closet.

She selected a casual outfit and a set of underclothes which she folded neatly into a small bundle and stuffed into the bottom of her oversized, empty handbag.

Then she ducked into the bathroom and fished through the medicine cabinet, pulling out an item here and there. She continued her rummaging through the top drawers of the long and well-lit vanity. Maria selected some small items and dropped them into the handbag on top of the clothes, shutting them in with a snap of the bag's closure. She placed it by the desk to the right of the door so that if someone entered, the opening door would hide it.

Then Maria walked into the hallway and toward the supply closet where she began her day's work.

▼ ▼ ▼ ▼

"That brilliant insight of yours is starting to tarnish." Dan lifted his head to project his voice over the wall divider that separated his work space from Lindy's. He had just taken a long slow pull from a strong cup of coffee and his voice had a bit of morning croak still in it.

They had made a dozen calls the night before to follow up on Lindy's intuition that somewhere, someone on the Governor's staff would be an unwilling volunteer for drug testing and might just be protesting about yesterday's announcement.

But they had struck out on each call. There was simply nothing on the grapevine, so Dan had gone back to his coffee and resumed a project that was already nearing deadline.

"My Chinese grandmother always said, 'When true knowledge flows, then knowledge and action advance side by side.' So far we haven't had much advance in either category. Maybe your insight of last evening wasn't very true."

"Dan, your problem is that you make those sayings of your Chinese grandmother mean exactly what you want them to mean." Lindy reached for a scrap of paper and began lettering the saying on the blank side with a felt-tip calligraphy pen. It was bound for her philosopher's gallery.

Dan's head slowly rose above the wall divider, his face plastered with a broad grin. "But that's the way my

Chinese grandmother used them. They're still great, aren't they?" He reached out his hand, a yellow pushpin between two fingers, waiting impishly for Lindy to finish lettering the saying. At 6 feet 4 inches tall—another endowment from his Anglo ancestors—he could make the reach easily.

And he knew Lindy couldn't resist adding this one to the collection.

She half stood, just enough to place the card in Dan's hand, and retorted, "Yes, but that's all the more reason to accord them the meaning that was intended."

Dan's phone rang as Lindy leaned back in her chair, rolling her instincts around in her mind like a squirrel rolls a nut over and over in its little paws, looking at it from every side, trying to decide where she should sink her teeth next.

Dan's hand appeared above the wall divider waving an old newspaper furiously to get her attention. Something good was happening.

Lindy jumped up, scurried into Dan's cubicle, and dropped into the chair next to his desk. Her partner punctuated the long conversation with affirmative grunts and little questions. The caller was doing a lot of talking and Dan was doing a lot of note-taking. "Yeah . . . Who's Gonzalez? . . . A blue Lincoln . . . Twelve-seventy-seven North Capitol . . . I got it . . . They saw who? . . . Did they find the woman? . . . Naw! Really? . . . Can't you tell me more? . . . Okay! I'm not pushing . . . Thanks a million . . . Yeah, I'm buying Friday. See you then." He hung up the phone and went right back to his notepad as if Lindy wasn't there.

She smacked his arm. "I hate it when you do this. Who was it and what did he say?"

"Action and knowledge may be flowing after all."

"What do you mean?"

"Well, that was Bill Smith, my buddy at State Police central dispatch. He was one of my calls yesterday afternoon, works the evening shift. It seems that after I called, fairly late in the afternoon, an unusual order came from on high."

"Unusual?"

"Yeah. An APB for a 10-16 on the female driver of a late model Lincoln, navy blue."

"What's a 10-16?"

"An order to pick up someone."

Lindy's face stated the question before she asked it. "What's so unusual about that?"

"That's not so unusual except that at the same time he was to issue an order for a car to stakeout 1277 North Capitol."

"So?"

"They were to watch the building to be sure the woman in the Lincoln didn't go *in*. Evidently the woman posed some threat to someone who lives in the building. Anyway, the jakes in the black and white had no idea *who* might be in danger and they had no idea *who* the Lincoln lady was or even what she looked like."

"Couldn't they just run the plates through DMV and get a name for this person, or at least some idea what kind of person they were looking for?"

"No plate number. Just a physical description. Smitty even mentioned that."

Lindy's exasperation was beginning to show. "What does this have to do with my hunch?"

"Maybe nothing."

Lindy rolled her eyes.

"Wait, I'm not finished yet. He said that Gonzalez called back thirty minutes later with an order for another car to watch the offices of the *News* for the same lady."

"Our offices?"

"The very same."

"That *must* mean that someone wanted to talk to the press."

"Or," Dan interjected, "someone *thought* someone wanted to talk to the press."

"Did we have any night visitors?"

"I have no idea, but I intend to find out."

"What else did your friend say?"

"What makes it so tantalizing is what my friend told me what his supervisor *didn't* say."

"What do you mean?"

Dan was growing more animated. When he got excited he used his hands more, punctuating sentences and acting out drama in the air.

"He said the order came straight from Gonzalez, the chief duty officer and the guy who's also standing in for Chief Brown while he's away for some conference. The order came through a call from Gonzalez who was in his *office* at the time—not on the duty floor or in the street. His *office!*

"And Smitty said that there was something funny about the whole deal, like Gonzalez knew who the woman was or that she was some muckity-muck from a family way up the pecking order." Dan finished with his hand above his head measuring the appropriate place on the imaginary pecking order he had laid out for Lindy.

She just leaned back in the chair and crossed her arms. "I have no idea what relationship this has to the possibility of someone on the Governor's staff complaining about drug testing."

Dan, too, leaned back and grinned like Alice's Cheshire cat. He hadn't played all his cards. "When the jakes on stakeout called in at nine, they gave the usual grumble about no action and then made an off-the-cuff comment that made Smitty's ears perk up."

"What comment?"

"They said that the only action all evening was a certain black woman they both knew who appeared at the door to the condo. 1277 is one of the posh condominiums on North Capitol. She was dressed to kill—about brought the officers through the windshield. She went down the block, bought a bag at the liquor store, and was back in the building inside of five minutes.

"The squawk on the radio was the officers on stakeout expressing how very much they would like to help Ms. Minnis empty the contents of the little brown bag."

"Minnis?" Lindy said, the features of her face sharpening as she focused on trying to place the name. "That's familiar."

"It was to me, too. She's the special events coordinator for the Governor. She serves on his campaign committee *and* in his administration."

"That's why the state police guys would recognize her."

"Sure, they're constantly being hit on to come to receptions or to volunteer to do stuff."

"But Dan, what does a cop seeing her have to do with what we're working on?"

"One more item. Just before Smitty went off duty, they found the Lincoln. It's registered to Franklin Justice."

Lindy was dumbfounded. "The Governor?"

Dan savored the moment. He loved to drop bombshells on Lindy. She amazed him so often with her keen insight and her uncanny intuition that honestly, she intimidated him. He felt that when he came across a piece of info that surprised her as much as her hunches sometimes surprised him, it meant that he was contributing a little more equally to their team effort.

"So the woman in the Lincoln," Lindy asked, still trying to make this peg fit, "was it Mrs. Justice?"

"They don't know. Picked up the car on the west side. Some low-life was driving it. He'd removed the plates and hung a piece of cardboard in the back window with *Lost Tags* written on it. Claimed that the car belonged to his uncle until DMV confirmed the registration. When the jerk found out he had stolen the Governor's car, he cracked and admitted that he had lifted it from a parking garage downtown—the eleven hundred block of, get this, *North Capitol.*"

"Eleven hundred? That's—"

"—in the right neighborhood! The lady gets the prize."

"Dan, did the stakeout team see anyone else they recognized? I mean, what's the outcome there?"

"Smitty either didn't know or wasn't telling. I got as much as I could this trip to the well."

"But what's the connection?"

"I have no idea! Maybe there isn't any, but it has all the makings of a heckuva good story on its own—and it's ours for the writing. I think we should talk to Tomass and get a go-ahead to work on this."

Lindy beamed. She mentally filed away her interest in the maybe-story about the Governor's drug initiative and embraced the very real story that had laid itself on their doorstep. She rose from the old metal chair and said, "Look, skip Tomass for right now. We need a little more to go on before we approach him with this. There's nothing worse than a male-menopausal editor taking his hormones out on us because of *his* deadlines." She picked up her briefcase and set it on the chair. "I say our first move is to have a talk with Ms. Minnis."

Dan looked at her skeptically. "Maybe you're right," he said, with a good measure of hesitancy in his voice. "Okay, we bypass the boss for the time being. You find Annie Minnis. I'm going to see what I can find out about the Lincoln lady."

Dan stood up from his desk and lifted an open right hand, waiting for a high-five from his partner.

Lindy smiled, raised her right hand and met Dan's with a hearty smack as she left his cubicle, excited. "Later."

▼ ▼ ▼ ▼

By break-time on Wednesday morning, the three teams of state police detectives assigned to Gonzalez's high-priority case had been on the job for almost twenty-seven hours—a regular shift, an emergency all-nighter, and morning cleanup. One pair discussed what sort of a bribe they'd have to pay for the E.R. docs at Memorial Hospital to set them up with an I.V. drip of coffee, or better yet, straight caffeine.

Two more cabbies and then back to their posts for brief reports. And then to bed.

A fiftyish man with a scraggly brown cap on his head entered the small room at the cab company's main office which the detectives were using for their interviews. "Thanks for taking time to drive by this morning, Mr. Jones," the lieutenant said to the hack in a tired but pleasant voice.

"No problem."

"We're trying to locate a missing person. Think she may have hired a cab last night, probably between six and eight. A white female, mid-forties, average height and weight, dark slacks and a light sweater, may or may not have been wearing an overcoat."

"You got a picture?"

"Sorry, no photo."

The lead cop began to brief the taxi driver . . . .

▼ ▼ ▼ ▼

A surge of adrenalin coursed through the cabbie's system as the trooper gave a perfect description of the crazy lady from the previous evening. It left the tips of his ears burning as the trooper finished and waited for his reply.

Jones looked up toward the ceiling, eyes first, his head following obediently. It may have appeared to the troopers that he was searching his memory banks, but there was no memory searching necessary for someone he remembered so clearly. He was looking up at the ceiling to decide what he should do.

The night before, after he came out of McDonald's and got back in his cab, the lady had given him an address in a Hispanic neighborhood. When he pulled up in front of a small, fairly well-kept apartment building, she paid him the fare, then pulled out two twenties and a ten. As she extended them to him, she said, "You never saw me tonight. Pick me up here in forty-eight hours and there'll be another fifty dollars for you. Thursday at seven. I'll be ready."

But what to do now? She hadn't seemed like a criminal—a little odd, but no criminal. And a lady as nice as this one could make up her own mind as to whether she wanted to be missing or not. Fifty dollars was the biggest tip he'd ever gotten.

The cabbie peeled his eyes off the ceiling and looked at the exhausted lieutenant who was patiently waiting for a reply. "No, sir. I didn't pick up anyone like that last night."

"You sure?" the cop asked, plainly frustrated that the grinding routine was not more productive.

"Yup," Jones said.

"Okay. Thanks for your time." The lieutenant looked down and scribbled something on the clipboard in front of him.

The cabbie got up and headed for the door.

"Send the other guy in, will you?" called the other trooper, who had said nothing up to that point.

Jones didn't look around, but gave a single wave of acknowledgment as he passed through the open door into the hall. He looked at his co-worker, who was slouched in a dirty leather chair smoking a cigarette and motioned toward the door. "Next," he said casually, and headed down the hall toward the main entrance and his waiting cab.

His ears had stopped burning.

▼ ▼ ▼ 6 ▼ ▼ ▼

Annie Minnis made the best of her unexpected day off. She made two calls just before 8 a.m., one to her office to let them know she wouldn't be in and another to the Governor's secretary. "No, he needn't return the call, Rosemary. I won't be in the office today. Just tell him that I have an important lunch meeting and that I'll need his input."

The first time she had left that message, years ago, Franklin had called her, perplexed. "I thought we were getting together today. I didn't realize you'd scheduled a business meeting."

In her most titillating voice, Annie had replied, "We are getting together today, silly. You're my important lunch meeting and I'm expecting input from you on some very nonbusiness matters." Her unintended double entendre had pleased her.

From that time on, that simple message had become part of their lovers' code. She knew that this morning, Franklin would know exactly what she meant. And this morning, she was more than a little anxious to find out from him exactly what had happened the previous evening that had her behind locked doors today.

After her calls, she fluffed and stacked three pillows underneath her head, pulled the flannel sheets and warm comforter up under her arms, and spent the next hour and a half in the latest Danielle Steele.

Just after nine-thirty, she rose and changed the bed. Flannel sheets were her favorite, but Franklin loved silk, so she dutifully redressed the bed in red silk with no comforter or spread. "Give the man what he wants," she said to the bed, admiring the tightly made corners. "He's paying the bills."

She showered and dressed in clean white sweats. In the kitchen she put on a pot of cold water for pasta and then chopped vegetables for a simple sauce. She'd boil the fettucini when they were ready. In the meantime the flavors in the sauce would be blending. Neither of them liked heavy lunches.

Annie expected the Governor at around eleven-thirty, their usual time, so just after eleven she selected an appropriate ensemble from her closet and went into her private bath to change.

Franklin loved black nightgowns on her because "it's the only color that brings out the incredible warmth of your skin."

Annie grew up on the streets during the time when the "Black Is Beautiful" consciousness was sweeping the African-American community. She didn't like it. As far as she could tell, the whole movement was just a reaction to the blacks of the sixties who wished they were white.

She thought that if black really was so beautiful, it wouldn't be the activists who'd make such a big deal out of it. People would just see. As far as she was concerned it was just one more example of people with an ax to grind. She didn't particularly like being black. But she didn't really want to be white.

To Annie Minnis, one skin color was no more beautiful than any other. She just wanted to dissociate herself from her past in every possible way.

But when Governor Franklin Justice kissed her ebony skin and saw real beauty in it, not the horrors of the street, it made her feel wonderful—and secretly, very proud that she was black.

She slipped into the almost-transparent negligee she had chosen, then pulled on silk stockings, the kind that require a garter—black, of course. She brushed her hair once more, then stood and looked long and admiringly into the vanity mirror at her body. With the sassiest of her old street accent she said to the woman in the mirror, "God only gave you one break in life, girl . . . but was it a *fine* one!"

Then Annie sat back down and pulled out her hand mirror, placing it face up on the vanity. She opened a lower drawer, took out the four or five items strewn across the bottom, and set them aside. She pulled the drawer out further, almost all the way, reached to the back of the drawer and pushed gently down on its wood bottom. The bottom panel gave way to her pressure and the front part raised up.

Annie lifted out the leather clutch, then pushed sideways on the false bottom of the drawer to skew it enough that it would remain raised. She opened the clutch's mouth and pulled out a small plastic square filled with white powder, a single-edged razor blade, and a one-hundred-dollar bill.

Private time with Franklin always was wonderful, but private time with Franklin while she was flying was beyond words.

The cocaine did have its side effects. Sometimes she didn't even want to see food, sometimes it was like she had a bad case of PMS, sometimes like she hadn't slept for days. She'd also had trouble with her nasal passages—"do-er's disease" is what she called it.

But when that puff of white dust rose off that mirror to meet her troubled nostrils, all concern for side effects was swept away.

Annie rolled the hundred-dollar bill and expertly sucked in some of the white powder.

She lifted her head, eyes closed, and breathed deeply, savoring the smell and the taste that soon would bring a high upon her. She lay her head all the way back and moved it from side to side as if she were trying to work stiffness out of her neck. Then she raised her head, opened her eyes, and met her own gaze from the vanity mirror with a knowing look.

The snow was beginning to fall.

At that moment, the doorbell rang. Franklin was early. She jumped up, closed the drawer with one foot and tucked the mirror—razor blade, bill, and all—under the pile of cosmetics she had taken from the drawer.

She took a long, black, transparent gown from its waiting hanger and slipped into it as she took one last look at the mirror.

"You are what he wants, girl!" she said to her reflection, and hurried off to answer the door.

▼ ▼ ▼ ▼

"I'm sorry. Ms. Minnis is not in," the receptionist said.

"Oh, I see," Lindy said. She had intended all morning to call to get an appointment with the Governor's special events coordinator, but Paul Tomass, her managing editor, had interrupted her with a rush project. She had pleaded that she was on a hot story and that this project would be a poor use of her time, but when she hesitated to give her editor details, he insisted.

It had eaten up the bulk of her morning.

Now it was eleven-twenty. She knew when she dialed the phone that if Minnis had a lunch appointment she'd be long gone by now. She had expected the secretary's response.

"When do you expect her this afternoon?"

"Ms. Minnis is out of the office all day today."

"Do you expect her back in town tomorrow?" Lindy knew better than to ask where she was. Secretaries get very defensive when you ask direct questions. But it always amused Lindy that if she asked a question that added something the secretary hadn't said, the secretary often would volunteer the very information that she would have hidden if asked directly.

Lindy had pried into people's schedules before. In fact, she had pried into more than just their schedules.

"Ms. Minnis is not out of town. She's home sick today and yes, we do expect her tomorrow. Would you like to leave a message?"

"Yes. Tell Ms. Minnis that Lindy Blakely of the *News* called. I'm researching a story and I'd like very much to interview her. I'll call back tomorrow."

"Yes, ma'am. I'll give her the message."

A look of determination pursed Lindy's face as she hung up the phone. How would she get in touch with Minnis now? This was too hot to wait till tomorrow. She knew it was useless to try the phone book. None of the Governor's staff would carry a listed number. She could fish around the State House or try to pull a few strings, but if there was something hot going on with the Governor, her questioning might pull on the strings attached to bells and whistles. She didn't want attention.

Just information.

She stewed on the problem, then with a flash of insight, she remembered. Dan! He wrote down the address! Lindy jumped up and ran into the neighboring cubicle. Like radar, her eyes scanned the desk for the notepad and locked on like an F-14's targeting system.

The top page was blank. Dan had taken it with him.

Just like a man, she thought as she picked up the pad along with a pencil. Thinks only of himself. Lindy turned the pencil sideways and made broad strokes with the side of the lead until the page was gray from her marking.

The address stood out clearly along with his other notes. Just like a man, she said to herself again, smiling. Beats the poor paper to death while he writes.

Lindy tore the page from the pad, went back to her cubicle to grab her coat, and headed for the street. Twelve-seventy-seven North Capitol was only five blocks away.

"Blakely," she heard behind her as she passed through Editorial with its rows of desks with no wall dividers.

She recognized the voice but ignored it. If she pretended she didn't hear, maybe he would go away.

"Blakely!" The voice was much louder this time.

She stopped and looked straight ahead, shoulders sagging.

It was Paul Tomass. "There's not enough meat in this story to make hamburger, Blakely," he said as he marched out of his corner office toward her with a handful of paper. "I want this piece rewritten by two-thirty. This is important and I am on a deadline!"

By this time he was standing directly behind her, talking to the back of her head. She turned around resignedly and with an intentionally disinterested look, held her hand out to take the printout.

"No way, José," Tomass said. "I'll keep this. Send the rewrite to my terminal ASAP. I want it on my screen by two-thirty—and don't screw around this time. This is important!"

Shoulders still drooping, Lindy tramped back to her cubicle, her slave pit. "I'll have to get back to you after two-thirty, Ms. Minnis," she said to her notebook as she flipped a switch and brought her computer screen to life.

▼ ▼ ▼ ▼

Annie caught herself just before she grasped the doorknob. She pulled her hand back and rearranged the black gown on her shoulders until it felt perfect.

Then she opened the door.

Franklin Justice pushed on the front of the door before she had it all the way open and charged into the living room of the luxuriously furnished apartment like a beleaguered bull hounded by a band of matadors. "It's deep this time, Annie," he said, as he dropped his light overcoat and headed for the wet bar, not even looking her way. He picked up the tongs and as he spoke, dropped two ice cubes into one of the waiting glasses. "For the first time in my career, I have a problem." He selected a tall bottle of single malt scotch. "A *real* problem." He unscrewed the top and poured the golden liquid over the two ice cubes. "A major problem." He raised the glass toward his lips.

Annie crossed the room as he spoke. She put her left arm around his waist, pressed herself full length into his side, and raised her hand to his arm to stop the glass before it reached his mouth.

"Here. I have a better way." She took the glass and set it back on the bar, moved in front of him, then wrapped his arms around her waist. She picked up the glass again and held it between them.

Annie reached into the glass and pulled out one of the ice cubes. She opened her mouth slightly and, looking into his eyes, rubbed the ice on her lips, first on the bottom one, then the top, until the melted crystal shone like clear lipstick. Then she dipped two fingers into the whiskey and coated her lips again. A bit of the liquid trickled down the inside of her lip and into her mouth.

"Scotch and water, sir. Just the way you like it."

Franklin brought his hands together on the small of Annie's back and drew her very close as he bent his head and kissed her.

Just as Annie was losing herself in the warmth of the embrace, Franklin pulled back. "You make it difficult for a man to concentrate on his problems."

Annie was undaunted. "Remember our pact," she whispered. "This will never be a place for problems."

Franklin pulled completely away this time. He grabbed the glass from her hands, downed the scotch in one burning swallow, and strode into her bedroom.

"Franklin?" Annie called after him in a wounded tone.

In just a few seconds he reappeared holding a lush, white turkish-towel robe. He draped it over her shoulders, then looked longingly at her elegant ebony body as he drew the curtain of cotton around her. "I have a problem, Annie," he said softly, apologetically. "A problem that I need all my faculties to deal with. And dressed like that, you are more potent than the whiskey."

He drew her close again and this time kissed her forehead.

Then he put both hands on her left forearm and led her to an overstuffed chair.

He didn't seat himself. Instead, he paced silently.

Annie sat without speaking for what seemed like a very long time as she watched her lover. It was obvious that he was trying to find words.

She felt a little fear along with a yearning to help him. Finally, when she could wait no longer, she broke the silence. "Franklin, what is it? Tell me. You're frightening me."

Franklin stopped pacing. He turned slowly toward her. "Annie, I have a problem—a major problem. In fact, I may have two problems and both involve you."

This did frighten Annie. In ten years she'd never seen Franklin this way. In making his big push on drugs as a public policy, had he discovered her secret? Or was it Evelyn, that neurotic waste of a woman?

She was frightened, but with the cocaine lifting her above the fray, she experienced the fear in a different way—she felt the fear more intensely but it wasn't as threatening. In fact, there was even a weird hint of pleasure in it.

"I'll help you solve your problem if I can, darling."

Franklin crossed to her and knelt by the chair, taking her hand in his.

"I was hoping you'd say that." He gave her a long, appreciative look, then stood and resumed his pacing.

"It's Evelyn. She's suspected for years that I've been involved with someone, but she never has pursued it. Been afraid, I guess. But recently she hired an investigator, and he's found us out. I don't know. Maybe she's suspected us all along.

"Anyway, when I stopped at home on the way here last night, I found her standing in the kitchen in a trance of some kind. She was holding a knife in front of her face. When I took the knife from her, she started shaking. I picked her up to carry her to a sofa and she went into convulsions, then fainted. When she woke up, she overheard me calling you and it all came out."

"What do you mean?" Annie said, the fingers of fear gripping tighter at her chest.

"I mean she exploded in anger. I've never seen her that way. She *clawed* at me, Annie. She screamed and threatened that if I didn't cut off my relationship to you within twenty-four hours, she'd expose us."

With that, the hand of fear wrapped itself around her insides and yanked her back to earth. She felt sobered— roughly, rudely, cruelly sobered. There was no distance between her and reality now. And for the first time since the earliest days of their relationship when she didn't really trust him, she felt her wall rising to stand between her and her lover as a protective barrier.

What a fool she'd been, to allow herself to feel secure in a relationship in which she was the only expendable party. Fool, she thought. Fool! Doesn't it always come to this? When push comes to shove, won't a man always go back crying to his mommy?

She didn't speak a word. She just stared at the empty space in front of her as if that emptiness would be filling her soon.

Franklin rushed to her and knelt in front of her. "Annie, I know how you feel."

Annie's stare changed from empty to icy as she turned her eyes on his.

"I do. I really do. You are the world to me."

Annie continued to drill her eyes into his.

Franklin stood again and composed himself. He stood over her and in a most serious tone pronounced, as if at a press conference, "I really do know how you feel, Annie. And I want you to know that no matter what Evelyn says, I'll never leave you."

Then he turned and resumed his pacing. "I told you I have a problem. That's only part of it. I have to finish telling you before I can tell you what I think we can do about it."

Annie looked back into her empty space and struggled to breathe as the fear maintained its oppressive grip on her insides. Her wall continued to rise.

"After Evelyn's outburst, I had to go downstairs to let the doctor in. By the time we got back to Evelyn's room, she was gone. The crazy shrew actually left through the back door of the house. I saw her driving off."

He turned back to Annie. "Baby, I have no idea where she went. I've had the state police on this since last night and they've come up blank. I think that she's gotten so desperate since her suicide attempt, and she was such a mess last night, that she just might do something to ruin me—us!

"I need your help."

Annie didn't look at him this time. She just concentrated on relaxing inside, on trying to breathe more deeply.

"Look," Franklin pleaded. "This doesn't mean an end to our relationship." He lifted an ornate wooden chair from its place beside an elegant table and set it down directly in front of Annie, just in the path of her empty gaze. "I have a plan, but I need your full cooperation."

Now he spoke excitedly. "Evelyn is sure to contact me some way in the next few hours. I'm going to tell her that you and I have broken off our relationship. I think if I can convince her of that, she will return home. At that point I can get her sedated and back in treatment. Then I think it's just a technical matter to have her committed to an institution, maybe right after the election. She's been depressive for years, she was suicidal late last year, and now she's run away. I believe that with this history I can have her put away for some time, maybe even for a long time. Then you and I can continue where we left off."

He had stopped directly in front of Annie, but she still wasn't looking at him. She couldn't see him now for the wall. And the cocaine.

"Annie, will you help me? I'm talking about cutting contact for just a few weeks—a month or two tops—until I'm sure."

She didn't respond.

He dropped out of the wooden chair and onto his knees in front of her. He buried his chest in her knees, took both her hands in one of his and with the other, tenderly touched her cheek, directing her face toward his. "Annie."

This time she looked.

"Will you help me?"

She heard him, but he was a long way away. Or maybe he was on the other side of the wall and it only sounded like he was a long way off. But she did hear him. With a blurred, distressed gaze, she looked at him and painfully shook her head. "Yes," she said in a rasping whisper, straining. "I'll help you."

In an obvious flood of relief, Franklin Justice lay across her lap and drew close to her. "I knew I could count on you." He squeezed her again, raised slightly to give her a peck on the lips, then stood and began to pace again.

He blabbered on about how this might be the best thing that ever happened—Evelyn out of the way and maybe even some public sympathy for him.

He talked on and on, but Annie didn't hear him. He was too far away again. The wall was now all the way up. She was breathing easier and she felt more secure, but behind the wall she was starting to feel a pain and sorrow that she hadn't felt for a very long time.

A loss.

Like somebody was dying.

Or going to die.

Her heart began to shed tears, but her eyes just held on fast to the emptiness.

Until Franklin mentioned Bruhof Distributors.

She shook herself and looked at him again. "I'm sorry. Would you mind repeating that?"

"Oh, no, Baby. Not at all. I know this whole thing has shaken you. And I wouldn't even bring this up if I didn't have to. But since we're not going to have contact for a while I just have to. Barney insisted."

She could feel the fingers of fear tightening again, and it was harder to breathe.

"It's no big deal. At least I hope it's no big deal. Barney has uncovered a discrepancy in the campaign books. You've been buying expensive European gifts for our donors from a company that hasn't made the first dime in campaign contributions. He's afraid that if word gets out, some of our faithful supporters who are Bruhof's competitors might not be too happy."

Annie felt relief begin to loosen fear's grip on her.

"We just want to stop doing business with them. Will you find another source for your champagne and perfume, Babe?"

The relief was so welcome that she actually smiled, weakly. "Surely, darling. I'll be happy to."

The Governor's face erupted into a bright smile. "Wonderful! This all may work out better than we ever dreamed."

He picked up his overcoat and draped it over his arm as he approached her again. Again he took her hand and said with kindness, "Look, I know this is as bad for you as it is for me. Take a couple days off if you want. Take a week if you want it and get a change of scenery. Just remember, it won't last very long, then we'll be able to resume the life we love so much."

Annie looked at him over her wall and for the first time since she'd known him, felt a tinge of bitterness toward him as undiluted as the drops of whiskey that had accosted her tongue only minutes before. The life we love! she thought sardonically. She wanted to scream, *I love you, but I don't love the life of a high-priced whore.* Her sorrow seemed to fill the emptiness between her and her trusted wall. She felt swallowed by the realization that her people were right after all: White plantation "massah" or white gilt-tongue politician, powerful men would have their slaves.

She didn't say a word.

Exuberantly, like an excited child, Franklin prated on, "—and when you get back in the office, check in with Barney. I'll let him know that you won't deal with Bruhof anymore. But he's got a few questions for you about what might be irregularities."

This time Annie's voice was low and cold: "What do you mean?"

"Oh, he came by my office this morning—and yesterday—and had a few questions I couldn't answer."

"What questions?"

"Well, he said there's no paper trail. Nothing but unsubstantiated invoices. He's also worried because the amounts are always the same and they're for luxury items from Europe when Bruhof doesn't even do business in Europe. You know bean counters. Don't worry about it. I'm sure you'll iron it out. Just get by to see him when you come back in."

Fear's fingertips were cold.

Franklin leaned over and slipped his hand behind her head. He pulled her toward him so that their eyes were only inches apart. His voice was serious now. "This will all be over soon. Just remember, I love you." He leaned closer to give Annie a long and grateful kiss goodbye.

A knock at the door stopped him short.

▼ ▼ ▼ 7 ▼ ▼ ▼

Franklin always closed his eyes to kiss Annie, to allow his other senses to more fully enjoy the pleasure of her lips. But the knock at the door forced his eyes open in a flash.

He froze, lips almost touching Annie's. His facial features instantly transformed into a chiseled hardness of suspicion and defensiveness. "Who is that?" he whispered harshly through clenched teeth, his now-wide eyes drilling holes in hers for the answer.

She didn't speak. She just shook her head from side to side with a surprised look.

He relaxed slightly, then stood up and looked at the door. He looked again at Annie and said coldly, "Get rid of whoever it is!" It was his voice this time, not a whisper. It was low, quiet, and full of menacing authority.

Franklin turned and strode toward Annie's bedroom. He took the two steps up from the sunken living room in one stride and disappeared behind the door of her bedroom.

Annie sat still as she watched Franklin withdraw, and as she heard the door to her private bathroom close behind him. She was numb from the last few minutes with him and didn't really care, at least not the way he did, about who might be at the door.

So she sat.

Until the knock came at the door again, this time a bit louder.

She stood and gathered herself together inside the robe Franklin had draped around her, then walked purposefully toward the door, assuring herself with every step that she'd benefit from this mess in the long run.

Annie peered into the security peephole and to her surprise, saw a co-worker from the state office with a large manila envelope under his arm. It was Larry Fredricks, a computer geek who did troubleshooting on the administration's mainframe. She had seen him around. He'd even tinkered on the hardware in her office.

But what was he doing here?

Annie suddenly became self-conscious that she was supposed to be home sick, not home to play around with her lover. She let herself feel the stress and the sadness of the last few minutes with Franklin and she actually became crestfallen. She began to look like she wasn't well.

Then she opened the door.

"Larry?"

"Hi, Ms. Minnis."

"What are you doing here?"

"Would it be all right for me to come in?"

"Well, not really. I'm not feeling well. What are you doing here?"

"I want a piece of the action."

A look of surprise dispelled the look of sickness on her face. Annie was truly perplexed and it showed. "What do you mean?"

"Come now, Ms. Minnis. We're both adults and at least one of us is not stupid." He spoke with a hick accent of some kind, colored by an irritating nasal mewl in his voice—cheap and mercenary. He slipped around Annie and into the living room of her apartment.

She didn't close the door. She didn't move except to face him.

She could feel anger kindling. She hated it when men thought they could go wherever they wanted to go and do whatever they wanted with their insufferable arrogance. It was bad enough to have to tolerate that from Franklin on occasion, but she simply would not endure it from some office bum.

Annie also felt something else rising as the man surveyed her apartment. This unusual situation also was beginning to frighten her. She was glad Franklin was in the other room.

But there was something in the man's demeanor—an *I know something you don't and I'm going to use it on you* attitude. She'd seen that enough in her lifetime to recognize it. Franklin's comforting presence might also be a threat to their relationship, depending on what this jerk had on his mind.

Deal with him, girl, she thought to herself as she let her rising anger choke down the anxiety.

Her normally cordial demeanor chilled, and she spoke, issuing instructions as if he were in her office to repair her PC. "Larry, you've made your way into my apartment on a day I'm home sick. Now you'll tell me what you're here for and then you'll leave." Annie spoke as if she were accustomed to being obeyed by subordinates like him.

She was.

As Annie spoke, Larry took the envelope from under his arm and twittered with it as he looked around the apartment again, this time more casually. When she was finished he turned slowly to her and said, "Home sick, huh? I ought to try liquor and silk stockings when I take my next sick day."

A flash of indignation ran through Annie's body. She spoke very deliberately, "You will leave now or I will call security."

"Naw, I don't think you will. Not after I show you what's in my envelope." Larry walked to the bar and placed the envelope on the counter. He picked up the glass Franklin had used only minutes before and lifted it with a twinkle in his eye. "Do you mind if I help myself to some of your home remedy?" He poured himself a healthy portion of the fine scotch over the slowly melting ice still in the glass.

Annie pushed the door enough to close it most of the way, then stood in front of it, both hands gripping the door handle behind her back. She raised her head to indicate the distance between her and the geek in the same way she distanced herself from the brothers in The 15th Street Pub. But she didn't speak.

Fredricks downed the whiskey in two swallows instead of one and made a terrible face at the burning in his throat. "Whew! That's good stuff!" He set the glass back onto the counter and turned to her. "Nope," he said, slapping the envelope, "you won't want me to leave after I give you these. In fact, you'll probably ask me to stay and share the afternoon with you." He looked her up and down suggestively.

To Fredricks's great surprise, Annie, always the woman of action, marched straight to the bar, her long legs making quick strides. She snatched the envelope from the counter, ripped open one end and reached inside for the contents.

She was dumbstruck.

She held a handful of pictures, at least a dozen—of her! Inside The 15th Street Pub. Sitting or standing with the Frog. Accepting an expensive-looking leather clutch from the well-dressed, ugly, black man.

Rage welled up in Annie and she exploded. "You worm!" she screamed as she started pummeling his head with the handful of photos. "You miserable, stinking, slimy little worm. How dare you come to my home and try to blackmail me!"

Fredricks covered his head with his hands and tried to back away from her, but Annie kept coming, hammering at his head and shoulders, photos fluttering from her grip.

Finally Fredericks ducked low and backed toward the door, leaving Annie heaving for breath and struggling to contain her fury.

"*Annie, Annie,*" Fredricks taunted, obviously daunted but his manly swagger returning. "You think about it. Hear?" He punctuated the air by pointing to her with a macho jerk of his arm. "Think about it. If I don't get a piece of the action, little Miss Humpty Dumpty could just come tumbling down."

In one deep breath, Annie brought herself under control. She turned slowly, picked up the torn pictures, and with wrath burning her face, walked deliberately to within whispering distance from her accoster.

Fredricks squirmed, but continued. "What with the Governor announcing big plans for a drug program, not to mention an election just around the corner, it surely wouldn't do for any of his uppity staff to be usin', now would it?"

Annie's expression didn't change. She held the photos in front of her, as if to give them back to him, and drew as close as the photos allowed. She took a long, deep breath and pulled her tall body fully erect, now standing so that her eyes were just higher than his.

Very slowly she said, "You listen to me. You take these pictures, and if you know what's good for you, you burn them and forget you ever saw my face." The anger in her voice was rising. "I survived a drunken father. I survived growing up on the streets in a neighborhood you wouldn't even show your face in. I survived the snakes in white society. If you think some pathetic white boy like you can frighten me, you're even sorrier than you look."

She was swelling with indignation now, but was beginning to relish it because it was obviously having its effect. "If you so much as whisper a threat to me again, if you even *look* at me like you recognize me, I'll have selected parts of your male anatomy removed and shipped to your sorry white mother with deepest regrets for her failure in life!"

Annie ended her diatribe in Fredricks's face with him shrinking backwards.

He stood silent for a moment in the face of this unexpected tigress, then straightened himself up, as if gathering his wits. "Yeah, I hear you. You're tough. Real tough." He shook his head up and down nervously as he spoke. "I know how tough cokeheads are. Let me tell you this, *Ms. Minnis.* You'll be sorry you ever talked to me that way. I'll soften you up some, then you'll be sorry, sorry enough to give me what I want."

With that, he turned and opened the half-closed door, pausing as he passed through it. "Hey—keep the pictures. I got plenty more where they came from."

He slammed the door to put an exclamation point on his last word.

The reverberations of the slam had barely died away when Annie's knees began to turn to jelly. She drew the pictures to her breast as if they were a life preserver and she was a drowning sailor. She closed her eyes and hung her head, breathing with difficulty from the stress of the encounter. Why is there cruelty in the world, and why did she always feel it?

As she turned to find a chair to drop into, she heard the rattle of the doorknob from her private bath. Franklin!

A surge of adrenalin hit her impotent limbs and she darted for the manila envelope and the pieces of torn photos littering the bar area. In only seconds, she had scooped up all but the scraps and had stuffed the torn pieces of photos and envelope under the cushion of a wingback chair she used for reading. She then stood nervously beside the chair, her hand on one wing for support, looking in the direction of the bedroom and her lover.

Franklin emerged from the door of the bedroom like a bear stepping out of his den after a winter of hibernation—slowly padding forward with a wrathful, hungry, glowering face. His shoulders seemed to have swollen in size, even though they were hunched angrily forward.

His light overcoat was still draped over his left arm, but he was no longer empty handed.

With both hands he gripped a mirror like a tray, a small ornate tray that bore a leather wallet, a curling hundred-dollar bill, and a single-edged razor dusted with a white powder.

Annie froze in horror. How could she have been so careless?

Franklin neither moved nor spoke. He simply stood still, an angry bear whose peace and security had been disturbed.

Finally Annie spoke, weakly. "Darling, I can explain." She dropped her hand from the chair and moved toward him.

"Stop!" he ordered.

She froze again. Franklin's voice lit up an inner screen with dark, vivid images that flashed across her consciousness as if projected on her inner wall. She saw a mother cowering in a corner with arms raised above her head to protect herself from the buckle of the belt with which her drunken husband was beating her because the meal she'd cooked didn't please him. She saw girls, sisters, hiding behind dirty beds in their rat-infested apartment, desperately searching for some way to protect themselves from the angry blows of brothers who wanted to make sure that the next time, the girls did exactly what they wanted. And she saw a lone girl, standing in terror before an uncle who was filled with heroin and hungry to take out his anger and appetite on a female.

She remembered.

Annie would *never* cower in fear before a man again.

The terror was dispelled, the void filled with resolve. She stood tall and didn't speak.

"You betrayed me," Franklin growled. "I trusted you and you betrayed me."

Annie neither spoke nor moved.

"What did you stuff under that cushion?"

Her first response was to lie. Instead, she didn't answer at all.

He gave her one long look, then flung the mirror across the room with his left hand as he continued to stare at her. It crashed into the glasses behind the bar. The leather clutch fell to the floor in front of the bar and the hundred-dollar bill dropped to the carpet just in front of him.

Then he walked deliberately to the chair and jerked out the stack of papers. With shoulders hunched over, he thumbed through the top three photographs, pausing a little longer on each. When he reached the fourth, he stared at it long, then slowly raised the hand filled with photos above his head and hurled the stack toward Annie with such force that they scattered all over the room.

Annie didn't move.

Slowly, in a very low, very angry voice, Franklin said, "I lifted you out of a dirt job and put you at the top of this city and then this state. I took you out of your nothing past and made you somebody. I gave you money, security, and love. I protected you from the wolves that wanted to chew you up and spit you out. I risked my career and my family life to keep you. I trusted you and you betrayed me." When he finished, his voice was no louder nor his words any faster than when he had begun.

Annie still didn't move. Instead, as he spoke she raised her head higher. She was peering over her wall now and she felt safer.

Franklin took the two steps down into the sunken living room and continued until he was about four feet from her, the appropriate distance for the task at hand. He kept his head down, his bushy eyebrows lowered till they interrupted her view of his eyes, but with a deep breath raised up to his full height.

"This is the way it will be," he continued, his voice as low and slow as before. "As of this moment, you are out of my life. You will not show your face again in any office associated with my administration. You will not call or in any other way have contact with any person in my administration. You will never, I repeat *never* attempt to have any communication with me again. You *will* pack your clothes and be out of this apartment by five o'clock."

And these final words were drawn out even further, deep pauses punctuating the angry tone: "Is that perfectly clear?"

As Franklin spoke, Annie's confidence stirred. For the first time she realized that for eight years she had lived a white version of her own black life as a child on the streets. She had more money, more status, more contacts, yes. But she still was a powerless woman dependent on the whims of a man for her security and her sense of worth.

How could she have been so blind?

Annie stared at him with the look of one serenely aware of the realities of the situation. She kept her head high and spoke as quietly and as slowly as Franklin had: "Who do you think you are?"

Franklin didn't respond. He just glared at her in anger, his head still lowered.

"You pompous oaf! You've been ordering people around so long you think it's your birthright!" Annie's head and shoulders began to move back and forth to punctuate her words. "*You* trusted *me*? You think I didn't trust you? And here you come parading around my

apartment like some white fool, asking me to trust you
again while you dispose of your neurotic wife so you can
get back to 'the life you love so much'! " She quoted his
words with disgust.

"And you say you risked something for me, boy? I not
only risked *everything* for you, I actually gave up most of
my life for you! I left my people, the job I earned on my
own merit, contact with friends, and a lot more just so I
could be at your beck and call!"

She was hot now, her voice rising to an occasional
shout. The anger and frustration of the day and of her life
fueled the flames. "And now you think that just because
I've done something that you don't approve of, you can
stand there in your self-righteous anger and make pro-
nouncements that will take away all the life I have left in
this world?"

Franklin didn't speak. He simply looked away from
her and toward the door and began to walk purposefully
toward it.

Annie closed on him, moving sideways to keep up with
him as she shouted into his ear. "You don't seem to
understand, *Go-vern-or!* Let me make myself clear." She
grabbed the cloth of his suit at the upper arm and pulled
hard, enough to make him stop near the door and turn
and look at her.

She leaned toward him and put her face in his face. "I
can ruin you!" She didn't flinch, but exhaled loudly
through flared nostrils as if to expunge all the fury from
her heart and lungs. "I will *not* leave my home! I will *not*
leave my job. I will *not* allow you to ruin my life!"

She could see in his eyes that Franklin was burning.
They'd never had an argument, not even harsh words, so
she had no idea what to expect.

He just burned, one powerful man staring down one
strong-willed woman.

Then he turned toward the door again, and without a word, opened it to leave.

Annie leapt at him and screamed in his ear as he walked through the door, "I can ruin you!"

Franklin swung round, grabbed the lapels of the turkish towel robe he'd wrapped around her only minutes before. "Don't play with fire, little girl," his voice was even lower, more deliberate, more filled with fury than before. "You *will* get burned."

With that he released his grip on the robe, turned, and stormed down the hall toward the elevator.

Annie watched him leave with an almost engulfing sensation of loss, but she shook off the smothering feeling by rallying herself.

"I will ruin you, Franklin Justice." Her shouts bounced off his back. "If you carry out your threat, I will ruin you! I'll be in my office at eight o'clock tomorrow morning and if things aren't as they should be, *I will ruin you!*"

She stood rocking on her toes as if to help her words find their mark as Franklin moved down the hallway and toward an open elevator.

The elevator door closed as he approached. With his back still toward Annie, he pressed the call button and waited. Annie's adrenalin was being spent rapidly and she could feel her anger-born confidence waning. Her anger was fast giving way to an anxious, disorienting trepidation that came straight from the realization that she was in a terrible mess.

The elevator bell rang and its doors opened lazily. Franklin stepped toward the waiting car, placed one hand on the rubber break to force the doors to stay open, then turned back and gave Annie one final glare.

Then he stepped into the elevator and disappeared.

When he was gone, she turned back into her apartment and staggered—anger, fear and emotional exhaustion crashing against her senses as reality once more became all too real. She leaned on the doorknob with one hand and grasped the end of the door with the other so she'd have some way to hold herself up.

"Oh, God," she moaned as she began to weep. Her head dropped back on her shoulders and she cried bitterly. Through her tears she whimpered, "Oh God of my poor dead mother. Don't You leave me alone, too!"

Annie felt broken as she used the last of her waning energy to close the door with both hands.

As she moved, forlorn, toward her bedroom, the phone rang.

▼ ▼ ▼ 8 ▼ ▼ ▼

Evelyn Justice sat on a worn but very clean couch in the well-ordered living room of Maria Arvizu, her arms draped over the couch's back as she stared out the picture window onto the street of a nuevo barrio, Midwest style.

The scene that presented itself was identical to one you'd see in any of a thousand other working-class neighborhoods in this country—older cars dotting the street; yards littered with toys and fallen tree limbs, enlivened by an occasional meandering dog; and row houses that looked like chorus lines of dance-hall girls who, tired of fighting the battle with time, had just stopped trying to make themselves look pretty anymore.

Even inside the houses there wasn't a great deal of difference between the Greenhills neighborhood now and when it had been predominantly Irish Catholic. There were still statues of the Virgin Mother adorning mantles in every other house and still the ever-present mementos of an old country left behind, but while the icons were more colorful than those of the Irish and the pace of speech a little quicker, things really hadn't changed much.

The only real difference between this neighborhood and any other of its kind in the Midwest was the people— the hair of those Evelyn watched moving about on the street was jet black and their skin glowed with the beautiful shade of umber that Hispanics share. This was a neighborhood past transition, completely reoccupied by the growing Spanish-speaking population of the city.

She had spent a good part of her day right there at that picture window. Evelyn had learned long ago in her battle with depression that if she could soak up the brightness of the sun, the conflict wouldn't be nearly as fierce.

And she was in a battle now, not just with the depression but with a gaggle of conflicting emotions that defied her attempts to bring them into some kind of order.

The one saving grace for Evelyn Justice was that she was *feeling* again. For the first time in years, she had a knot of anger deep inside. It pulled on all the strings inside her, took up all her inner slack, and made her tighter. It focused her emotional energy. She really *felt* the anger, felt it centered in that one place.

Feeling it felt good!

For years she had been so anesthetized by her depression that she couldn't really feel anything. Her pain had been spread evenly throughout every molecule in her body so that it seemed she was existing in a dense fog. She felt the pain, but it was vague, amorphous, diffused throughout her being so she could never define or conquer it.

It was the same with the drugs they gave her. They, too, spread throughout her body like a killing fog, numbing her pain just enough to enable her to function one more day but blurring the rest of her being.

As far as she was concerned, the drugs and the depression were cut from the same cloth. And both of them blanketed the real Evelyn Stark Justice.

Sitting in the light always helped. Sometimes when the glorious rays of the sun bathed her, she almost could imagine the heat burning off the fog and leaving her mind as clear as a country morning.

But it never burned off. Just day after day of the same clinging, smothering fog of depression.

But yesterday changed everything. Now she could *feel* something again, something specific, something sharp and well defined. She was angry, angry almost to the point of hatred. Her husband was a lying, cheating two-timer, and his mistress had been a friend, if you could use that word in the world of politics and government.

She had loved Franklin. She knew she hadn't been the kind of wife he needed. He was a high-powered, high-profile Type-A personality whose sex drive had always been consuming.

She knew she had never satisfied him sexually. Early in their marriage she could see it in his eyes after their intimacy, like a famished man looking up from an ill-spread table wondering when the main course would be served. Later in their marriage, as she began to fall into her depressive state, the ever-present reminders of her inadequacies drove her ever lower on the downward spiral as she became less and less his marriage partner.

Even more stabbing was the memory of the previous night's confrontation with the dark side of her soul.

She *was* a gentle person, a good person. A moral person. She never had done violence or harm to anyone. Even when she had slashed her own wrists it had been an act of mercy.

But she had become someone else when in her depraved hallucination of the previous evening, she had envisioned burying a knife in the throat of her husband's lover and felt triumph in the act.

Evelyn had thought about that dreadful dream on and off for most of the day. The sunshine that helped fight back the depression also kept calling back the horrid sense of blackness, of the pit she had fallen into in her dream. She knew what that place was. She knew why her own subconscious had delivered her into it.

She knew she deserved it.

But the one virulent idea that really gnawed at her sanity—the one idea she didn't want to allow the morning's sunshine to fall on for fear she'd see the truth—was the notion that the dreadful dream was not a dream at all.

Had she *actually* killed Annie Minnis, dreamed Franklin was talking to the woman on her bedroom phone, and then fled her husband in fear? Or had she hallucinated, *actually* awakened to hear the phone call, and then fled her husband in anger?

She just couldn't see clearly enough through her fog to know for sure. She thought the incident was just an ugly surfacing of her true self, but she wasn't sure, especially because of the clinging guilt.

For her sanity, she had to believe that it was all a dream, in spite of the guilt she felt. She had to believe that the anger, which was much stronger than the guilt, was the real motivator that had precipitated her actions of the night before.

When the cab driver had come back out of the McDonald's restaurant after fifteen minutes or so, she ordered the man to drive her to the Greenhills neighborhood and the home of Maria Arvizu.

She didn't know what she needed from Maria, or even what she wanted. Evelyn just knew that Maria would welcome her.

Maria had worked as a maid in the Governor's mansion for a dozen years, long before Evelyn and Franklin moved in. From the beginning of their stay in that great house, Maria had been gracious in a genuine way. Evelyn had seen herself only as a guest there. She believed that her hosts were the good people who, like Maria, spent most of their days, year after year, giving time and care to the historic residence and the people who lived there.

Maria served as Evelyn's personal maid, tending to her quarters and any special needs. When Evelyn lay in bed until one or two in the afternoon, wrestling with depression, Maria would often sit by her side. Sometimes Maria would hold Evelyn's hand. Sometimes she'd read from the Bible. Sometimes she would simply sit in reassuring silence to let Evelyn know that someone cared. The women's relationship was by no means close, but rather comfortable . . . trusting. It was the only such relationship Evelyn had.

It was to Maria—gentle, understanding Maria—that Evelyn had come when she fled her home the night before.

When the taxi had pulled up to Maria's address late in the evening, Evelyn paid the driver, tipped him fifty dollars and asked him to forget she'd been a passenger. "But remember this: Pick me up in two days, at exactly 4 p.m. If I'm not here, this should make it worth your while." She handed him another fifty. "If I am here, I'll take care of you again."

Then she got out of the cab and told him to wait until she was sure this was the right house. She'd wave him on.

When Maria answered the door and saw the mistress of the Governor's mansion standing on her porch, a surprised smile splashed across her face. "Mrs. Justice! What a surprise! Come in." She stepped back, opening the door wider to receive the First Lady.

Evelyn was brief and direct. "Maria, I need your help," she said as Maria closed the door on the departing taxi. After a quick but careful glance at the small hall and the living room it opened onto, Evelyn turned around to meet her squarely. "I can't explain tonight—I just can't. But I need your help. May I stay with you tonight and tomorrow night? I promise, tomorrow I will tell you everything."

With a look of mild confusion on her smiling face, Maria replied, "Certainly, Mrs. Justice. You stay as long as you want. You are welcome in my home."

The warmth of Maria's voice and the beauty of her rich Spanish accent flooded Evelyn Justice with gratitude. She stepped forward and embraced her maid. "Thank you, Maria. I knew I could come to you."

Maria expressed her concern with this surprise visit and its unknown motivation by fluttering about Evelyn to help her settle and to care for her needs. She wanted to get her bag, fix her something to eat, make her comfortable. But Evelyn would not be babied. She explained that there was no bag, she had no appetite, and that the most welcome thing Maria could do would be to allow Evelyn to sit with her in her cozy living room for a short time, then show her a bed where she could be alone to think and to rest. Maria did exactly that.

In the morning, quite uncharacteristically, Evelyn awoke early and met Maria in the kitchen where she was preparing a lunch to take with her to work. "Maria, you are a godsend. Thank you for your hospitality and your patience."

Maria just smiled and nodded her acknowledgment.

"I have one more favor to ask you, then I promise that this evening I'll explain everything."

"Yes, ma'am. How can I help?"

"I need for you to get a few of my things when you do the bedrooms and baths today. I need a change of clothes, some makeup."

Maria agreed to do what Evelyn asked, then seated her guest at the kitchen table and busied herself setting places for two.

"Maria," Evelyn said as she sat and watched her hostess, "you've been so kind to me. I just realized that I've never even asked about your family. Last night I didn't even consider that your family might not want a stranger in their home."

With a sober look, Maria turned back to the counter and the fruit she was slicing. "I am alone in this house," she said, without looking up.

"How long have you been in the United States?"

"For a long time. My husband was an official in the government of Anastazio Somoza in my home of Nicaragua. When he saw that the Sandinistas were growing in power, he arranged for our son, Jaime, to come to the U.S. for school"—she turned to Evelyn—"to keep him safe from the guerrillas." She pronounced the word "hair-REE-yahs," trying to use her hard-won English vocabulary but belying the fact that such words came from her reading and not her conversation.

Maria stopped and looked out the kitchen window. She stood motionless.

Evelyn didn't violate her solace. She realized that she had intruded, uninvited, into more than just Maria's small apartment. After several long moments, Maria looked back at the bananas and grapefruit and began cutting again. "My son's papers expired only three months before Somoza left and the government crumbled. He returned to Managua at the worst possible moment.

"My husband was taken prisoner as a collaborator with Somoza. I never saw him again, but I received news that he had been tortured and killed by the death squads.

"My son was forced to join the Sandinistas. He was nineteen years old. Because he had schooling, they put him in the *alphabetización* and sent him to the countryside." Again Maria turned to Evelyn, half-sliced banana in hand. This time there were tears in her eyes. "*Alphabetización* is the Sandinista program for teaching *campesinos* how to write and read." She turned back to the fruit. "In his fifth month in the countryside, Contras attacked the village where he worked. My son was shot as a Sandinista.

"Then I took my daughter and drove north across the border and into El Salvador. I hoped we could find safety, but when in mistake we drove toward a Contra camp, we were stopped and interrogated. I explained our trouble. Then the *Jefe* told a soldier to take me someplace while he questioned my daughter.

"The soldier took me away from the camp, into the edge of the jungle, and put me in a—it was like a jail of sticks." Maria looked up again from the fruit and assumed her statuesque pose. She began to speak again, but she didn't move a muscle besides her mouth as she gazed off through the kitchen window. "There I heard my daughter scream. I tried to get through the sticks, but they were tied tight. I begged the soldier to let me go to her. Finally she stopped screaming." Maria sighed deeply.

"But still they didn't let me out. The soldier checked the door to the fence once more, then turned and hurried back to the camp. I was alone.

"It was hours, then another soldier came to me. I was frightened for my dear Irenea. The soldier led me back to my car, not through the camp this time. I think it was so I would not see the other soldiers, or they would not see me.

"When I could see the car, I see that my Irenea was waiting so I ran ahead of the soldier. When I came to the car, my Irenea was lying against the door, uh . . . loose, like a rag. She was not awake. Her clothes were torn. She had cuts and dark places all over."

Maria's voice had been quivering. Now her previously unmoving shoulders slumped and began to move up and down as she struggled to control her emotions.

Evelyn stood up and crossed the room. She put her hand on Maria's shoulder. It helped steady her. Maria reached for a tissue, wiped her eyes, then took a deep breath and stood erect again.

"Maria, please don't feel that you have to tell me these things. I certainly didn't want to cause you pain."

Maria looked into Evelyn's eyes. "I'm sorry. On normal days, I don't talk of my grief. But yesterday, on the day off from my work, I feel my family and my great loss. It comes out to you because you ask. God sends you to me in the same way He makes me here for you. Your visit comes in time of need for both of us."

Evelyn reached across Maria's back and placed one hand on her far shoulder and her other hand on Maria's near shoulder, then squeezed. Without speaking, she released her hands and reached for the grapefruit knife, beckoning to Maria to move aside so she could take over the cutting.

As Evelyn slid the grapefruit knife around the citrus membranes to release their juicy pulp, Maria turned and leaned against the counter, this time looking into the kitchen and fingering the crumpled white tissue as she spoke. "When I looked back at the soldier who take me to my car, he shook his rifle to make me leave.

"I drove away. My dear child was not moving. Not too far I stop at a river and take her out to wash and refresh her. She opened her eyes, she was breathing, but my Irenea was not there. It was like someone reached inside and took my child out of her body, but left her body alive.

"Irenea began to shake before I got her again into the car, so I hurried to drive to a city for a doctor. But the car stopped as we drove and I could not get it to drive again. It was almost dark and we were in the Salvadoran jungle without food or water or shelter."

Maria paused for a long while before she spoke again. "My Irenea was dead before the sun could warm her again."

This time it was Evelyn who stopped and looked up and out of the kitchen window into nothingness. Tears filled her eyes. It was at that moment, that morning, when Evelyn's perpetual emotional fog began to clear. The first sharp pain she felt through her haze was Maria's rather than her own. It was the first time in her life Evelyn had entered into the suffering of someone other than herself.

She dropped the knife and wiped the grapefruit juice from her hands as she turned to watch Maria.

"I buried my dear child with my own hands in a lovely place in that jungle. That day a kind man in a truck filled with vegetables stopped and helped start my car again. He didn't know my Irenea.

"I drove to San Salvador and made for passage on an airplane to Puerto Rico and the home of my sister. She took me, but I could never stay with her. Her family left Nicaragua together long before the Sandinistas make their trouble.

"They were very happy in San Juan, but while I live there I feel only the loss of my husband and my children. So I called this city and spoke to the professor at the University where my Jaime studied."

"Your son came here to school?" Evelyn queried.

"Yes. I could not return to Managua near my dead husband or my dead son or my old life. And I could not go to the jungle to be near my dear child. So I thought to come here to be near where my son found escape from the trouble of our country that took us all."

Evelyn looked at her hostess with sorrow and respect. "Maria, I'm so sorry." Evelyn's expression of sympathy came from a deeper place than she'd been in touch with for a very long time.

"No. Don't be sorry for me. It is the place of people to suffer in this life, but it is the place of God to love and comfort. In my suffering I have come to know my God."

Evelyn wanted to say something else to Maria, to protest against the idea that there was any good to be had from such terrible loss. She wanted to rail against cruelty and misfortune and a God who would let it all happen.

But Evelyn simply pulled her lips taut and embraced Maria. She didn't say a word.

Not long after that tearful encounter, Maria gathered her things to catch the bus into the city and the Governor's mansion. She made sure that Evelyn knew where all the necessities were—food, towels, toiletries. Then she twittered between Evelyn and the door several times, torn between her sense of punctuality and her concern for Evelyn's well-being.

After Maria left, Evelyn alternated between her post at the picture window and a self-imposed stint at tidying up Maria's already spotless, if humble, home.

She wasn't just angry at Franklin now. She was angry at the injustice of life that Maria had suffered so painfully. She felt guilty for wasting years of her life sucking her babyfied thumb and complaining about stupid, selfish, almost mindless problems when her maid, the woman who cleaned her toilet, had endured almost unendurable anguish—and yet could still smile and find good in the suffering.

The depression was still there, just outside of her peripheral vision, like a shadow that vanishes when you turn to look at it directly. She knew it was still there, lurking.

But it was lifting. Her sky was beginning to clear.

She could hardly wait for Maria to return.

▼ ▼ ▼ ▼

"Yo, mama. Word!"

Annie winced with disgust as she recognized the Black Frog's voice on the other end of the phone line. The

revulsion she felt toward him as a person was exacerbated by his vulgar croaking voice and his idiotic use of
street slang. She hated him and the culture he represented. "We have no business to discuss," Annie said in
a curt tone, leaning her head slightly away from the
receiver in an involuntary reaction.

"Yo, we do have business! My people got a call from
your people this mornin' and my people aren't happy.
Your people don't want to pay for the last couple of
deliveries I made to you. My people want me to make a
house call to collect the rent. In person."

Annie froze. She knew these people. She knew exactly
what the Frog meant by "house calls."

She slammed down the phone and began to rock back
and forth, steadying herself with an iron grip on the
receiver. As her mind searched for her next step, she
could feel the panic rising.

Not enough time to call George Barnett. Wouldn't
matter anyway.

Not enough money in her accounts to cover the last two
deliveries, and they might want more.

No weapon in her apartment, nothing to protect her
from the Frog.

Oh, God, what do I do?

Annie broke through the ice of fear that was holding
her and rushed to her closet. Run. Get out. You can't be
here when he arrives.

As she reached for a coat, she realized she was still
wearing the lingerie. She looked down at herself with fear
and disgust, cursed herself, then ran into the bedroom
and stripped off the fragile clothing.

Without pausing to find underclothes, she pulled on
the sweatpants, then the sweatshirt she had lounged in
that morning. She swung around to her closet, stepped
into a pair of deck shoes, grabbed the purse from her
dresser, and ran back to the front door.

She grabbed the knob and swung the door open, ready to sprint down the hall to the elevator.

He was standing in the doorway, leaning on one arm against the doorpost, chewing on a cigar, a smart little cellular phone in his free hand. The Frog didn't say a word for a few moments, just allowed a sick smile to spread across his face.

He lowered his arm from the doorpost, flipped the cellular phone closed and dropped it into the inner pocket of his suit coat. He grasped his cigar with his now-free hand, chewed two or three more times, then drew it slowly from his mouth.

"Yo . . . mama . . . ," He spoke the words with machismo grunts, pausing between each word for effect. "I didn't even ring the doorbell. You and I must have some real chemistry."

Annie was so filled with terror that the only part of her that moved was the stinging acid rising in her throat. The Frog eased into the room with slow, swaggering steps, a hideous smirk disfiguring his already malformed face. Annie backed away.

He gripped the door with both hands behind his back and, with his eyes still bearing down on her, backed up slowly until the door came to rest gently in its frame.

▼ ▼ ▼ ▼

Lindy Blakely hated rewriting. It was a tedious chore. Every time the managing editor insisted on a rewrite, she felt the same frustration and resentment she had felt when, as a child, her mother had insisted she redo a drainer full of dishes that still had little specks on them.

There was always something more interesting and important to be done.

It was 2:20. She had grabbed a quick bite from the vending machine in the lunchroom, made a few calls to verify sources, conducted one brief interview, and rewritten the story. All that was left was running the spelling checker on the piece and sending it to her boss's terminal via E-mail.

The phone rang as she was punching in the commands to run the spelling checker program. She ignored the phone's bleating. Stupid phone sounds like a sick sheep, she thought as **PLEASE WAIT—CHECKING DOCU-MENT**** showed up in amber letters on the black screen. After the third bleat, she lifted the phone from its cradle. "Blakely," she said matter-of-factly, still watching the screen.

"This Blakely?" the voice said, sounding a bit frustrated and colored with a touch of nervousness. Or was it impatience?

Lindy rolled her eyes in a great upward sweeping arc. "Isn't that what I just said?" The only thing she hated more than rewriting was when people like this guy called her.

"I have a tip for you. You interested, or not?"

Lindy knew this voice. He'd called before. Her mental picture file had him pegged as thirtysomething, probably not married, definitely somebody's underling. She was usually right. She got enough of these calls. The receptionists thought that she was always up for either a good lead or a good laugh. But she hated these calls.

"Sure," she said resignedly. "What have you got?"

"Well, I don't know exactly."

A mama's boy. She had him nailed.

"Tell you what," she said. "You tell me what's on your mind and I'll ask you questions if I don't understand."

"Okay."

The message line on her screen lit up:

@TAG 1 = ** *7 UNMATCHED ITEMS—BEGIN RE-VIEW (Y/N)?* **

She pressed the *Y* key to bring the first misspelled or mismatched word to the screen.

"It's like this. I can't tell you who I am."

She'd heard that before from this guy.

"I can't tell you how I know what I know."

She'd heard that before, too.

"I just want someone to know, in case there's really a problem."

That was a new one.

@TAG 1 = *SYMPOSIYM* *** *(U)pdate, (S)kip, (E)dit.*

Lindy pressed the *E* key and fixed the word.

"You there?" the caller asked.

"Uh-huh," Lindy grunted, looking at the next word— *VERONICA.* She pressed *S* to skip it.

"There's this state employee who's been involved with the wrong crowd, if you know what I mean, and . . . "

"No, I don't know what you mean," Lindy said as *INTERNATIINAL* came up.

"You know what I mean!" he said with a little more enthusiasm, as if saying it louder would make the light come on for Lindy. "The wrong crowd. Druggies."

"Okay, go on." She pressed the *E* key and changed *INTERNATIINAL* to *INTERNATIONAL,* then pressed *ENTER.*

"Well, look. I saw her today. She skipped work. I dropped by her apartment and she was all out of sorts, like I had come at a very wrong time."

@TAG 1 = *FEEELING* *** *(U)pdate, (S)kip, (E)dit.*

Lindy hit the *E* again and fixed it. She was getting bored with this call. "Maybe she was having a lunch-time quickie with a friend and you came by at the wrong time."

"That's exactly what happened, and I know who it was with. You'd like to know, too. I hung around to see. Even got a picture."

Lindy looked up from the *MAMAGER* lighting up the screen. This might be interesting, even though she didn't like the idea of hearing it from someone who might be trailing this woman for who-knows-what reason. "Go on," she said nonchalantly, trying not to let her rising interest show through in her voice.

"Well, her lunch-time quickie was not with anyone from the wrong crowd. He was most definitely from the in-crowd."

Lindy rolled her eyes. How long had it been since she heard that phrase. This yo-yo probably had on a polyester leisure suit that his mother had pressed for him.

"Thing is, I knew about the druggies for a long time, but this one shocked me. I'm afraid she's in some deep trouble and she may not even know it."

"So what's the tip?" Lindy's voice was curt. She hoped to prod him a little to get him to the point.

"The tip?" he said excitedly, his voice rising either in mild or mock disbelief. "I just gave you the tip! Whadda you want?"

"You gave me nothing—as usual!" Lindy sounded like an old horsetrader. "All you gave me was that you're worried about a friend. You didn't give me who, what, when, where, why. I appreciate the call, but unless you can tell me more, at least a name, you'd have more luck with your priest or the cops."

"All right! Okay!" He paused, obviously trying to decide what to say and how to say it. "I'm going to give you a name and an address—*if* you promise you'll follow up and see if she's okay."

"I'm not a social worker."

"I know. That's not what I mean. I mean do some sniffing around and if she's in trouble . . . " he paused again. "Oh, just do the right thing, will ya?"

"I don't have a name yet."

"I'm gettin' there. Look, if you promise to do what you can to help, *if* you can help, I'll do something good for you."

Lindy was looking back to her screen again. She was losing interest. "No promises."

"That's good enough. You do what you can. I'll call you back later and if things are cool, I'll send you a picture of Juliet with her surprise Romeo."

She rolled her eyes again. A wimp trying to sound cool was one of the other things she hated more than rewrites. "I still don't have a name," Lindy said as she pressed the *S* key to skip the word *FIFATLY*. It was really no word at all, but she stuck it in every piece she wrote, a little joke. It stood for "Five Fat Ladies" and was stylishly-thin-Lindy's good-natured jab at the perpetual dieters in typesetting, none of whom really needed to diet.

"Annie Minnis. 1277 North Capitol. Apartment 1845," the geek said.

Lindy bolted upright in her chair, her mouth agape.

"I'll call you back," the man said.

The receiver clicked and the line went dead.

▼ ▼ ▼ 9 ▼ ▼ ▼

"Governor Justice's office. This is Rosemary."

"Hello, Rosemary, this is Mrs. Justice." Evelyn felt a bit awkward calling her husband's office. She felt sure that Franklin's pride would prevent him from telling his staff that his wife had run away, but she couldn't be sure.

She also felt awkward reiterating an ultimatum to Franklin, especially in the midst of her emotional roller coaster ride. But while sitting on Maria's couch, looking out on the procession of normal life in Greenhills, she had decided that she had to call. She had to let him know she was all right, and she had to let him know that she meant exactly what she had threatened the night before.

She wanted the illicit relationship halted immediately. Otherwise she'd never be able to rediscover the meaning of the word "normal."

"Oh, hello, Mrs. Justice. So nice to talk to you. How have you been?" They did know about her "problem" and her stay in the hospital.

"I'm doing just fine, Rosemary. Thank you for asking. I'm calling to speak to the Governor." Evelyn always referred to her husband formally. Earlier it had been "the mayor" and earlier still, simply "Mr. Justice." She was from the old school.

"I'm sorry, Mrs. Justice. The Governor is in a meeting right now. He, Chief Brown, and Mr. Barnett have been at it since he returned from lunch."

"That's fine, Rosemary. Please leave a message for me, would you?"

"Certainly."

"Tell the Governor that I called and that I will try him again late afternoon."

"Is there a number where he can reach you?"

"No. I'll call back."

"I'll see that he gets your message when he returns."

"Thank you, Rosemary."

▼ ▼ ▼ ▼

Lindy Blakely made the correction on the final word in her rewritten story, and then excitedly punched in the *SAVE* command. She sent the file to her boss's E-Mail box, then punched up the *TOSS* program so she could leave her partner a message.

TO:Dan Li-pong
RE:Hot lead

Got a call from an informant re: Minnis. Guy's called before. Lovelorn type, evidently shadowing her. He was by Minnis's apartment at noon and got some negative vibes. I'm on it. Apartment #1845. I'll call.

LB

The computer automatically added the date and time as the message was saved, and Lindy shut down her terminal. She might not be back today.

She grabbed her coat and headed for 1277 North Capitol for the second time that day. This time, though, she chose not to use the elevator because she'd have to walk through the open, dividerless area that comprised Editorial. It would be too easy for Tomass to see her and hold her up. Instead, she headed in the opposite direction and the little-used back stairs which would disgorge her onto a narrow alley.

Up the alley, west for a block-and-a-half to Capitol and north to 1277.

The building she entered had been an elegant hotel in earlier days, the Imperial. In the early eighties, some enterprising developers had banded together to convert the old Imperial to pricey condominiums.

The lobby reflected both the elegance of an earlier age and a style of its own. It had once been a cavernous room, the front desk guarding the front door with the expanse behind the desk forming a huge open area that functioned as lounge, meeting place, reception area, et al. The developers had built a beautiful glass and steel wall just behind the front desk to provide more security for the building and to define the boundaries of the restaurant which had been opened in the great vaulted room.

The developers had wanted to emphasize the exclusiveness of the new condo and the status its residents would enjoy, so they dropped the "Imperial" and named the new facility simply "1277 North Capitol." It had become *the* address in town.

Lindy knew how to get around security here. She marched right up to the sweeping semicircular desk and announced the name of a friend to a guard standing watch over a bank of TV screens. Actually, Lindy had interviewed a woman, a designer and socialite, on two occasions and knew that she lived at 1277—friend enough for her purposes today.

"I'm sorry, Ms. Zanetis is out. May I take a message?" The guard was very businesslike, but definitely handpicked for his looks. He was a high-class seatwarmer.

"No, thank you. I'll call later. Where is your ladies' room?" Lindy knew exactly where it was, but she wanted the guard's permission to enter the hall that led to the elevators. The restrooms were in the end of that hall, only twenty feet or so past the elevators.

Lindy thanked the guard and moved in the direction of the hall. She stopped at the windows of two of the posh lobby shops, looking at the displays to kill time, then entered a third shop, a hairstyling parlor, and quizzed the receptionist about a product that would make her perm a little fuller. After a five-minute discussion, Lindy thanked the woman and said she would think about which of the recommended products she would purchase next time she was in.

Then she headed for the ladies' restroom. Lindy went inside, made sure there was no one else in the facility, then stood with the door cracked so she could watch the bank of elevators. You had to have a key to use the lifts on this floor, so Lindy either would have to step on with a resident or enter as a resident was leaving. Coming back down would be no problem—no keys needed above the ground floor.

The old floor indicator mechanisms, the kind that had clock-like faces with hands that swept across the numbers of the floors, would be her clue as to when to move. She'd just have to wait and hope for someone coming or going in the middle of the afternoon.

Several minutes passed as she kept her vigil from the ladies' room door. No movement of the indicator's hands.

She didn't worry about another female dropping in from the lobby. Not at this time of day. But she was getting tired of leaning into the cocked door, so Lindy released her grip and let the door close to the "sssssssssssh" of the pneumatic arm. She stood up against the smooth coolness of the old marble wall tiles and laid her head back.

She closed her eyes, rotated her head to loosen the tensing neck muscles, then placed her hand back on the door handle.

The elevator bell dinged. Without looking, Lindy yanked the door open and stepped out into the hall. She walked briskly along the left side of the hallway.

An elderly couple made their way out of the now-open doors of the elevators, heading in the direction of the lobby. They didn't see Lindy as she ducked into the waiting lift even though she almost brushed against them in her desire to avoid the security cameras.

She pressed the worn black button marked *18* on the shining brass control panel and the doors closed her in. The old manual control lever was still there, a remnant of the days when each elevator had an operator to control it. Lindy stood up straight, grasped the lever in her left hand and turned to look at a group of imaginary passengers in the empty elevator. "Next stop, eighteenth floor," she said playfully. "Ladies' secrets, reporters' lifeblood. Watch your step, ple-ahs."

As the doors opened onto the eighteenth floor, she pressed the *OPEN* button so she could have enough time to read the signs indicating which direction she'd have to go to find 1845. She wanted to step into the hall purposefully and walk directly to the right apartment. The security cameras would give her away if she wandered, looking as if she didn't know where she was going.

1801 > 1825

1826 < 1850

Lindy stepped out and turned left.

Now to get in, she thought. It was 2:55. Surely any lunch-time suitor would be gone by now.

But so might Annie Minnis.

She walked up to the door marked *1845* and let her right hand fall onto the heavy wood in a fairly loud series of knocks.

No response. No voice, no sounds of movement. Nothing.

She knocked again.

Again, nothing.

Lindy turned around, leaned her back against the heavy door, and crossed her arms in her own version of "The Thinker."

After a moment's concentration, she realized that if someone was watching the security cameras, she'd be suspiciously conspicuous. "Then be innocently conspicuous, rookie," she whispered to herself as she pushed her back off the door and walked briskly down the hall, directly toward the camera scanning this end of the eighteenth floor hallway.

She stopped ten feet in front of the unblinking eye and began waving her arms. "Yoohoo. Mr. Guard."

Only a man would believe a woman could be this helpless and stupid, she thought as she addressed the camera, looking like she was expecting some kind of answer.

With a silly, innocent-as-can-be grin on her face, Lindy flipped open her leather notepad and wrote, *I NEED HELP!* in large letters on the topmost page. Hastily, she tore the page from the pad, dropped the binder, and waved the paper in front of the camera.

She stopped waving and held it as still as she could and as high as she could so the robot eye could read it. Like a schoolgirl, she peeked from behind it and looked to the camera as if again waiting for an acknowledgment.

Either this guy is going to be here any minute, or I've got time to figure out another way to get into that apartment, she thought.

Lindy had started the wave, hold, peek cycle for a third time when she heard the ding of the elevator behind her. She turned to see the hunk of a security guard step off the elevator and look in her direction. "You okay, ma'am? How did you get up here?"

This might not be so bad after all, she told herself as the tall young man strode toward her. "Well, yes. But, no," she said, raising as much mock dumb-blonde bewilderment as her professional cynicism and her dark brown hair would allow.

She picked up her notepad and moved toward him, wanting to intercept him in front of the door to Minnis's apartment.

"What seems to be the problem?" He'd moved faster than she and was further down the hall than she'd hoped for.

"Well, nothing," she said, then added in a singsong, "I hope." She slipped her arm into his, turned him, and walked toward 1845. "*You* know I came to see Cynthia Zanetis, and *I* know that she's not in." She looked at him and giggled, "You told me that downstairs."

The guard was extracting his arm from hers.

"Anyway, when I came out of the ladies room, I saw one of the elevators open and I thought to myself, 'Why not go up and check on Annie while you're here?' You don't know about Annie," she said, poking his muscular upper arm with a playful finger. "Well, you *do* know about Annie, but you didn't know that I knew Annie 'cause I didn't ask you about her when I asked you about Cynthia downstairs."

A skeptical look was rising on the guard's face.

"Anyway, Annie is Annie Minnis here in 1845." She'd maneuvered them to the door. "Annie called in sick this morning. Lucy—that's Annie's secretary—said she talked to her, to Annie, just before noon and Annie said she felt rotten and that she wasn't going anywhere all day."

"Now look, lady—"

Lindy could see that this was the critical moment in her little play, so she pushed harder. "Anyway," Lindy interrupted, making a face that mildly rebuked the guard for his interruption, "I'm here to see Cynthia and it dawns on me that while I'm here I should check on Annie, see if she needs anything, so I came up here and pounded on her door and nothing! Not one thing! She didn't answer the door and I don't hear anything inside."

"Maybe she's trying to get some rest," he said, his pride in simple common sense showing.

Lindy jumped on it: "And maybe she's puking her guts out in the bathroom right now while we stand here and talk about whether or not she's taking a nap! Or maybe her fever's so high she can't even dial the phone, let alone get up and answer the door when I'm knockin'. And maybe if you'd stop arguing with me and open the door we'd know for sure whether or not she needs us. Wouldn't we?"

Her closing flourish was to cross her arms and flash a defiantly expectant look as she asked, "Wouldn't we?"

"If you think I'm going to let you in this apartment, you've—"

Again Lindy jumped in, this time with arms still crossed and her look changing to a scowl. "Did I ask you to let me into Annie's apartment?"

The guard started to object again, but Lindy dropped her arms dramatically and at the same time huffed, "Look!" She gave him a frustrated shake of her head. "I'm just here to see if this woman's all right. And by the looks of things here it's a good thing I thought about it as I was leaving the ladies' room. Just open the door and stick your head in—no, she might not be decent. Let me stick my head in and make sure she's okay. That's all. Just let me check and see if she is all right!"

She could see he was going to do it, so she shut up and waited. The guard looked at her for a long few seconds, then turned to the door as he fished for his keys, muttering. "I guess it wouldn't hurt," he said to himself, then looked at Lindy and added, "but you don't go in and you definitely don't stay. In fact, you ride the elevator down with me." He paused, key in lock, waiting for her assent.

In response, she just gave a single decisive nod. When he turned back to the door again, Lindy allowed a smile of victory to spread across her face.

The key turned in the lock and the guard levered the door unlatched. Without hesitating, Lindy stepped in front of the man and pushed the door open.

"Ms. Minnis?"

▼ ▼ ▼ ▼

Dan Li-pong reentered his cubicle feeling a growing excitement inside. He had struck out in his attempt to identify the Lincoln lady, but in the process had uncovered some fresh tracks which he was sure would lead him and Lindy on an interesting chase, even if a story never materialized.

Dan first tried to track down his friend Smitty in the dispatcher's office. He wasn't at home and his shift didn't begin till three o'clock. He finally called around to enough people in the dispatch office to find out that Smitty was not on duty that day. He was in a meeting on soon-to-be-installed new technology that would allow all emergency and law enforcement agencies to share the same central dispatch. Most of the younger officers were excited about the change, but most of the older ones were hesitant. Smitty was in the former category, which was one reason he'd been chosen for the seminar. He would be back tomorrow.

Dan also tried to find something on the case and the woman's identity at both the Prosecuting Attorney's office and the Public Defender's office, but nothing on the Lincoln lady.

He then drove to the Governor's mansion in hopes of catching sixty seconds with the First Lady, but she was either out or security was keeping the peasants at bay. But he did bump into a man dressed like a cook who apparently had strolled to the garbage receptacle at the back of the property to make a deposit and have a smoke. The First Lady enforced a strict no-smoking policy indoors.

Dan had parked his car near the back of the driveway and had knocked on one of the two side doors. On his way back to the car after being rebuffed by security, he saw the cook and struck up a conversation.

A very interesting conversation!

Back in the office, he checked to see if Lindy was in—he couldn't wait to brief her on what he'd discovered. When he found her cubicle empty, he swung into his, dropped into his chair and played out his communications ritual, a set of habits developed over several years. First, he'd sit down in his chair, fire up his computer terminal, roll the chair to the left side of his desk so that the wastepaper basket was between his legs, and then check the regular and interoffice mail he had picked up from his box on his way through editorial. He always leaned over the waste basket, his elbows on his knees, to look through the stack, one letter at a time.

Dan evaluated each letter by its envelope—if he liked its looks he opened it; if he didn't, down it went into the circular file. He didn't like the looks of most letters, and he never opened interoffice mail from anyone but his boss. It was a fetish.

After the envelope ritual, he'd always swing back to his now-ready computer and select the *TOSS* option on the opening menu. *TOSS* was a program that allowed anyone in the building to leave a written message for anyone else in the building. He liked this kind of interoffice mail because he could read and write messages during his sometimes endless phone marathons tracking down stories.

This was interoffice mail he'd read. In fact, sometimes a message in *TOSS* referred to material sent through regular channels that required his action, and he'd have to fish through his wastebasket to find it. But he still had something against opening regular interoffice mail.

The first two screens in *TOSS* were routine notes from other staff about in-process projects. The third screen was an invitation to dinner from the redhead in typesetting, one of Lindy's FIFATLYs. He typed in a gracious "thanks but no thanks," then sent it to her terminal. He didn't like redheads.

He did like Lindy.

Dan scrolled to the fourth screen and there was a brief note from his partner. 2:32 p.m. He looked at his watch. 4:05. He scanned the note, burst into a smile, and shouted "Yes!" with a wiggle of his arms and hips in the chair like a running back celebrating his touchdown in the end zone. "My main woman!"

Quickly, Dan punched the series of keys that backed him out of his program, shut down his machine, and headed for the street. He took the route through editorial that Lindy had avoided. He was done for the day and nobody would hound him.

On the street, he moved at a very quick walk until he turned the corner onto North Capitol. What he saw at first slowed him down to allow a careful eye to take in the scene, then quickened his step to move him toward the scene even faster than intended.

In the middle of the next block, the street was lit up with the rotating blue and red beacons of police cars. They appeared to be parked in front of the old Imperial.

As he drew closer, he saw that he was right. There were three black and whites; two unmarked vehicles with the portable beacon flashing on the roof of the driver's side of the car, cable dangling into the open window—the detectives usually drove these; and an Emergency Medical Services ambulance, doors ajar and gurney missing.

Dan slipped into the front door without pausing for a look-see and headed for the security desk. "Got a stiff?" he asked the guard, who appeared fairly agitated to Dan.

"Yeah."

"From the looks of the artillery outside, it must be murder instead of a gray-haired thrombo. Anybody I know?"

The guard was distracted, his head bobbing slightly back and forth. Something's eating him, Dan thought.

In response to the question, the guard looked insolently at Dan, still bobbing his head. He raised his eyebrows and gave him a full-powered glare.

Dan got his wallet and fished out his press I.D. In a more cheerful tone, almost as if he were changing the subject, he said, "Say, I'm press. My partner had an interview with one of your residents. Can you get me in?"

"What's the name?"

"Minnis. 1845."

The guard shrugged nervously. "Sorry. Eighteenth floor is sealed off. Eighteen-forty-five's where the body is."

Dan didn't like that news. If something screwy was going on related to Annie Minnis, Lindy might have been in the middle of it. "Is it a resident or a guest?"

"CPD gave me orders to keep my mouth shut."

"Gimme a break."

The guard didn't answer. He just looked away and again became engrossed in whatever it was that had him agitated.

"Where's the elevator?"

The guard motioned with his head in the direction of the elevator hallway. "Cop's there."

"Thanks," Dan said bitterly, and he strode across the lobby. Around the corner, he saw a familiar face under the black police cap. "*Ni hau mah.*" His greeting bounced off the marble walls and into the ears of the Asian cop standing guard by the elevators.

"Oh, Dan. *Ni hau!* What brings you here?"

"Business. I hear you've got a dead fish in the tank. Anybody I know?"

"Sorry."

"Look, I know that eighteen is sealed off. My partner, Lindy—remember Lindy? She left me a message that she was coming over to interview a resident in 1845. Annie Minnis, a staffer for the Governor."

The Asian cop looked long and hard at Dan, then spoke slowly. "We've got a stiff in 1845, black female, and a live female, white. The detectives are quizzing her right now."

"1845 is Minnis's apartment. She's black. Lindy's white. Gimme a break, will ya? She's stepped into the middle of something that we're both onto."

The cop didn't respond. He just looked like he was processing the request.

"Come on." Dan was pleading mildly.

The cop reached for the microphone of his radio, attached with velcro to a special patch sewn into his shirt just below the left shoulder, and brought it to rest on his upper lip. He looked at Dan one more time, then keyed the mike. "This is Chung. I got a visitor down here who's connected to the woman you're questioning. Her partner at the newspaper. Should I send him up?"

The mini-speaker in the handset crackled with the static of another mike being keyed. "Forget it! One reporter in the middle of a murder scene is five too many. If he wants to see her he can wait till we're done with her."

The cop shrugged at Dan. "You heard the boss."

"I guess that means he won't go with me to the senior prom." Dan had heard that line in some B movie and always had wanted to use it. He winced inside at how stupid it sounded when the words escaped his lips, but they'd served their purpose—they'd effectively broken off the conversation regarding the murder scene and now he was free to cut loose from his friend.

Dan smiled and thanked the cop, then turned and moved back in the direction of the lobby, looking around in hopes of finding the stairs.

▼ ▼ ▼ ▼

Franklin Justice bustled back into his office just past four-fifteen with an aide in tow, her arms wrapped around a stack of reports. He stopped in front of Rosemary's desk and plucked the stack of phone messages from her extended hand.

"Chief Brown is waiting in your office, and Mrs. Justice called for you."

At that news, Franklin's head jerked up from his messages. "What did she want? Did she leave a number where I could reach her?"

Rosemary didn't know what was happening.

"No, sir. She didn't say. She just asked me to let you know that she called and that she would try again late this afternoon."

The Governor thumbed through the message slips looking for the one from Evelyn in hopes that there really was a number.

"I didn't bother making out a slip, sir."

Franklin looked up and out the window behind Rosemary with a scowl. He froze in thought for several seconds, then looked back at his secretary. "Hold my calls." He handed her the message slips. "Call these people back, the important ones, and tell them I'm not available until Monday. No interruptions." Justice started toward his office door, but paused and turned. "Except for Evelyn. Put her through immediately if she calls again." Then he strode into his office, leaving his aide standing flat-footed with the armload of reports.

James Brown, chief of the state police, was sitting in one of the leather wingback chairs facing the wide desk when the door swung open and the Governor strode in. He sat up straight and wiggled forward to get a grip on the chair arms so he could stand up. He knew where he fit in the pecking order of life.

Brown had been raised poor white trash—the wrong side of the tracks. He'd lifted himself out of that background through a distinguished stint in the army, earning a G.E.D. and a ranking of sergeant along the way. He left the army, joined the state police, and worked his way up through the ranks by a combination of political savvy (Army style—sucking up to superiors) and merciless competitiveness.

But still there were vestiges of the background. His attitude toward his own name, for one. He hated it because either way you said it, James or Jim, some smart mouth associated him with a famous black stud. He hated it. He'd had the name before either of them.

Another vestige was the racist tendency that led to that resentment. He fought it, partly because of a mild sense of guilt, but mostly because he was in a dangerous position to be holding on to any remnants of childhood bigotry.

He loved his hard-won position too much. He loved sitting in his boss's leather office chairs. He loved being on top.

Most of the time, that is. He wasn't sure this was one of them, given the mood that flooded the room as the Governor stormed in.

Brown had become fairly fat, even for a late-middle-aged desk jockey, so he had to scoot forward to the edge of the chair and lean out in order to be able to stand to attention for his superior. He often wished he had a little portable hoist he could hook onto the back of the wide leather gun belt that he wore more as a girdle than for a gun. That way he could get up out of chairs a little more easily.

The Governor was behind his desk before Brown made it all the way up.

"Chief," Governor Justice said curtly in greeting as he scanned his desktop and settled into his chair. He, Brown and Barnett had gotten together briefly in Barney's office shortly after lunch. Justice had been back from Annie's apartment for only a few minutes when he called the impromptu meeting. He wanted to be briefed on the State Police effort to find Evelyn, and he wanted Barney in on it to make sure he kept up to date.

But there was nothing new. No leads, even after interviewing dozens of people in the transportation-related fields. "Sir," Brown had barked hoarsely through vocal cords more used to smoking than to talking, "she's just disappeared. My best guess is that she's either holed up in one of the downtown hotels or she arranged for a friend to pick her up."

"She didn't have time to call a friend," the Governor had responded. "She must be downtown."

"Should I send men to question the desk people at the downtown hotels? The evening shift will be on duty by the time I can dispatch my men."

"No. Not now." Justice had nixed that idea from the beginning. All he needed politically was a bunch of troopers parading around the downtown hotels flashing a picture of the Governor's wife and asking about her as if she were a missing person. The press would be on that like a flock of vultures. He simply had ordered Brown to continue his investigation as initiated the night before.

But now, barely three hours later, Brown was back and executing the part of his job that he hated most—bearing ill tidings to the king. "Governor, I'm afraid I have bad news." He paused, trying to get more comfortable with the situation.

"What is it, Chief? Has my wife been in an accident? Did you find her at a hospital?"

"No, no," Brown answered quickly. "Nothing like that. There's still nothing new on your wife. It's about one of your staff, Miss Minnis, the lady that helps you out on special events."

"Well?"

"Well, sir, city police found her dead in her apartment earlier this afternoon." He dropped his bomb and waited.

Shock filled the Governor's face.

The chief sat still until the awful quiet prodded him to speak again. "Seems a young reporter went by to talk to her and found her. A security guard at the building called it in."

Justice responded by leaning slowly against the chair's tall back for support. "Annie? Dead?" The Governor looked at Brown for some confirmation that he'd really heard what the chief had said.

"I'm afraid so, sir. It was murder, plain and simple. I spoke briefly with the city's Chief of Detectives before I came to your office. He didn't know much, but he said it might have been drug-related. Signature murder."

"Annie." His voice trailed off. "Annie." He lowered his head and was staring into the vast blotter that protected his desk's expensive finish, calling her name as if to summon her back from the world of the dead.

Both men sat without speaking for several moments, the Governor shaking his head. Brown squirmed in the leather wingback trying to screw up enough courage to spit out the next part of what he had to say.

Finally, Franklin lifted his head without looking at Brown and spoke. "That's tough news to swallow, Jim." He continued slowly, pensively, "It's bad enough that one of your staff dies. Cancer or a car wreck's bad, but it's natural. But this!" He shook his head slowly from side to side, then looked into the chief's eyes, "What do you mean, 'signature murder'? "

"I mean that the woman was killed in a way that a certain drug ring usually dispatches their victims. We've seen this one before, an M.O. of a local ring, a gang of blacks and Latinos in bed together to crack a Jamaican stranglehold on local trafficking. That's why the city C of D thinks it might be drug-related. A regular kitchen knife, usually right out of the victim's own drawer, stuck into the victim's brain, slid in between the spinal column and the skull on the left side of the back of the neck."

Brown relaxed a bit as he described the murder. He was a lot more comfortable with such business details than he was with what he had to get to with the Governor. "That's what they think it was, sir. Drug-related."

While the chief had been reporting the first round of suppositions, he noticed that the Governor's emotions were a lot closer to the surface than he'd ever seen before, especially in his face.

"I had no idea Annie—" the Governor looked up, "—uh, Ms. Minnis, had any involvement with drugs. Are you sure about this 'signature murder'? We're a pretty close staff, and I'd never had the slightest suspicion of her in this regard."

"Sure as we need to be, sir," Brown responded. "It's possible that whoever killed her stuck her in the neck because of the circumstances, but most stabbings are to the torso and most aren't fatal. A neck stabbing is pretty unusual outside of the drug and organized crime scene, except in the case of ritual murders with some sicko religious connection.

"No, sir. This one's either the signature murder or a fluke. And right now, I bet on the first horse. They found a stash of cocaine in the woman's bathroom."

Justice's face turned pale with alarm. Defensively, he spat out, "I assure you, Chief, if I'd had any idea, she'd have been dismissed long ago. My administration has stood firmly against the drug problem since the beginning." His tone grew officially indignant as he made his pronouncement. Then he seemed to realize how pompous he must have sounded to the chief and the wind visibly left his sails. He added, self-consciously, "Of course. You know what my administration has stood for. You're a part of it. You know exactly what I'm talking about."

And Brown did know. He had been appointed as chief of the state police by the man seated across the desk from him. He owed him his current position, along with a lot of respect.

That made it even harder for him to get to his point.

He swallowed hard and bit the bullet. "Yes, sir, I do know. And I'm proud to be a part of what you're doing for our state. And that makes it real hard for me to ask you what I have to next."

Justice looked at him through a puzzled haze. "Go on."

"Well, sir. It's just that while it looks like a drug murder at this point, things aren't always the way they seem. I don't have many of the facts yet. I'm trying to say that sometimes the worm turns on a man, if you know what I mean."

"Cut to the heart, man. What are you trying to say?"

"What I'm trying to say is that we never make a determination this early, especially if it's not cut and dried."

"What do you mean?"

"It's just that when Gonzalez came on duty at three o'clock, he heard the news and came to me. He told me that last night, when you called him about your wife being missing, you also told him to send a unit to watch 1277 North Capitol."

"And?" The Governor leaned his head forward as his mouth opened for the word to escape, almost as if he were helping the chief along.

"And," Brown parroted, elongating the word a little, "1277 is the site of the murder."

Silence. The puzzled look remained on the Governor's face. Finally, "Your point, Chief?"

"Well, sir . . . ." It was desperately difficult for Brown to get to his point. He'd never had to do anything like this before. "It seems more than coincidental that you'd give this address to Gonzalez in connection with your wife's disappearance and then someone on your staff shows up dead there less than twenty-four hours later."

Justice sat up straight and in a burst of anger, slapped both hands against the top of his desk. "What are you trying to say?"

"I'm sorry, sir. This is very tough for me. But I just want to know why you had Gonzalez station a unit at this address last night. Did you have any reason to believe that Mrs. Justice might have posed some threat to the victim?"

"Evelyn has never posed danger to anybody but herself. I told Gonzalez to watch that building because Evelyn liked Annie. I thought since she headed down-town out of our driveway that maybe that's where she was headed."

Brown swallowed hard and asked, somewhat timidly, "Then you have no reason to suspect any foul play?"

"What did I just say?" Franklin barked, angrily. "Did I not make myself clear?"

Brown sat up in his chair and laid one hand on his rotund stomach, just north of his gun belt girdle. He groaned to himself as he pressed hard on the spot. He had suffered from an ulcer for years and he knew when he walked through the door of the Governor's office that it would flare up on him again before he passed back through the door. He could feel it coming while he was beating around the bush earlier, but with the Governor's outburst, the ulcer caught fire with a vengeance.

"Yes, sir, you did," he said, this time aloud and to his boss. "Perfectly clear. It's just that I have a responsibility in the post you gave me to make sure that I don't leave any strings dangling in an investigation as sensitive as this one, what with a reporter smack in the middle of it."

Again, Justice looked back at the chief without speaking. It appeared to Brown that he was thinking through the whole situation, so he kept quiet.

"I'm sorry for my outburst, Jim. Of course you're right to look at every eventuality. I'm a bit on edge now, in light of the stress of not knowing where Evelyn is . . . " he paused, " . . . and then this." Justice looked off into nowhere again.

Brown just sat with his mouth shut.

His boss's face wrinkled in thought. "Evelyn? A murderer?" He looked back at the blotter and shook his head as he spoke, slowly, almost as if giving word to his thoughts, "She's been very unstable lately. . . . But could she be capable of this? . . . She did use a kitchen knife when she cut her own wrists, but . . ." Justice sat up straight and looked at Brown. "No! Not possible! I know this woman too well, and she is not capable of such an act. You do what you need to do, but you'll find that what I've said is true!"

"Yes, sir. And I certainly don't want to make things worse for you. You'll have no objection if I have a little talk with Mrs. Justice when we find her? Just to see if she can shed some light on the situation?"

Justice rose. "Of course not, Jim. As long as you let her rest up before you question her. She's in a very fragile state right now."

Chief Brown rose in response. "I'll be sure to consult you, Governor." His discomfort had melted once he said his piece and the Governor used his first name. He felt better, but his ulcer didn't.

Justice walked around the side of his desk to usher the chief to the huge oak door that opened onto the hallway, the de facto private entrance. As he patted Chief Brown on the back, his phone rang its intercom tone, then Rosemary's voice came on the speaker.

"Sir, could you pick up?"

Chief Brown pumped the Governor's hand hurriedly and excused himself, glad to get out of his boss's way.

▼ ▼ ▼ ▼

Justice returned to his desk as Brown disappeared into the hallway. He raised the phone and spoke, "I'm alone, Rosemary. What is it?"

"It's Mrs. Justice, sir. Line two."

"Listen, Chief Brown just left through the private entrance. Hurry into the hall and stop him. I want him back in my office. Now."

"Yes, sir."

Justice looked down at the phone for a long moment, then took a deep breath and pressed the flashing button labeled *0002*. "Evelyn?" His voice sounded like that of a stern father calling for an errant child to appear before him.

"Hello, Franklin." Her voice was gentle, rational, somewhat tentative, but with a hint of smile.

An awkward silence.

"Evelyn," Franklin said with authority. "I have three questions for you."

"That's fine, dear. I have only one for you."

"Are you all right?"

"I'm better than I've been in a long time. And I expect that before you see me again, I'll be even better."

"I don't understand."

"Oh, I've had a revelation of sorts—about myself, my life. I'm sifting through clutter that I didn't even know I had inside."

Franklin Justice reacted with the most bitingly sarcastic tone he was capable of. "Well, I'm certainly glad you're having a therapeutic holiday. You've thrown me into a panic and dozens of state troopers into overtime. I hope your little escapade has been worth it!"

"Don't you dare try to make this into a guilt trip for me," Evelyn said, her voice shifting from gentleness to sternness. "I'm not the one who was unfaithful."

Silence.

"Fine," Franklin finally said, roughly, the frustration showing through.

The door from Rosemary's office opened and Chief Brown stepped into the room, closed the door, and stood just in front of it, not wanting to intrude on the phone call.

The Governor motioned to him to sit down in the wingback. "My second question is, where are you?" His voice changed after the chief entered the room. It was kinder now. He scrawled *Mrs. Justice* on an envelope as he asked her the question, then showed the envelope to the chief and pointed to the phone.

Brown leaned forward as if by doing so he'd somehow be in on the conversation.

Evelyn responded to the question, "That's none of your business."

Another pause. Franklin was not accustomed to assertiveness from Evelyn. This was a delicate situation and he was trying to handle it carefully.

"All right, have it your way," he said. "But you must give me a specific answer to one question."

"*After* you answer my one question."

"Fair enough."

"I gave you an ultimatum, Franklin. Have you cut all ties with that woman?"

"That woman," he said somberly, "is dead."

She gasped. "What do you mean?"

"I mean just what I said. She's dead. She was found murdered."

"Murdered?" Evelyn's voice was unbelieving. "Who would murder her?"

"I assure you, my dear, I have no idea. Now my question. You *must* answer me!"

Evelyn didn't respond.

"When are you coming home?"

"I don't know."

She seemed to be thinking. "Maybe tomorrow." Her answer came slowly. "I was planning on tomorrow, but . . . I'll see. I have to think about it some more."

"Evelyn, I insist that you either tell me where you are right now, or promise me that you will be home when I arrive there this evening."

Another long pause. "I'm sorry, Franklin. I can't do that. I won't do that. For the first time in years I've had a glimpse of what normal life is supposed to be, and until I can see clearly what that means for me, I can't come home."

The Governor looked at Brown and sighed heavily, expressing with his eyes the frustration he was feeling.

"Very well," he said. "I'm not in a position to change your decision. But you must understand that when you do come home, we have some things to settle."

"Yes, Franklin, we certainly do."

"And Chief Brown of the State Police, who is here with me now, will also need to speak to you."

"Why would he want to speak to me?"

"He has his reasons."

"What reasons? What possible reasons could he have?"

Justice thought for a moment, then responded, "I'll let him answer that."

The Governor looked toward Brown and said plainly, so the First Lady could hear, "Chief, my wife would like to know why you wish to speak with her when she returns home. I'm going to put her on the speakerphone so she can hear for herself."

Justice pressed a button and then laid the handset into its cradle. "Evelyn, Chief Brown."

"Ma'am," the Chief huffed.

"Jim, what conceivable reason do you have for wanting to speak to me? Have I done anything wrong?"

"No, ma'am. It's just the coincidence of you disappearing about the time one of your husband's staff is murdered."

"What possible connection could there be?"

"None, I'm sure, ma'am. It's just that your car was reported found in a parking garage only a block away from the victim's apartment. You might have spent the night with the victim and could shed some light on the investigation."

"Well, I assure you, I did *not* spend the night with that woman and I have no knowledge whatsoever of anything that might have happened to her."

"Yes, ma'am. But just the same, I'd like to ask you a few questions when you return."

"Oh, you can ask me questions all right. And I will be all too happy to tell you exactly the way things are!"

Justice scooped up the handset and brought it to his ear, cutting off the speakerphone. "Darling, the chief is just doing the job I appointed him to do. What with your recent illness and your relative instability and the awful coincidence of your disappearance with the murder—"

"Franklin. You listen to me. I don't know what's going on. But this I know: You committed adultery with that woman over a period of years during a time when our marriage was deteriorating. *You* were unfaithful to *me*. And now, you will see to it that I am not harassed by any policeman because *your* mistress is dead. I don't know what you've told that officer, but I know what I'll tell him if he asks me so much as the first question."

She dropped the threat in his lap and waited.

"I understand clearly, my dear," he said in a cordial voice when he finally answered. "That's no problem. I'm just concerned for you and want you to come home."

"I'll be home when I'm ready to come home. And don't send your gestapo looking for me."

The receiver banged in Franklin's ear as his wife slammed down the phone.

"Just remember, Evelyn," Franklin said to the dead receiver. "I love you. Please take care and come home soon."

He slowly lowered the phone back to its cradle.

▼ ▼ ▼ 10 ▼ ▼ ▼

Dan Li-pong was only in his late twenties, and he was proud that he was in great shape. But he had to admit that he had forgotten just how many polished marble steps there were in eighteen flights of stairs.

He took the first couple of flights at a quick pace, two or three steps at a time. By the fifth floor, he had shifted to one-step-at-a-time gear, and by floor seventeen, he had to stop to recover his breath and his energy. He didn't want to try to talk his way into apartment 1845 while passing out from oxygen deficiency.

When his chest had stopped heaving, Dan mounted the last flight and stepped into the hall. There was commotion to his left, where he was headed, but he glanced back in the direction of the elevators to see if they were guarded on this floor. He didn't want any unpleasant surprises from the rear. His eyes and the guard's met at the same instant.

"Hey, you!"

Dan turned to his left, away from the guard, and walked briskly in the direction of the noise and the people as if the guard didn't even exist.

"You from the stairwell!" The voice was louder, more threatening.

Dan picked up his pace. He could hear the heavy muffled footsteps behind him as the guard began to jog on the posh carpeting.

Dan didn't look back.

Before him, just ten yards down the wide, richly colored hall, were a half-dozen police and fire rescue personnel. By this time they had turned their heads in Dan's direction to see what the shouting was about. At the same time, as if stirred by some unseen force, they moved together to form a wall to trap Dan between their thick arms and the jogging policeman.

Three feet from the massive barricade and four feet from the door to 1845, Dan felt two hands seize his shoulders from behind. The guard from the elevator lifted up on Dan's jacket, swung him to the side, and buried his face in the flocking of the wallpaper.

Dan felt the abrasive synthetic material in the flocking dig into his cheek as the guard held him to the wall, then the sharp pain of a boot striking the inside of his ankles, one at a time.

"Spread 'em!"

Hands flew over his body to check for weapons, then the same hands lifted him again, spun him around and pressed his back into the same flocked wallpaper.

"You better have a good story, buddy."

Dan looked directly into the eyes of the officer who had him pinned to the wall. The man's eyes were wide open and he was breathing a little faster than normal. Not enough exercise or too much adrenalin. Or both.

With his eyes riveted on those of the guard, he turned his head slightly, toward the open apartment door, and shouted so those inside could hear: "I'm press, reporter for the *News*. My partner is in 1845." Then he turned calmly back to the cop.

A questioning look came across the guard's face, as if to say, *I don't know what you're up to but I don't trust you.*

Before the guard could respond, a thin, strained voice emerged from the door to the apartment. "Dan?"

It was Lindy.

Dan kept his eye contact with the guard.

"Dan?" Louder this time.

The guard turned his head in the direction of the door, as if deciding what to do, then Dan saw a look of resolve spread across his face. He pulled Dan off the wall, turned him and was beginning to escort him roughly back in the direction of the elevators when Lindy burst through the door, followed by a trim, well-dressed man who stepped into the scene with authority.

"What's going on out here?"

The wall of officers parted to let their boss through. Lindy took advantage of the breach and headed straight for her partner.

"Dan!" she said in a voice colored by both relief and stress.

Dan gripped her shoulders and looked in her eyes. He loved her eyes, but he could see in them the stress he heard in her voice. And there was more—anxiety, or fear, or pain. He wasn't sure.

He *was* sure that she was shaken, badly, and that he wanted to embrace her, to let her know that he was there for her.

But Lindy was self-consciously professional and would not appreciate being patronized that way. "You okay?" he asked instead.

"Who are you?" the well-dressed man asked Dan as Lindy breathed "Yes, okay," to Dan in answer to his question.

Dan looked up from Lindy's eyes and over her head to the detective. "Dan Li-pong from the *News*. I'm this lady's partner."

"I thought I made it clear to the officer downstairs that I wanted no more company, especially another reporter."

"Yeah, it was clear—to him. But I had reason to fear that my partner might have been in trouble, so I used the stairs. Wouldn't you do the same for your partner?"

"Take her outa here. We're done with her. For now."
The chief of detectives turned to Lindy. "You stay available. I *will* have other questions." He swung around and
strode back through the watching officers and into the
apartment.

"I have to get my notepad," she said to Dan as she
turned to follow the detective.

Dan moved to follow her, but the human barricade
closed to stop him. His heart was racing, filled with the
excitement of his partner's incredible good fortune at
having been first on the scene of a sensational—and
headline-grabbing—murder. He lifted his head to look
over the blockade and caught a glimpse of the corpse, a
delicate-looking black female in a white sweatsuit. She
was crumpled face-down in a heap on the floor, almost
as if her body was a rag on the bottom of a pile of dirty
clothes, the sweatsuit on top. The entire left shoulder of
the heavy cotton shirt was stained deep red in a rough
partial circle that emanated from the neck area.

As he looked closer he could see the source of the blood.
The handle of a knife rose out of the back of her neck, just
left of center, like a mutant mosquito feeding on a victim.

His stomach turned.

He wanted to look away, but the reporter in him forced
his eyes to take in all he could. His view was limited, but
he could see that the room was in shambles. A man was
bent over a sofa poking at its fibrous guts as they exuded
from long horizontal slashes in the white fabric of the
sofa's seats. A low table was overturned, its glass surface
shattered across the floor. The left arm of the body was
draped over one corner of the upset table, and the
woman's left side lay on much of the broken glass. Two
men squatted on either side of the body in the midst of
other debris that littered the floor.

"Gettin' your eyes full?" barked one of the officers.

Dan just looked at him with a smug grin, then turned back to the door in time to see Lindy walk back out. Her shoulders were hunched and she looked to Dan like a fast-moving turtle. She had pulled her head as far down into her shell as she could and was trying to turn her back on the apartment as she left.

Lindy slipped her arm into Dan's as she moved through what was left of the human barricade. He put his other hand on her arm and squeezed.

Lindy looked up into his eyes. She was fighting back tears.

▼ ▼ ▼ ▼

In her maid's living room, Evelyn Justice also was fighting tears.

She just had hung up the phone and was feeling the coldness of Franklin's words to her, an emotional distance she'd never felt before. On the phone, it sounded as if he actually didn't care that the police wanted to question her, or even that they might somehow suspect her of murder.

It was hurting more than the sting of the slap the evening before.

Evelyn looked through the sparkling glass of the picture window in the direction of the main street where the bus passed every forty minutes. As she sat, she felt the looming presence of depression that continually hung over her consciousness. She felt her confusion and insecurity pulling on the dark curtain, like a long arm pulling down on a roll-up shade, trying to loosen it and draw it down to shut out the light.

As she sat, she watched for her maid and protectress, as if by watching intently enough Maria would return sooner.

▼ ▼ ▼ ▼

Lindy clung to Dan's arm as the pair padded down the thick carpeting of the hall, away from the police and the open door of apartment 1845. She needed his arm, his strength, his presence. She'd never thought about needing Dan before. She was having too much fun as a reporter and enjoying too much career advancement to think more than twice about anything beyond friendship with a man.

By the time they reached the elevator, she was shaking. In a matter of a few dozen steps, she'd gone from a cool, if stressed, professional to a trembling mass. Dan lifted up on her arm as they stepped into the waiting elevator and they both stood tall as the doors closed like curtains on the scene in the hall.

"Lindy, are you all right?"

"Yes." Her eyes stared in concentration. "I just need a minute."

The trembling began to spread from her arms to her neck and head.

When the doors opened, Dan escorted Lindy into the large open entry hall and sat her on one of the luxurious couches that helped define the style of the lobby. "Sit. I'll get a cab and be right back."

He hurried to the security desk. "Can you call a cab for us?" he asked the young guard at the desk who had watched him crossing the lobby.

"I'm no hotel clerk."

"Do me a favor. This woman's been through the wringer upstairs. I need to sit with her. Just call a cab, will ya?"

The young guard shrugged his assent and reached for the phone.

"Thanks," Dan said as he turned to walk back to Lindy. The couch was empty.

▼ ▼ ▼ ▼

"Oh, Maria! I thought you'd never get home!" The strain in Evelyn's voice was apparent as she greeted Maria at the open front door. It was early spring, a warm early spring, just past six o'clock, and the sun was casting long shadows as it peeked out from behind trees in the west. The stress and the feeling of aloneness she'd felt increasingly over the past several days was only exacerbated by her concern for Maria. It seemed to her that it was too late for her to be coming home. She feared something had happened.

Evelyn had tried all day to busy herself, but there simply wasn't anything to do but cook a meal. Maria's small home was immaculate. Evelyn had tackled the evening meal only because she needed to be *doing* something. It certainly wasn't because she was a cook. The only time she'd been in her own kitchen for years was to get a snack or to oversee the preparation of food for a dinner party.

The worries of the day and of her life came through in her voice as she greeted Maria.

"Mrs. Justice," Maria responded, her thick Spanish accent making the title *Mrs.* sound like *Meesus.* "It is a long bus ride from the city, and I didn't leave work until after five o'clock." She took off her coat and, as she hung it in the tiny hall closet, continued, "I'm so sorry to be later than you expect. I will have dinner ready for you very soon."

Evelyn looked at her maid with surprise, and then with guilt. "Oh, no, Maria," she said with tears welling in her eyes. "You misunderstand."

Maria turned from the closet with a puzzled look on her face, and immediately saw the strain in her mistress's

face. She put a hand on Evelyn's shoulder to steady her
a bit.

Evelyn felt the welcome touch and reacted to it. "Oh,
Maria!" She took a step forward and almost fell onto
Maria as she sought a warm, secure embrace.

"Mrs. Justice! What is the matter?"

Evelyn buried her face in Maria's shoulder and just let
go. She felt the tears washing away the awful confusion.
She felt the heaving in her lungs as she sobbed and could
sense the tension and stress being dissipated. She felt the
real Evelyn, the lonely one, rise up from deep within,
recognize a friend in Maria, and bond with her as they
embraced.

For the first time in years, Evelyn felt, really *felt*, that
someone cared for her. Whether the feeling was accurate
she didn't know—couldn't know—and didn't care.

Maria, with an arm still around Evelyn, turned her and
guided her to the living room and the sofa that had been
her waiting place for most of the day. They sat down
together and let several minutes pass while Evelyn col-
lected herself. Evelyn took a tissue from a box on a table
and wiped her face.

"Maria, I'm so sorry."

"For what, Mrs. Justice?"

"I'm sorry that for even a moment you thought I'd
expect you to come home from a long day at a thankless
job and then go straight to fix me a meal." She laid the
tissue on her lap and reached for Maria's nearest hand.
"I'm so sorry. You have opened your home to me in the
most gracious way, made me feel welcome, and have
accepted me just as I am in the midst of turmoil without
so much as asking why. I'm sorry that in the past our
relationship has been the kind that would lead you to feel
like my servant instead of a trusted employee ... and
now, a trusted friend."

"Truly, there is no sorry needed. I am happy to open my home to you and to care for your needs as my guest."

"Well, that won't be necessary. I'm not much of a cook, but I have prepared dinner for us." She stood up, eyes red and swollen, her hand gripping Maria's, then lifted on that hand to invite Maria to stand also. "Besides," she said as they moved toward the kitchen, "I have some explaining to do. I promised to tell you why I'm here."

"You cooked for us?" Maria asked with a wide smile of appreciation. "It has been a long time since someone prepared food for me in my own home."

Evelyn smiled back, the strain easing from her face. "Then that will only make it taste better—and my cooking needs all the help it can get."

▼ ▼ ▼ ▼

Dan swung back to the security guard who had just begun to identify himself to the cab company he had on the line. "Where'd she go? Did you see where she went?"

The guard mumbled "Just a minute" into the phone, then covered the mouthpiece and lowered the receiver to the top of the formica counter he sat behind. "What now?"

"The girl I brought in here. Did you see her get up and leave?"

"Look, buddy. I ain't no babysitter. I ain't no hotel clerk. I'm here to take care of this building, not people like you who come into it." He held the phone up between them. "You still want this cab?" His voice was surly.

Dan turned to the empty couch. He hurried to the front entrance and pushed hard to make the revolving doors move faster. On the sidewalk, he looked both ways frantically. No Lindy.

He pushed back through the revolving doors and hurriedly moved from one of the small lobby shops to another, stepping in just long enough to scan the room, then moving on.

The fourth of the four shops was on the end of the lobby nearest the elevators, and with a foreboding flash, Dan wondered if she'd gone back upstairs. His cop friend was not in the hallway and all the elevator doors were closed.

Dan moved down the hall until he stood in the middle of the bank of elevators. From this vantage point, he could see the floor indicators above each. One of the antique hands rested on 7. Another rested on 1. It must be sitting at the ready. The third was moving upwards past 13, and the fourth pointed to the *B* underneath floor one. His eyes caught a piece of paper taped to that door: *Out of service for repairs*.

His eyes jumped back to the single moving needle-like hand. Past 15, 16. It slowed. Past 17. It stopped on 18.

"Whatta you doin' Lindy?" he said aloud as he pushed the old brass button with the arrow pointed upward.

Nothing happened.

He glanced up at the indicator lights and saw that one in-service elevator was on the first floor, ready for duty, but the door wasn't opening. He pushed the button again, harder this time, as if a little extra pressure on the call button would open the recalcitrant door.

Nothing. No doors opening.

Dan swung in frustration and lay against the shine of the old brass doors for the elevator car that had stopped on 18 as he realized that it didn't matter how hard he pushed on the call button. You couldn't enter the lifts on this floor without a key!

He crossed his arms and ran through his options: Get to an upper floor via stairs, get the guard to key one of these open, stand around and wait for someone to come along and enter with them—he didn't like any of them. One and two had him dealing with the guard, whom he'd already miffed. Three had him killing who-knows-how-much time.

He had to try to coax the guard.

Dan dropped his arms and tensed to pull himself away from the face of the doors when a bell rang above him and he felt the brass begin to slide under his back.

He flashed a huge smile to lady luck, then turned and watched the doors open the rest of the way.

"These things are as slow as the seven-year itch!" he said to the lady who stepped off. His already anxious posture made his "impatient resident" charade all the more likely to be true.

He smiled at the woman and wished her a pleasant afternoon, then stepped into the lift car and pressed *18*. The doors ground closed, creaking against each other, and Dan began the climb.

"Come on, come on!" he coaxed the old elevator to climb a little faster. "Come on." He bounced nervously.

The light behind the *18* on the brass control panel finally lit up, a little *ding* sounded, and the two doors heaved a sigh as they opened again, like an old man grunting when he's asked to perform a strenuous task one more time after he'd done it for a lifetime.

Standing in the hall, waiting for the elevator, were four men, a woman, and a gurney loaded down with a black plastic body bag. Three of the men were uniformed police; the other man and the woman were EMTs.

"Didn't we just get rid of you?" asked one of the jakes.

"Did my partner—the woman you were questioning—did she just come back up here?"

"Nobody but us stiffs," one of the cops said as he laughed to himself and jabbed his elbow into the female EMT. She rolled her eyes.

"Thanks," Dan said as he pushed the button marked *1*.

"Hey! Hold on." The doors closed as the jokester cop stepped toward the elevator.

"Sorry." Dan smiled. "Next car please." He loved to antagonize cops.

The elevator opened onto the first floor again and he darted back to the security desk. The guard was sitting erect, the picture of alertness, but he was watching the local news on a tiny TV he'd pushed up under the over-hanging counter. "Did you see her?"

The guard just looked up and shook his head from side to side.

Dan swung back to the entrance and out onto the street. Again his eyes scanned the sidewalk for signs of Lindy. She must have gone home, he thought, and he started south at a slow jog. His car was parked in a lot just midway between 1277 North Capitol and the offices of the *News*, two blocks away.

▼ ▼ ▼ ▼

Back in the lobby of the condo building, Lindy stepped out of the ladies' room much more calm and composed than she had entered it five minutes before.

She was coherent again, and she had to get back to her world, her order, her own little cubicle and try to make sense of what she'd seen. And, she insisted to herself once the shock had begun to settle, to focus herself on what was obviously one killer of a story.

But where was Dan? Men are never around when you need them, she muttered to herself.

▼ ▼ ▼ ▼

This time it was Evelyn's turn to lead Maria to a seat. As they neared the kitchen, Maria raised her nose to the aroma, took a long draught of the scented air, and ex-haled pleasurably, "Ummmm! Mrs. Justice. This is a pleasure."

"Good!" Evelyn said as they moved toward the kitchen table, set with pieces which were clearly from Maria's Nicaraguan homeland. Evelyn was feeling much better now. She'd gotten so much of the churning upset out of her system through her tears.

Evelyn stepped around Maria and pulled her chair back from the table for her to be seated. But Maria had slowed down, staring at the place settings, and had stopped at the corner of the table.

Evelyn held the back of the chair for a moment, then realized that Maria was frozen at the sight. "Maria?" she said gently.

"Maria?" she said as she let go of the chair and reached for her friend's shoulder. "Are you all right?"

She didn't answer immediately. Instead, she lowered her fingers to the rim of the nearest plate, a brightly colored dish decorated with orange birds outlined in black and flowering plants in yellow and green. She gently traced the orange rim of the plate with her finger, then touched one of the bright birds—reverently, closing her eyes, almost as if connecting herself with the world that plate represented.

As Evelyn held on to her shoulder and watched her, she saw tears.

"My Irenea," Maria said quietly, her voice straining against the emotion.

Evelyn said nothing. She just waited.

"My Irenea and my dear family. Oh, that *Nuestro Señor* would have taken me when He took them."

Evelyn realized what she'd done. "Maria. Again I'm so sorry. I found these lovely dishes and thought you'd enjoy them. I didn't even think of how they might make you feel or why they were at the back of the cabinet. Please forgive me."

"Mrs. Justice," Maria turned to Evelyn, "you are a good woman. Why do you always apologize for doing good to people? I've watched you during the years and I see that same thing. You take time to make a meal for us and you want to please me with your kindness. You have no way to know my sorrow. You don't need to apologize for a kind act."

"But Maria, I'm so selfish. All day I've watched for you to come home so I could unload my grief on you. On someone. I never even thought that you had enough grief of your own without being further burdened with mine."

"Mrs. Justice, do you have a friend?"

Evelyn drew back from Maria. The defenses she'd cultivated during years in the public eye kicked in, and she felt her sensibilities react as if offended. "Of course I have friends," she said, her voice still mild but with a hint of reprimand in it.

"I did not ask if you have friends. I ask if you have *a* friend." She said the *a* very distinctly to make her point. "Is there someone who loves you the way you are and someone you don't need to apologize to in order to feel accepted?"

At first, Evelyn listened in disbelief at the pre-sumptuous question Maria was posing. Who does she think she is? was the thought that her defenses first telegraphed across her consciousness. But the confusion of her life and the stress of her day, especially the conversation with Franklin, melted the arrogant First Lady's response and Maria's words actually sank in.

She dropped to the chair she'd held for Maria, set her elbow on the table and rested her chin in her open hand. "No," she admitted. "No, I don't. Not even Franklin."

Maria pulled one of the other chairs to her and poised herself across the corner of the table from Evelyn, directly in her line of sight so Evelyn had to look at her instead of off into space. "May I ask one more question?"

"Certainly."

"Are you a friend to yourself?"

A puzzled look came across Evelyn's face. "What do you mean . . . " She didn't finish the question. Instead, she bowed her head and shook it. "No. You know. You sat by my bedside when I was recovering from my suicide attempt. If a friend is someone you love and someone whom you'd never even dream of doing harm to, then I'm not a friend to myself." Her shoulders sagged. "Or anyone else," she added in a self-deprecating tone.

"Mrs. Justice, you are a good woman, a kind woman. It is not meant for you to carry the pain of life by yourself. In the Bible there are two sayings. One says that in this life, we are to carry our own burdens. The other says that we are to carry one another's burdens. How can we carry our own burden and someone else's? Or how can we carry our own burden and let someone else carry it? These two sayings from God make me think and make me smile."

They didn't make Evelyn smile, but they certainly made her think. "That seems like double-talk to me. And believe me, I've been around politicians enough to know it when I hear it."

Maria's smile was unaffected. "I believe that it is our place in life to carry our own burden. It is right for us to care for ourselves and our family. People are troubled when they do not carry their own life's burden."

"I've seen that enough in the welfare state."

"True. But in life we also have weight added to our burden that makes it too great for us to bear alone. If we try, we fail. We become sad, or angry, or troubled. It is *not* right for us to bear those burdens alone. So Mrs. Justice, you have been a friend to others in your kindness, but you have not had a friend for the kindness you need and one to help you love yourself again."

Evelyn's thoughts ran through the list of terrible crushing burdens that had driven her unmercilessly toward depression and suicide only months ago. She hadn't had a friend. No one had shared her burden. She unloaded it temporarily on her psychiatrist, but he didn't really care. It was no loss to him if she killed herself and no gain if she got better. She hadn't had a friend. Not even her husband who was so preoccupied with public policy— and his private whore.

But at the same time, Evelyn realized that her life's burdens were not greater than those of her gracious hostess. "Maria, you've been through far worse pain than I. Have you such a friend?"

"Yes," she said confidently. "And no."

"You sound like my husband again." There was real disgust in her voice. "He's a decisive public leader, but he's still a politician. There is never a clear yes or no with them."

Maria laughed softly. "Oh, Mrs. Justice. I am no politician. I am just a maid. I give you both answers because both are true, not because I'm afraid of the truth."

"Can you explain?" Evelyn asked.

"Yes, yes." She smiled. "But first, may I serve you dinner?"

▼ ▼ ▼ 11 ▼ ▼ ▼

Evelyn sat bolt upright. "Oh, dinner!"

She stood up and began to buzz around Maria like a guard bee taking care of the hive. "Here," she said as she picked up the two brightly colored plates. "Let me set these aside. We'll eat from others." She set them in the middle of the table, one on top of the other.

Maria rose too. "I'll help."

"No!" Evelyn said sternly from the storage cabinet as she pulled out two white, plain pieces of dinnerware. "I cooked. I get to serve."

Evelyn could tell that Maria was uncomfortable in the situation, but she seemed pleased nonetheless. Maria relaxed more in her chair, then leaned forward and began to massage her right knee.

"Did you do something to your knee?" Evelyn asked as she reset the table.

"It is arthritis. My legs miss the warmth of Nicaragua."

"And I've assigned you to take care of the upstairs?" Evelyn asked as she lifted one of the baked chicken breasts out of the baking dish and onto the milk-colored plate.

"It is not a problem."

"But it will be changed when I get back." Evelyn shook the tongs at Maria to emphasize her point.

"We can talk about that later, Mrs. Justice. For now, let me finish the answer to your question."

"Okay. I'll serve up the food, you serve up the answer."

Maria began. "I would like to go back to my life in Nicaragua before the Sandinistas, but I never can go back now. There is nothing in Nicaragua for me but ghosts of my life before. Here, in this city, I am near what might have been. It is a greater comfort."

Evelyn went to the coffeemaker and poured two cups. "Then your friend is here?" she said as she carried the cups to the table and sat down.

"Yes. He is here."

"He?" Evelyn thought, caught off guard. The idea of Maria entertaining a male friend somehow surprised her. But she said nothing.

Maria saw the mild surprise ripple across Evelyn's face. "My friend, the one in whom I have found peace, is the Lord."

A little knot formed in Evelyn's stomach, an *Oh-no, not that* knot. She didn't mind discussing God at dinner parties. In fact, she rather enjoyed it. There was no doubt in her mind of His or Her or Its existence. Any thinking person could see that there was something beyond the mere existence of humans and this world. Truth be known, she found the ideas of other well-educated people as stimulating on this subject as on the many others discussed around the Governor's table.

But Evelyn always had been uncomfortable with talk that personalized this divine force or being. She associated any reference to knowing God or relating to God or knowing God's will with a certain class of person.

Like a maid.

Only twice in her life had that association ever been challenged. The first time was several years ago, at a bash Franklin's law firm was hosting as a thirty-year anniversary of the partnership. Franklin had been inducted as the newest full partner only months before, so the whole weekend was a milestone in more ways than one.

The senior partners at that time invited stars from their own constellations to share the big weekend in private suites, high-powered dinners, and opulent parties.

Evelyn was much younger then. The thrill of rubbing elbows with personalities from many different fields was something she had never forgotten.

At dinner on Saturday night, in the ballroom of the old, exclusive downtown club, she was seated between her husband and a famous actor. She was delighted.

Evelyn turned her charm on both men. It was one of those nights, long before the trials of marital loneliness, depression and suicidal behavior, that she believed she was charming. She felt like Cinderella with handsome princes on both sides and her fairy godmother behind her, guarding the clock to prevent its striking twelve times.

It was late in the dinner, dessert to be exact—she remembered because the incident was so out of the ordinary. Their waiter had just served a chocolate mousse cake with raspberry cream icing—she could still see it—and the conversation turned decidedly somber. She had chattered on about the movies her famous dinner partner had made, pumping him for behind-the-scenes stories from her favorites. But when she asked him what box-office plans he had in store, the answer shocked her.

"None," he said matter-of-factly. "I'm dying."

Evelyn was stunned.

Her mind raced to cope with what to say, what to do next, but she was at an utter loss for words. She quickly lifted her napkin from her lap to her lips and made a show of removing some blot that obviously prevented her from speaking. But her sudden squirming gave her away.

The man noticed her discomfort, laid down his dessert fork, and turned to her, patting her on the forearm. "It's all right. I'm cool about it. I'm sorry if my bluntness disturbed you."

"Oh, no. That's all right." She felt incredibly relieved at his words. "I mean, of course it's not all right that you're ill." She paused. "You *are* ill?" He didn't look it to her. In fact, those gorgeous eyes and his captivating presence had made her lose her manners more than once during dinner. She wanted to know all she could about him.

"Yes. The doctors say I don't have much longer. That's why I'm so glad to be here this weekend with my old friend Pence." He looked in the direction of one of the senior partners. "Old college buddies," he said with the impish grin that had made her heart skip a beat when she'd seen it on the wide screen.

Evelyn replaced her napkin in her lap and folded her hands primly on top of it. Then she turned and said to him in the most sincere way, "How have you, so full of life and known by so many people, been able to handle that news so calmly? So stoically?"

"It's not stoicism, I assure you," he said as he turned back to his fork and the chocolate mousse cake. "The simple truth is that until recently, only the last several months to be exact, I'd have been terrified and angered by that news. I was a hellion most of my life and I never took bad news well."

He leaned forward and planted both elbows on the table, then cocked his head toward Evelyn. "But while I'm not happy or excited about the situation in any way, I have found peace and contentment." Then he smiled and added, "In my old age, you might say."

Oh, that grin. Much longer with him and she'd just melt, no matter how dispiriting the conversation.

"Years do change us," she said, trying to affirm or support him.

"Wasn't years that made the difference," the actor said. "I met Jesus Christ and He changed the whole show."

That was the first time that anyone on her social level or above had ever spoken of God in a personal way in her presence.

To this day, she didn't really remember how the evening concluded. Her shock over learning of the terminal illness of this cultural icon, and the disturbing personalization of God in that situation, blurred the remainder of the event for her.

That was the first time this God-talk had ever hit home, and it was reinforced when she learned of the actor's "untimely death," in the words of the press. She wondered how it was for him when he actually closed his eyes that last time, and she wondered where he was now, and . . . well, she wondered.

That was the first time. The second time was now, with Maria, her former high-official's-wife-turned-maid-turned-respected friend, and it was causing the knot in her stomach to tighten. The knot was there because ever since the gala dinner with the dying actor, the trueness of his words had sunk in, even though she didn't really know exactly what his words meant.

"Maria, I must be honest with you. When I hear people saying things like 'God is my friend,' I must confess that I normally just ignore them. I've always felt that sort of talk trivialized the idea of God, and the source almost always was a lower-class type of person."

"Like maids?"

"Oh, no! No! That's not what I'm saying at all. In fact, just the opposite. I was going to say that I normally ignore the talk because it doesn't come from people I respect or look up to. But with you it's different. I feel that we are more like sisters—what you've done for me, how you've taken me in.

"I've always respected you. I deeply appreciated your quiet presence during those long days when I was struggling with depression. You were the only one who talked to me instead of avoiding me. I appreciate that. Maybe it's because of that, but I feel like you are my sister. You've been in government service, higher than I've been because your husband was an official on a national level. You've known pain and sorrow, much more than mine."

Evelyn's words were slowing. She was thinking, trying to get to her real point. "And you care for me. I can tell."

Maria didn't speak.

"What I'm trying to say is that I've ignored such God-talk in all other instances but this one, and one other. I want to hear what you have to say about it."

Maria responded with a big single nod, a nod not only of her head but of her shoulders and even part of her upper body. "Very well, Mrs. Justice. First, I will thank the Lord for this food, then we will eat the lovely meal you made, and I will tell you."

Maria bowed her head modestly and addressed God— He, She, or It—in Spanish. Evelyn didn't bow her head. She thought that was more a response of brainwashing than of reverence, and the last thing she wanted to be was a hypocrite. Instead, she watched her friend and listened.

Evelyn didn't understand Spanish. She recognized the *Nuestro Señor* which began Maria's prayer, but after that the words were incomprehensible.

But Evelyn *felt* them. Ever since Maria had walked through the front door, Evelyn's tumultuous emotions had been calming. But as her maid addressed this unseen Friend in words she didn't understand, Evelyn felt the calm.

" . . . *el nombre de Jesus,* amen."

Evelyn knew that last word. She was watching as Maria raised her bowed head.

Then Maria picked up knife and fork and said, "First, I feed me your food, then I feed you my story."

The fork had just pierced the juicy meat of the chicken breast and the knife had just been touched to the crusty seasoned coating, ready to slice, when the doorbell rang.

"This is a surprise," Maria said, looking up from the plate of food. "One guest in one day makes me happy. Two guests is like getting gifts on my birthdays. Excuse me, Mrs. Justice."

Maria rose, crossed the kitchen floor, and disappeared through the old swinging door into the tiny hallway.

Evelyn heard the mumble of voices, Maria's and a man's. She raised her spoon and dipped it into her cup. She stirred, then scooped a spoonful of the dark liquid and sipped. "A little cream to soften the harshness of my brewing technique," she said aloud, to the spoon. She heard the singsong intonation of her words and remembered the tea parties she had hosted for her stuffed animals as a little girl.

Evelyn allowed the memory of that carefree, secure time to warm her as she poured a thin stream of cream into the coffee. The cream lightened the dark coffee, just like the warm memory of her childhood lightened the dark foreboding inside her. She wrapped both hands around the cup and lifted it to her lips, reveling in one more warm connection.

Evelyn heard the front door close and Maria's steps approach in the tiny hall.

She thought again about her childhood tea parties. "Oh, God," she said, aloud but softly, in barely more than a whisper, "You may be no more real than the stuffed animals I shared a table with as a girl. But if You are, I am grateful to You for Maria."

The door to the kitchen swung inward. Evelyn set her coffee back in its saucer and turned to Maria with a smile.

Maria stood in the doorway, one hand extended to hold the door open. A state trooper stood behind her, wide-brimmed hat under his arm. "Evelyn Justice?"

▼ ▼ ▼ ▼

Chief Brown clearly was nervous as he entered the Governor's office to brief his boss on the preliminary report from City Police on the Minnis murder, and to update him on the status of his department's search for the Governor's wife. Brown was a lifer in law enforcement. Few things rattled him. But facing his boss in this situation was one of them.

"I'm telling you, Frank," George Barnett was saying as Rosemary ushered Brown into the inner sanctum, "this whole situation stinks. I don't like it. There's something very wrong here and you're the one who's going to suffer for it."

Brown hadn't seated himself. Instead, he just stood by the other leather wingback. He thought the situation a little too tense to just drop into a seat, especially since he had nothing new to bring to the conversation since he had appeared before the Governor only—what? An hour or two before?

"Sit down, Jim," Justice said as he gestured the chief to sit. "Barney's a bean counter and he's worried that the beans are adding up to trouble. I'm not in too much agreement with him and his feathers are ruffled. What about you?"

"Me?" Brown responded.

"Who do you think I mean?"

Brown had been afraid of this. Like all the Governor's closest staff and department heads, Brown knew that Franklin Justice's personality was a pendulum that swung in two different directions. Coming into the office, he had been afraid that with the events of the past day or two, the pendulum would be swinging his way.

"I'm sorry, sir. I am not qualified to make evaluations of your political situation."

"Neither is Barney, but that doesn't stop him."

Barnett rose, picked up a sheaf of papers and files, and leaned toward his old friend. "Frank, I'm not interested in sitting here and being ridiculed. I told you what I think and what I believe to be the most important aspects of this problem. They're yours now. If you want me, you know where my office is."

Barnett turned to Brown. "Chief," he said as he shuffled the stack of papers in his arms, "check out Annie's connection with Bruhof Distributors. There's a skunk in that closet. I'd stake my reputation on it." With that, Barnett stepped between the two wingbacks and walked out of the office, through the regular entrance that led back into Rosemary's office, a route he never took unless he wanted to make a statement.

Brown was feeling very uncomfortable and his instincts told him to keep his mouth shut.

He did.

"Don't mind him, Jim," the Governor said. "He's a very close friend, but sometimes he takes himself too seriously."

Brown didn't get that impression from what he had witnessed of the conversation.

"What do you have for me?"

"Sir, I have a preliminary report on the Minnis murder from the C of D over at the city."

"And?"

"No change in what I told you before. They still think it's drug-related. The new information I have bolsters that judgment. They found a stash of cocaine. She'd been using for a long time, even had a false bottom drawer in her bathroom vanity. The apartment was pretty well torn up, like a muscle job meant to send someone a message."

"Is that all they found, no other material evidence? Records, photos?"

"None that he was willing to tell me about, and I think he was up-front with me."

"It seems to me that there should have been some other corroborating evidence in the place. Are you sure they didn't find any pictures or other such data?"

"No, sir." The chief answered. "To the best of my knowledge they did not. Should they have?"

The Governor just shook his head and grunted, then asked, "What else do you have?"

Chief Brown decided that his boss was in as good a mood as he was going to be in for a while, so he swallowed hard and opened his mouth. "They're pressing me about the incident with Mrs. Justice. I tried to keep it in the department but as usual, someone had loose lips."

"Why are they worried about Evelyn? You didn't ask their help in finding her, did you?"

"No, sir. But they know about the disappearance and the dispatch of the car to the Minnis condo building. They want to talk to her a lot worse than I do."

"Jim, I just can't imagine Evelyn doing anything like that." His voice trailed off and he was silent for a while, looking away from the chief and obviously thinking about something. Then he added, "But a few months ago I couldn't imagine that she could ever attempt to take her own life." He looked back at his chief law enforcement officer and asked, "How are you handling it?"

"I told Ben Wheeler at homicide to let me handle this end, at least until he gets further into his investigation of the possible drug link. They have no suspects yet. They're working on tracking her supplier now. We might know more in the morning after forensics has had a crack at their material, but it does mean we have a little more time to find Mrs. Justice and resolve the question of exactly where she has been."

"Good! Let me know as soon as you hear anything."

"Yes, sir."

"Does the press know yet?"

Brown felt the fire in his ulcer flare up. He hated this part. "That's the bad news, sir. Minnis was found by a reporter for the *News,* woman name of Blakely. I'm afraid she knows all too much."

"Can we put a lid on her?"

"Not likely, unless you want to whip up a storm. We aren't talking to any press about what we know, but no telling what she's got already."

"I'm sure we'll find out in the morning," Justice said as he swung his chair to the side and rested his chin on intertwined fingers. He stared off into space, as if he were processing Brown's news.

The chief kept his mouth shut for a reasonable period, at least long enough to feel like he'd been respectful. But he wanted to get this over with and get back to the bad guys. He felt a lot more comfortable among them.

"Sir, a question if I may."

Justice looked at the trooper with a turn of his head, not of his chair.

"What did Mr. Barnett mean about Bruhof Distributors?"

"Barney's paranoid about Bruhof because Annie—Ms. Minnis—was buying expensive items from them."

Brown looked puzzled.

"The problem had a couple of sides. They'd made no campaign contributions. The paperwork wasn't in order. And he was worried because the items we *were* billed for were expensive European goods, but Bruhof only trades in the Orient and South America." Justice turned back to the wall. "At least as far as we know."

Silence. Brown was determined to say no more than necessary. Justice raised his chin from its spot atop his intertwined fingers, and without looking in Brown's direction said, "Jim."

"Sir?"

"Keep on this. I want to know what the city police know, and I want to know at 8:00 a.m."

"Yes, sir."

"One other question."

"Yes, sir."

"You've told me what CPD thinks but you haven't told me what you think."

The ulcer burned hot again. Brown paused to try to swallow the pain, then answered. "I think it's too early to give you a judgment on what City has."

Justice looked at him hard, as if trying to decide whether to challenge him in light of his earlier statements.

Instead of pumping him, the Governor said, "Back to Mrs. Justice."

Brown felt a twisted kind of relief. He had no better news to give regarding the whereabouts of Mrs. Justice, but he was much more comfortable with a status report on the Governor's wife than on another round of tough questions about his wife's potential culpability.

"Sir, I'm afraid we know nothing new. There's no warm trail anywhere, so we're backtracking. We've monitored the downtown without talking to hospitality industry people. We've covered transportation. And I have men out now, questioning the staff at the mansion and trying to turn over stones in other areas in hopes of finding a fresh lead."

"Is that it?" Justice said brusquely, looking back to the wall.

"I'm afraid so, sir."

Again, Justice looked off into never-never land for a quiet two or three minutes. Brown just preserved the quiet and struggled against the pain in his gut.

Finally, Justice spoke slowly, still looking far away. "Jim, I guess I don't have to tell you that the events of the last twenty-four hours could mean deep trouble for me. Barney knows it, all too well. I brushed him off because I can't deal rationally with a situation when I'm fighting down the demons of fear for my own political life."

The only thing Brown hated more than being the bearer of bad tidings to his boss was being his confidante. His ulcer flamed.

But he kept his mouth shut.

"I know I'm not telling you anything you don't already know, but here's what my gut tells me. First, I think you should call off the dogs in the search for Evelyn. The more waves we make there, the more likely we'll get a back-wash of trouble. I believe she's all right, just trying to make a statement. And she *has* contacted me once."

Brown just kept quiet.

"As to the Minnis affair," Justice continued, "I want you to be on this personally. You, and you alone, are to stay in vital touch with CPD. I want reports three times a day, every four hours, beginning at 8:00 a.m. In the meantime, I'm going to put Barney onto damage control. He's the best for that.

"We must face the realities of the current situation and deal with them head on. Do you agree?"

Brown breathed a sigh of relief to himself, then drew a long breath back to be able to speak. "Governor, I believe that course is the wisest."

Justice turned to the chief. "Then do it!"

▼ ▼ ▼ ▼

The security guard in the lobby of 1277 North Capitol had had no idea where Dan was. He had mumbled a complaint about how Lindy had gotten to stay in on the action upstairs, and how blowing other people's noses was not supposed to be part of his job. Lindy had changed her mind about the hunk. He was cute, but also an overgrown baby.

She left the building.

She wanted to be with Dan, but she knew he would know where to find her when he finished whatever he'd gotten into.

Lindy thought about hailing a cab for the short trip back to the office. Her knees felt like they'd been replaced with gelatin.

She decided that the walk would do her good in more ways than one, so she'd make it back to the *News* building on her own. She stopped at the coffee machine and poured a cup of late afternoon brew that was so thick she almost had to yank it out of the pot with a fork. Then she headed straight for her cubicle, her own little three-tiered world where she and the coffee could get her act back together.

"Lindy, where on earth have you been?"

Dan yelled across the rows of desks, computer terminals all lined up like one-eyed plastic soldiers at the squat. He wove in and out of the desks, hurrying as quickly as these barriers would allow, to get to her.

Lindy just stopped when she heard the commotion and stared in his direction.

Dan cleared the last desk and ran to her, taking her shoulders in his hands and shaking gently, meaning it as a mild reprimand. "Lindy, where were you? I was in a panic."

"Dan," Lindy said, craning her neck to look upwards into his eyes. She wasn't used to looking at him from this close. "Why are you so excited? Why'd you go off and leave me?"

"What?"

"Why did you go off and leave me? When I came out of the ladies' room, you were gone."

Dan's mouth opened as he dropped his jaw. "The ladies' room?" But there was a smile now.

"Of course. Where else would I be in that frame of mind?"

"You were in the ladies' room?" He began to laugh.

This made Lindy angry. "Stop it, you jerk." She hit him on his shoulder. "I had to compose myself, and the middle of a lobby is no place to do that."

She was angry. She made a quick flip of her other hand and sent the contents of the coffee cup splashing across his upper chest and underneath his chin. Luckily the late afternoon coffee was as cold as it was strong.

Dan backed off instantly, wiping at his neck and his clothes. "What are you doing?"

"I told you to stop laughing and I certainly don't need a clown comforting me." She stepped out and headed straight for the far hallway that led to her cubicle.

"Lindy, I'm sorry." He started after her, then wiped at his shirt again. "Wait a minute," he said as he looked around for something to wipe up the cold coffee.

But she didn't wait. She swung around the corner and marched down the hall to her office. When she came to the opening in the movable walls, she paused, looked in, closed her eyes in relief and took a deep breath, then took the three steps to her swivel chair and sank in. The only place she'd rather have been at that moment was in a tub of hot, perfumed water.

▼ ▼ ▼ 12 ▼ ▼ ▼

Dan crept sheepishly up to the opening of Lindy's cubicle. He had walked very softly down the shiny linoleum of the hallway and stood in the doorway trying to select just the right words. Lindy's back was to the opening. She was leaning at an angle and rocking gently. He couldn't see her face.

"Stay away," Lindy said softly but firmly. "I'm mad right now and I don't want you to bother me."

"Good grief, Lind. Do all women have eyes in the back of their heads or do you have special powers?"

"It takes no special powers to hear a gorilla clomping down a deserted hallway in shoes that need a lube job."

Dan was still standing at the door, waiting to be invited in. He rolled his eyes at her comment, dreading the confrontation to come. "I'm sorry," he said. "I—"

"Nope! Nope! Nope! Shush!" Lindy rattled off the words like a machine gunner as she raised her hand to stop him mid-sentence. "I forgive you." She turned the chair to face him. "In fact, I owe you the apology." Lindy stood and walked over to him on the narrow path that was the only clutterless part of her floor. She brushed at the coffee stain on his shirt, then took hold of his collars and snapped them, as if trying to put some of the starch back into them. "Where's your tie?"

"Trashed it," he said, his heart beating a little faster. "Beyond reclamation." He had never stood this close to his partner, at least not this way, with her acting like a woman instead of a reporter.

Lindy let go of his collars and let her hands drop to his chest, palms stretched on the still damp coffee stains that had ruined his shirt. She looked up from the stains and her hands and his chest to Dan's eyes. "I'm sorry. I had no right. I just can't get the awful picture of that poor dead woman out of my mind, and your laughing set me off."

Dan's heart was racing. He was sure that she could feel it pounding underneath her palms, so he reached up, covered her hands with his, slid his thumbs between his chest and her palms and squeezed.

The quiet in the hallway seemed to him to draw circles around them, bands of silence that made him more aware of their aloneness, bands that seemed to contract in a way that moved him inexorably closer to her.

Dan had never felt for Lindy what that silence and her nearness were raising up in him.

Her eyes. Her glorious, round, sparkling, bright, intelligent eyes.

He wanted to be closer to them. To her lips.

"It was terrible, Dan," she said with a broken voice.

"I think you need to sit down and tell me about it," he said, pulling her away from him. "I want to hear." He guided her gently backwards on the bare strip of floor to her swivel chair and lowered her to the seat. He turned, dislodged the other standard office-issue chair from two inches of papers surrounding each leg, and planted it squarely in the bare patch in front of her.

He took hold of the arms of her chair, turned her to face him directly so that her knees touched his, then leaned back. "Now talk. I'm all ears."

▼ ▼ ▼ ▼

"Yes, I'm Evelyn Justice, Officer. What can I do for you?" The shock of seeing the state trooper had caused her insides to reel, but her finishing school training, the long years as a hostess in the most difficult of circumstances, and the subtle but definite change she'd undergone in the past twenty-four hours kept her surface unruffled.

She spoke to the young trooper as if he was a newly arrived guest at a late afternoon cocktail party.

Maria and the young officer couldn't have recognized it, but Evelyn did as the words came out of her mouth: She was poised. She was calm. In control.

In spite of the awful things that had been happening to her, in spite of the cold reception she'd gotten from Franklin on the phone, in spite of the shocking news of the tramp's death, she was calm. In control.

Not depressed!

She still could feel the dark shadow of depression lurking behind the officer, wanting to leap around him and down her tunnel of consciousness to take over.

She almost wanted it to. In some warped way, the darkness was comforting. It insulated her from the coldness and the pain of life. It was a powerful excuse for losing her husband's attention, her own youthful attractiveness, and her engaging social life. In fact, her depression had been like a pair of shears—she had pruned her life down to a painful stump and had castrated all Franklin's logic in trying to coax her out.

She almost wanted it to fill her again, to justify her in the face of a young police officer's question and to exculpate her from whatever rash action she might take.

She *almost* wanted it.

But she didn't.

She could feel her old self stirring, as if from a long slumber. The few hours she'd spent away from her life on public display and the few minutes of her real and meaningful connection to Maria's life of loss and aloneness had made a change in Evelyn. A little switch had gone off deep inside.

It seemed that for the first time in—how long had it
been? months? years?—at least the first time in months
that thoughts and feelings were beginning to flow outward instead of inward. She could feel that old self
stirring and it was enough to hold the depression at bay
and to respond to the trooper with her head held high.

"Mrs. Justice, we're under orders to question all personnel associated with the operation of the Governor's
mansion in order to determine your whereabouts. I must
report that I have found you. Please don't try to escape."

"Escape?" Evelyn replied, incredulous. A flash of
anger filled her. She stood slowly to her feet and drew in
a long breath through clenched teeth. "Young man, do
you know who I am?"

Maria walked toward her with a frightened look on her
face. She stood between Evelyn and the trooper and
motioned to Evelyn, as if to stop her from talking or to
calm her. Evelyn grasped her arm and gently pushed her
aside.

"Yes, ma'am."

"Good!" Evelyn responded, her eyes narrowed in
anger as her old self stretched to fill the empty place for
this encounter. "Then I won't have to remind you that I
am the wife of the Governor of this state. Do you have a
warrant for my arrest or any orders other than to invade
the sanctity of the homes of my staff and badger them
with your questions?"

Maria had a look of near-panic on her face. "Mrs.
Justice," she whispered, "please do not anger him."

"No, ma'am. I'm just to question those assigned to me
and to report back whatever I find."

"Has there been any criminal activity on my part or on
the part of my staff?"

"No, ma'am." The young trooper's voice was more
tentative than before.

"Then by whose authority do you intrude into this or any other home associated with my husband's administration?" Evelyn squeezed Maria's hand.

"Direct orders from Chief Brown. Now ma'am, maybe you misunderstand the—"

"No!" Evelyn said loudly and firmly. "It is you who misunderstand. I demand that you leave this house at once."

The trooper had shifted uncomfortably from one foot to another during Evelyn's tirade, obviously unsure how to handle the situation. When she finished, he said, in a half-challenging, half-questioning tone, "I'll have to report what I found here."

"You do that," Evelyn said. "You do just that. You go right now to your car and call Chief Brown and give him this message: If he wants to talk to me, he now knows exactly where to find me."

▼ ▼ ▼ ▼

"I don't know how to express how terrible it was, Dan!" When Dan leaned back in his seat to indicate that he was ready for her to talk, Lindy involuntarily mimicked him. She too leaned back in her chair, laid her head back on the cushioned fabric of the headrest area, and closed her eyes. But she wasn't in that position for more than two seconds when she shook her head vigorously, as if trying to dislodge water trapped in her ear. "Oh," she said, shaking her head a second time. "Eyes closed or eyes opened, I still see her. I've seen other corpses, other murder scenes. I've seen blood before. But somehow this seemed even more cruel."

Dan patted her hand gently. "Lindy, my Chinese grandmother always said, 'People are people because they have fellow-feeling. Without it, even though they have eyes, ears, nose—they are not really people.' " He stopped patting and let his hand come to rest on hers. "It's okay for you to feel this way."

She wanted to move on, to talk about something else. She needed to back off this for a minute.

"Let me tell you what happened after we split up today," she said, changing the subject. Lindy's body changed position as she began to talk, smoothly transitioning from the relaxed but pained expression of trouble to her forward-leaning professional self, ready to engage a task at hand. "I got a call just as I was finishing the rewrite on the article about that stupid symposium on European union at the university," Lindy began. "Some loser who'd called me a couple of times before beat around the bush about a tip he had on some state worker.

"He said this person, a woman friend, was connected to what he called 'druggies.' Don't know if he meant dealers or doers. But the call was about the person being in trouble, presumably with her lover—get this—who *wasn't* a druggie. He didn't say who the lover was or what the trouble was, but when I pressed him, he did say who the friend was."

"Annie Minnis," Dan said, the connection to Lindy's presence at 1277 North Capitol becoming instantly clear.

"Annie Minnis!" Lindy repeated. She said the words with a real note of sadness in her voice. "That's when I left you the *TOSS* message and took off."

"Did you go directly to the Minnis apartment?"

"No reason to do otherwise," she said, feeling better as she eased back into what seemed to her to be normality. "When I got to the apartment, I conned the security guard into letting me in. You saw what I saw, Dan. You looked in the door and saw the poor woman dead on the floor."

She paused again and rolled her head and eyes up to the left, toward the ceiling. "I ran to her and saw the hideous knife sticking out of the back of her neck and I knew it was too late. The guard felt for her pulse under her chin and in her wrist," Lindy touched those spots on her own body for emphasis, "but he couldn't find one. I could have told him.

"I looked up to find a phone and that's when I saw that the whole place was trashed. Top to bottom. Couch slashed, glass broken, tables overturned. The bedroom was in the same condition—well, not quite as bad. Stuff was out of drawers and a mattress was pulled off the bed, but nothing broken.

"The guard called 911 from a bedroom phone and reported what we'd found. I stayed in the living room to keep her company till the coroner came."

Lindy got a serious, distant look on her face again. "I felt like I needed to be with her . . . so she wouldn't be alone." She paused as if she were looking at the scene in her mind, then continued, her voice more intense: "When the police arrived, the guard came back in and was playing traffic cop, wanting me to move or to go in the hall and wait or to ask me questions. But I just sat there watching over her. Dan, I really felt for her. I felt sad, and frightened, and angry, and I felt a terrible loss for her."

Dan squeezed her fingers and smiled. "My Chinese grandmother would be pleased with you."

Lindy cocked her head slightly with a question on her face.

"Yes, she'd be pleased," Dan said. "You have fellow-feeling. That means you're real people."

She looked at Dan again. "One thing I do know." She leaned slightly closer. "It's put my life in perspective and made me much more aware of what's important." She leaned even closer.

This time Dan was leaning in too, like Lindy was a magnet whose attractive force he wasn't able to resist.

Just as she was about to speak, the shrill clamor of a phone ringing cut her off.

It was her phone, her sheep-bleating phone that sounded like a fire alarm in the stillness of the darkened offices. Dan looked in her eyes. "You need to get the phone, but remember," his voice grew softer, "this discussion isn't over yet."

She looked at him with a look that asked, what do you mean? The phone shrieked again. Lindy picked it up and raised it to her ear. "Blakely," she said in as routine a voice as she could muster.

"Did you do what I asked?" It was the geek, the informant.

"Did you check on Annie Minnis for me?"

▼ ▼ ▼ 13 ▼ ▼ ▼

"Rosemary, this is Mrs. Justice. Put me through to the Governor, please."

"Mrs. Justice. How nice to speak to you. I'm sorry, but the Governor is in conference with Chief Brown of the state patrol. They've been meeting on and off all afternoon, what with the death of Annie Minnis. He asked that I hold all calls."

"Brown? Is he still there? Put me through immediately. Brown will want to hear what I have to say, too."

"Yes, ma'am."

Evelyn cast a confident look at Maria, hoping she'd pick up on it and feel a bit more encouraged about all this police business. She covered the mouthpiece of the phone and said, "You'll see. This will all come out fine in the end. I'm sorry that I dallied and didn't tell you all that had happened to me in the past two days. But it didn't even dawn on me that you might be adversely affected. Selfish! Stupid and—"

She raised her head abruptly. "Franklin? If you don't know already, I am with Maria Arvizu, our upstairs maid. She has been kind enough to provide refuge for me as I've thought through this whole miserable situation."

"How kind of her." Franklin's voice was perfectly intoned to communicate appreciation, but Evelyn knew it was seething with sarcasm.

"It was indeed. I intend to reward her for that kindness. I have some things to say to you and I'll be brief. I know that you have Chief Brown in the office with you. Has he been holding your hand all afternoon?"

"Evelyn. The chief and I have had to meet regarding the tragic murder of Ms. Minnis. He's been in and out all day. You should know also that we're on the speaker-phone."

"Then pick up, please." She waited to hear the tell-tale click and the clearing of the sound from her husband's end of the line.

"Yes, what is that you want to tell me, dear?"

"Short and sweet. First, I'll be coming home tomorrow. Don't bother to come for me tonight. I have a great deal more I need to talk over with Maria before I come home. I'll catch a cab in the morning."

"That's fine, dear. My main concern has been for your safety. I'll rest better tonight."

"Franklin, your main concern is now and always has been for your own precious behind."

No response.

"Second, I want to see you at noon tomorrow and discuss our situation. I have some things to say that will hearten you, and some that will frustrate you."

"I'm sorry dear, I have an app—"

"Cancel it. I either speak with you at lunch, in our own house, or I have lunch with the press."

"Very well. I'll have Rosemary make the necessary adjustments to my calendar."

"Good. Third, please put me back on the speaker-phone."

The Governor didn't respond.

"Franklin, I insist on addressing both you and the chief at the same time."

"Are you sure?" he asked, doubtfully.

"You needn't worry. I'll watch what I say."

Another pause, then Franklin said, "Very well."

A click came through the line, then the tell-tale hollow sound of a speakerphone's microphone picking up the empty noise of an office.

"You're on the speaker, Evelyn. I have Chief Brown with me in the office."

"Thank you, Franklin. I have one final thing to say and both of you need to hear this. You both have been intoxicated by your positions to the point that you think the state patrol is your own private police force. I'm sure you're already aware of this, but I am spending time at the home of one of the women who works at our residence. Jim, one of your troopers came here this evening, came into this house uninvited, looking for me. He made intimidating remarks about my not trying to escape. Escape! As if I were some prisoner! He had no right. You have no right. I want you both to know that tomorrow morning, I intend to contact an attorney completely dissociated with your administration, Franklin, and bring charges against the patrol. You had no right."

"Mrs. Justice, I assure you—"

"Evelyn," Franklin interrupted the chief. "Of course, you may do what you want in this situation. I just ask you to be circumspect in that decision and think of what such action will mean to all concerned."

"Including the way you'll look in the press?"

"That's not what I mean at all, and you know it."

"Governor, could I say something to Mrs. Justice?" Evelyn heard decisiveness in the chief's tone.

"Certainly, Jim," Franklin responded.

"Mrs. Justice."

"Yes."

"I'd like to say something to you in the best interests of both you and your husband, but I don't want you to misunderstand me."

He paused for some response, but Evelyn didn't give him one. She wasn't sure what he wanted to say or why he wanted to say it.

"Are you still there, ma'am?"

"Yes."

"Uh . . . I *would* advise you to speak to an attorney sometime soon, but not for the reason you have in mind now."

"And for what reason *should* I seek an attorney's services, Chief Brown?"

"With the funny circumstances surrounding your disappearance and your link to the deceased, you're a prime candidate to come under suspicion in the murder of your husband's aid."

"You mean his mistress!" she spit out angrily.

"Well, uh . . . I . . . " the chief sputtered.

Evelyn could tell that she'd caught him off guard with that. She could just see Franklin's face turning red with anger. The little act of defiance felt good at first, then almost instantly it turned her stomach bitter and twisted the knot that already was growing there.

"Evelyn, stop muddying the water with your petty jealousy." Franklin barked the order like he was a drill sergeant and she was a recruit fresh in boot camp.

"My petty jealousy," Evelyn said, drawing out each syllable of each word in a tone of disbelief. She was furious. "How dare—"

"Excuse me," the chief interjected authoritatively. "This is the first I've heard about any mistress or any jealousy, but if what you just said is true, then that's all the more reason you should be worried about being a suspect, especially given your unknown whereabouts at the time of the murder. If you're going to hire an attorney, you'd better consult your husband and get a good one. And make sure he *is* a friend of the administration."

The specter of suspicion by the police was not one Evelyn wanted to deal with. She knew she wasn't guilty. She knew even if there was an investigation, it would prove her innocence.

At least she thought she knew it. She had been wrestling with the somewhat surreal events of the last months and especially the last few days, but . . .

No! She wasn't guilty. She wouldn't let this Midwestern Mussolini intimidate her! "I suppose you are searching for me because you want to haul me in and put me away."

"No, ma'am," Brown said. "Not at all. No, ma'am, City Police are handling this one. The state almost always lets them take the lead in their jurisdiction unless there's something unusual about the case." The chief was sounding more like an advocate to Evelyn every minute. "I'll be honest with you. They're real interested in us finding you so they can question you. So far I have been able to divert their attention from you for only two reasons."

"Which are?" Evelyn asked, her heart beating slightly faster as the drone of the chief's professional demeanor stirred her fear.

"One: We've handled your disappearance from the get-go. Asked them to let us do it all because of the sensitive nature of the problem."

"And the other reason?" she asked.

"Their first line of reasoning is that the death is drug-related. They're gonna bark up that tree till they find the raccoons or till their dogs get another scent."

"And I'm one of the other scents!"

"Looks like it. I didn't think so until what you just said, but you certainly will be if they can't find a solid drug link."

Evelyn had been listening intently as the chief spoke. She wasn't sure how to think or feel about what he had said. He sounded sincere, like he was telling her the truth, like he really cared.

But so had Franklin while he was cheating on her all those years.

"I'll think about what you've said, Chief, before I make any final decisions."

"Thank you, ma'am. I will have to speak to you—soon—but I appreciate you hearing me out."

"Franklin, we'll discuss this further at lunch tomorrow. I'll see you then."

Evelyn hung up the phone and went to Maria. She put her arms around her, patted her back, and said, "Thank you again, Maria—my friend."

Maria returned the embrace, then Evelyn turned them both back to the table and the cold chicken. "First, let's finish dinner. Then, I need some advice on what to do tomorrow."

▼ ▼ ▼ ▼

The Governor and the chief of the state patrol looked at each other long and hard as Justice leaned up and pressed the disconnect button on the telephone set. Neither spoke for a while.

Finally Justice spoke, more to dispel the uncomfortable silence than to communicate anything. "Stubborn woman!" He knew it was a stupid thing to say, but Evelyn's outburst about Annie being his mistress had him feeling very, very self-conscious right then.

"Uh-huh," Brown grunted, obviously thinking about something else.

"Governor, is it true what your wife said about your relationship to the victim?"

Justice squirmed uncomfortably in his leather chair, then decided that straight up and at it was the only way to respond. "Yes, Jim. It is. I've been seeing Annie for some time. After hearing Evelyn today, perhaps you can understand why."

"Well, sir, it's none of my business what you do in your marriage or out of it. But that fact certainly shines a whole new light on the situation."

"You seem to have something else on your mind."

"Yes, sir, I do."

"Say it, then. Don't waste my time."

"Well, sir. This whole thing could be bad for you, too."

"God help me, I know. The political fallout from this could be radioactive!"

"I don't mean politically, sir."

"Then what *do* you mean?"

Slowly, the chief said, "I mean that your relationship to the deceased *will* get out sooner or later, and if CPD's current line of investigation goes nowhere, you're as likely to come under suspicion as your wife is."

A long silence.

"One other question, sir."

Franklin looked at his chief and raised his eyebrows to grant permission for the question.

"Can you document where you were and what you were doing at the time of the murder?"

▼ ▼ ▼ ▼

Lindy covered the mouthpiece of the phone with her hands and whispered to Dan, "It's the guy. The guy who called this afternoon."

Dan stood up, clearly excited. He turned left, then right, like he was looking for another phone or a notepad or something that would help him participate in the conversation.

"You alone?" the voice asked.

Lindy hesitated. "Yes." She wasn't sure why he asked, so she wasn't sure how to respond.

"Then why'd you cover the phone?"

She hesitated again, looking at Dan for help. He still was nervously lifting himself up and down on the balls of his feet. When she looked at him, her face clearly reflecting her mini-dilemma, he just stopped the rocking motion and jabbed his head forward. *What?* he mouthed.

"Okay," she said. "My partner's with me. I covered the phone because I wanted him to know it was you again, and I didn't want to scare you off. I've told him all about your call this afternoon."

This time it was the caller's turn to hesitate. Several seconds went by, several very uncomfortable seconds for Lindy, and he still didn't speak. She could take no more of it and spoke up: "Okay? Is that okay?"

"Yeah," the voice came back. "As long as he's your partner."

"We work together on everything."

"So, did you and your partner check on Annie Minnis for me?"

"Yes. We did." Lindy motioned for Dan to go into his adjoining cubicle as she spoke. "Let me ask you a favor. Will you let my partner pick up an extension so he can be in on this conversation?"

Again, silence.

"It's okay if you don't want him to," she added after a pause, hoping she hadn't miffed him.

"All right. But I'm talking to you. He's listening. Just listening."

"You got it."

She stood up and lifted her chin toward the top of the wall dividers as if to help lift her words over the top of the carpet and stainless steel barriers. "Dan, I'm going to conference forty-seven. Be ready to pick up." She turned to the phone, looked at the rows of buttons to be sure she'd press the right ones in the right order, then spoke into the phone again. "Look, I'm going to conference us. If I cut you off, will you call back?"

"Maybe I will and maybe I won't."

She rolled her eyes. "Hold for a minute."

She put him on hold and rang Dan's line. When he picked up, she said, "You can listen in, but don't talk unless he talks to you or unless I ask you to. I don't want to lose him." Then she pressed the *conference* button, and the flashing button which indicated that a caller was holding on *1947*.

"You there?" she asked.

"I'm here. Now that you've got your cheering section, are you gonna answer me?"

"Yes. I—that is, we—did check on Annie Minnis."

"And?"

"And . . . " Lindy again wasn't sure how to answer the guy. She wished she could at least see Dan and his facial expressions to get some feedback. "She's dead."

"What?" the voice exploded on the other end.

"We checked on Ms. Minnis and found that your fears were confirmed. She's dead."

"I—I didn't expect this. Annie dead? Look, this changes everything."

Lindy could hear the surprise in his voice, and she was sure that he was about to bug off the phone and get lost. It sounded like all of a sudden he was in deeper than he expected. "I want you to know, as soon as we hung up this afternoon I went straight to her apartment. I talked a guard into letting me in. We found her dead on the living room floor. Murdered."

"Great deduction, Sherlock. Of course she was murdered. I told you she'd gotten herself mixed up with the wrong kind of people!"

"I know it. That's what you told me and you were right." Lindy was talking faster, wanting to keep the pace of the conversation going so he wouldn't hang up. "You also told me that you were her friend. I don't know what kind of a friend or what kind of a relationship the two of you had, but if you were her friend, you've got to help her now. You told me that she'd been involved with drugs. How do you know that?"

"That's none of your business how I know that. I just know it."

Before the guy had finished his sentence, Dan's head appeared over the wall divider. He slashed at his throat with one hand as the other held the phone, then waved a clear *No*. He didn't want her to pursue that line.

"I'm sorry," she said quickly. "Look. Let me say something, then ask you the question in another way. If you're Annie's friend, you want to see that whoever did this to her gets what he deserves. I'm a reporter. I have the power of the press behind me in this situation. I can take what you have and make it count to even the score."

"Yeah!" the guy said with a huff of derision. "I know about the press and settling scores. I was Annie's friend, but not the way you might think. And I was never friend enough to her to make me want to get involved in a murder. All the police and their questions. Forget it!"

"Just a minute," a third voice said. It was Dan. Lindy closed her eyes and breathed a sigh of relief. She felt like she was about to lose the guy. "This is Dan Li-pong, Ms. Blakely's partner."

"You're not in this conversation."

"I am long enough to clarify something." Dan always believed that it was easier to ask forgiveness than to ask permission, so he didn't even pause for the caller's approval. "You work with us to bring out what happened to this woman and we can make you two guarantees."

He stopped to let the bait wiggle just a little to entice the guy to swallow it. Lindy closed her eyes and crossed her fingers.

"Your guarantees probably aren't worth the ink it would take to write them down." The caller's words sounded final, like he was rebuffing the offer. Then he added, "but I'll listen."

Then it dawned on Lindy what Dan was doing. She'd approached the man as if he were Minnis's friend, somebody who cared about her. That was stupid. A friend never would have been secreting calls to a reporter about love affairs or doing drugs. This guy wanted something from Minnis, and he also wanted something from a call to the press. Dan had picked up on that right away and was about to save this call from oblivion. *Yes!* she exclaimed to herself as she pulled her fist down like a hammer the way an athlete does when he scores points. *Yes! Dan!*

"Two guarantees. First, anonymity. I don't know what you do for a living and I don't care. But in my business, finding and developing sources is what it's all about. You can write like a third-grader if you've got lines to people who know."

Lindy was shaking her head in approval. She could see Dan buttering this guy up.

"That means a smart reporter always protects his sources. If I screw you, I get screwed. It all comes back to roost and I'm history. That's the privilege of the press and nobody—not police, not lawyers, not the government—can make us talk. You tell us what you know, we guarantee your anonymity."

Dan waited for the guy to swallow the bait—and the hook.

"And the second guarantee?"

Dan phrased his next words carefully. "Like I said, I don't know who you are or why you called Ms. Blakely in the first place, but I'll guarantee that I'll—I should say we—will do all we can to see that you get satisfaction. If it's legal, we'll do our best to see you get what you originally wanted."

Lindy waited patiently now.

"Too late for me to get what I wanted."

Dan didn't speak.

Lindy's heart sank. She was sure they were about to lose him again, but she kept quiet, too, sensing that anything she'd say now would nix the whole deal.

"But you're right," the caller continued, "there will be some satisfaction in telling you what I know. If you keep quiet about where you got it."

Lindy sensed that and jumped in. "Listen. You called this afternoon and I believed you. I dropped what I was doing and went to check out what you said. Now you've got to believe us. We guarantee that you'll remain anonymous, and that you will get satisfaction."

A long pause. Then, "All right. Here it is. I told you Annie didn't show up for work today. Called in sick. I went by to check on her and found her decked out in sheer black stockings, wrapped in a robe and smelling of cologne and whiskey—my idea of a real sick-day! Anyway, she wasn't happy to see me and definitely didn't want to talk. I figured she had some guy with her for a lunch-time quickie.

"So I wandered back to the elevators and when one opened, I stepped in and shut it down. Figured I'd wait and see who Romeo was."

Lindy remembered the caller had used that tired cliché when he'd called before. She rolled her eyes again.

"And?" Dan asked.

"I'm gettin' there," the guy said. "I'm outa sight of the security cameras, so I relaxed and figured I would just wait. Well, I didn't have to wait long. Pretty soon a ruckus came from down the hall. I didn't really think it was coming from Annie's place, till I hear the word *Governor* real plain."

A shock coursed through Lindy, a bolt like lightning that burned her as it raced through her body.

"*Governor?*" Dan asked.

"That's what I said, isn't it? It was Annie, yelling. I peeked out of the elevator to have a look-see and just about that time her door opened and who do you think walked out, big as life?"

"Franklin Justice?" Lindy asked, barely above a whisper, more to herself than to the caller.

"The one and only. She was yellin' at him. 'I'm gonna ruin you,' she said. I was about to have a heart attack for fear when he swung around to her he'd see me. He was ticked!

"Well, I'd almost turned the elevator back on to get outa there, but when he turned around, I waited. They were yellin' at each other, but I didn't pay much attention. I had my camera with me and I was frantically fumbling around to get the thing set to take a picture."

"You got a picture of the Governor and Annie Minnis?" Dan asked.

"I hope I did. I shot one, but who knows whether you ever get a picture when you want one?"

"Wait a minute," Dan interrupted. "You're telling us that you were hiding in a dead elevator when Annie Minnis and Franklin Justice were fighting in the hallway of her building, *and* that you shot a picture of the two?"

"You take good notes," the caller said.

"You normally carry a camera around on your lunch hour?" Lindy asked.

"Not normally," the guy said. "But a lota times. I like takin' pictures. And I'm semi-professional. I sell a lot of the ones I shoot."

"What happened after you took the picture?"

"I don't know after that. I shot the picture, then hit the elevator's *Stop* button to turn it back on. The doors closed and I was on my way down."

"What did you do then?"

"I got off at the ground floor and headed straight for the men's room. I went into the last stall and hid out for ten minutes. I didn't want him seeing me coming or going. I work for the state!"

"Is that when you called me?" Lindy asked.

"No, I didn't call you for a long time after that. I hung around the men's room a little longer, then got feelin' guilty, like maybe I coulda done something, so I went back up to her place to see what I could do."

Lindy's skin crawled. She didn't know what it was, but she felt the caller was lying now. He was no friend to Annie and he was up to no good. Her intuition fairly shouted that to her. "How did you get back onto the elevator? In fact, how did you get on the elevator in the first place? Those old lifts are keyed so that only residents or security can operate them."

"I didn't say I got on the elevator on the first floor," the caller shot back. "I walked up to the second floor and got on there. The only place you need keys is on the ground floor."

"He's right, Lindy," Dan added.

She didn't like that. This guy was lying about something and Dan was over there agreeing with him.

"Anyway," the caller continued, "I went back up to Annie's floor and stepped off the elevator and what do you think I saw?" Neither of the reporters answered him, but it didn't matter. He was getting into telling the tale now and the pause had a great dramatic effect.

"I saw this black dude just standing in front of Annie's door, sorta leanin' on the door frame. He wasn't knocking or anything. He was just standing there, waitin'."

Lindy was beginning to feel dizzy. The comfort of Dan's presence and the surprise of this call had taken her mind off how she felt about Annie Minnis's death. But this guy was repulsive to her. He was crude and insensitive. She was sure he wanted to use Annie for his own ends, and that thought brought back all the horror of the poor woman's senseless, gruesome death.

She closed her eyes and began to breathe deeply to try to make things stop swimming in her head.

"What did you do when you saw the man?" Dan asked. "Did he see you?"

"You bet he saw me. It's one long empty hallway. How could he miss me? But I stopped at the second door from the elevator and knocked. So I knocked, and I knocked again, then went back to the elevator."

"Did you get a picture of the black guy?"

"You crazy? This guy was a pimp or dealer or something. He was dressed in a suit that would have cost me a month's salary. I wasn't gonna mess with him. I hit the ground floor button and got outa there."

Another long pause followed the obvious conclusion of the man's story. Lindy didn't want to talk. She felt sick to her stomach.

Dan was the one to speak. "That's some story, buddy. How do we know it's true?"

Lindy's eyes opened wide. That devil! That shrewd, wonderful devil! He was going to get the picture from this sleaze.

"Whadda you mean, how do you know this is true? I was there, that's why! Whadda you tryin' to say? You callin' me a liar?"

"No, no, no," Dan said in a detached sort of way. "That's the point. I don't know whether you're lying or telling the truth. It's a great story, but we wouldn't touch it with a ten-foot pole unless we knew there was some truth in it."

"This makes me mad! Didn't I tell the girl that there was something wrong this afternoon? Didn't she go and find out I wasn't lyin'?"

"Oh, yeah!" Dan said. "You weren't lying about Annie Minnis being in trouble. That's pretty clear. But who's to say that the Governor or this black man or anybody else was there? Seems to me that it's just as likely *you* killed her."

Lindy smiled. She was so glad Dan was twisting this guy around. *She* should be doing this, she thought. She really wanted to rip this guy, but she definitely wasn't herself at the moment.

"Wait just a minute," the caller said, slowly and suspiciously. "What are you doin'? What about your guarantees?"

"You've still got 'em, buddy. But if you think for a half-a-second that I'd take some crazy story about the Governor and sex and murder to my editor without some *very* substantial backing, you're wrong with a capital *W!* You give me what I need, then I give you satisfaction and a guarantee of anonymity."

"Huh!" the man grunted. "I guess you're right. It does sound risky."

A pause.

"Okay. I'll mail you a copy of the picture if it comes out."

"No way. If there is a picture, it's got to run in tomorrow morning's paper. We'll meet you to pick it up."

"Hold on. Now who's crazy? I'll talk to you on the phone, but I don't trust your guarantee that much. If we can't arrange a drop, then no deal."

Lindy was shaking her head *Yes* in big, dramatic moves. She could hardly believe Dan had this guy eating out of his hand.

"I have no problem with that," Dan said, like a banker about to get a customer to sign for a loan on his terms. "Here's how we'll do it. I don't know where you are and I don't care. You know where we are. Name a place that you can get to before us, where you can drop the film and not worry about it. Hang out and keep an eye on it until we come. You don't have to show yourself, just make sure we get it. Then call us tomorrow."

"Okay . . . Let me think . . . Okay, here it is. There's a post office at Edgewood and Meter Road on the south side, open twenty-four hours. They got cubbyholes full of tax forms in the lobby. I'll stick the film all the way in the back of the first cubbyhole on the bottom row on the far right."

"First slot, bottom row, far right. Got it."

"I'll be watching."

"Call us tomorrow." Dan hung up.

Lindy slammed the phone down and squealed "Yes!" as she grabbed the extra chair in her office and set it on top of the papers on her floor and against the wall divider. She jumped up into the seat, looked over the divider at Dan, and raised her hand for a high five.

Dan stood up and slapped her hand. "Come on, partner. We've got a story to tell, and this is just the beginning."

Lindy stepped off the chair onto the clear path and darted into the hallway. "What do you mean?" she said to Dan as he hurried into the hall.

"I mean you told me what happened to you today, and this guy told us what he knows. But you haven't heard what I found out this afternoon."

▼ ▼ ▼ ▼

"Maria," Evelyn said to her friend as she sipped the last of her very welcome cup of tea. "I'm simply exhausted— physically and emotionally! I feel like I've been on a wild ride for months, even years, and the last day and a half has been the worst for sudden ups and downs."

"Then you must go to bed now. It is good to have much sleep when you are very tired."

"I do want to go to bed soon. I am very tired. But do you know, it's because I'm *tired* that I want to go to bed."

"*Yes!* It is good."

"No, Maria. I'm not making myself clear. Do you remember after my suicide attempt, when you were so patient to sit by my bedside and spend time with me?"

"Yes."

"Do you remember that I was in bed most of the time?"

"Yes."

"I was in bed because I couldn't get out of bed, not because I was tired and needed sleep."

Maria nodded her head, acknowledging the meaning Evelyn was trying to get at. "I think I understand."

"I was depressed all the time. I didn't want to open my eyes. I didn't want to see a living soul. I just wanted to sleep and forget the troubles that were depressing me. I wanted to die."

"Mrs. Justice, it is as you say with me after I lose my Irenea. When I lose my husband and my son, I was very sad, very lost inside, but I had to be strong for my daughter. When she was taken from me, I had no reason to be strong. I just had reason to leave that country to save my life, but I am like you. I did not care to live or to die."

"I want to go to bed tonight because I'm tired, really tired. I'm terribly confused about all that's happened since yesterday, but I have a strange calm inside about it, and I can feel my long-lost confidence beginning to swell again.

"One last request."

"More tea?"

"No, thank you. I've had enough." She raised her hand, palm out, to reiterate. "Actually, it's a request for you to do something you did with me often when you sat by my bedside during those awful weeks. Would you read the Bible to me? It brought a calm to me then, and I would very much like its calming influence again now."

"It is good, Mrs. Justice. I am happy to read." Maria got up from the couch and walked to her bedroom. A moment later she emerged, Bible in hand. "In the Bible, God speaks to us. I find His voice when I have trouble and when I have . . . uh," she struggled for a word, then shrugged her shoulders, "when I have no trouble."

"I told you how I've always felt about God and the idea that a God could or would somehow communicate with people. But without any argument, when you read to me before, something was there."

"No, Mrs. Justice. Not some*thing*," she said as she opened the book, flipping through the pages. "Some*one* was there. God shows Himself to us in this book."

Evelyn felt the tiredness coming on strong now. She wanted to hear the words from the book, but she couldn't handle more of the talk. Not now. "Would you read? Just a little?"

Maria found the place she was looking for and began to read: "The Lord is my shepherd, I shall not want . . . ."

▼ ▼ ▼ 14 ▼ ▼ ▼

Franklin Justice was in his office before seven o'clock on Thursday morning. He had barely slept for the second night in a row, the previous night being one of the most miserable he could remember. He was all alone in the huge mansion which had been reserved for decades for the Governor and his (perhaps someday *her*) family, all alone with thoughts of Evelyn, Annie, and his political future.

But he wasn't early this morning because of insomnia, which he had, and he wasn't early because it was his habit, which it was. This morning, he came early to avoid contact with all but the most eager of the state worker beavers.

He had seen the morning paper.

He wanted to climb into his bunker, his command center, and from there direct his forces to combat the worst political nightmare of his career.

On the front page, upper section of the largest circulation daily in the state, was a picture of him walking away from an angry, bathrobed Annie Minnis in the hall of her condo.

The sight of the picture had shocked him to the core, first slamming his chest and knocking the wind out of him, then bringing panic like a flood over his already tired and stressed emotions. He absolutely could not believe this paper would print such a story without first requesting his comment. Either something broke late in the evening or he had a real enemy.

From the alarming picture, his eyes had raced to the headline: *Governor's Aide Murdered, Police Suspect Drug Connection.* He scrambled to read the lead story, but didn't get past the first line, *Less than twenty-four hours after announcing a major new drug policy for state workers . . . .*

Justice immediately called George Barnett and James Brown and ordered them to meet him in his office as quickly as they could get there. He also called his long-time friend, political advisor and campaign manager, Dave Frizzell.

"Dave, have you seen the paper this morning?"

"I have, Frank. I was going to call you. We've got a whale of an incident on our hands."

"I'm glad you said *we*, Dave. I really need you in on this one."

"I'll be in your office by seven-thirty."

Justice was so tired and alarmed that he couldn't even think straight or sort out what the issues were, let alone the priorities.

The phone rang as he paced the opulent oriental rug that graced the old hickory floors laid down in his office in bygone days, cursing the men he needed most for not moving faster this morning. The call was coming through on his private, unlisted line, not one of the switchboard lines.

"Justice here."

"Frank," a gruff, raspy voice said. "It's hit the fan this time for sure."

The rasp belonged to Rex Melton, state party chairman and political boss for more years than Franklin had been out of high school. The man was a legend. He had taken over the leadership of the state party in the early fifties after successfully managing Dwight Eisenhower's first presidential campaign in the state. Every one of his peers across the nation had been swept away in the turbulent sixties or before, but Melton had navigated those deadly political waters and came out stronger.

In the mid-sixties, he began to vest different groups and individuals with some of his power. He initiated a finance committee, entirely separate from the political organization and managed by a board of directors made up of business and professional leaders; he began "slating" candidates, a process that allowed the party's volunteer workers to select the candidates they would work to support in the primary elections, a sort of preliminary primary; and he created a structure to oversee the political patronage system, the structure that required state workers to contribute 2 percent of their salaries to the party coffers.

By vesting the hundreds of individuals involved in these programs with both a voice and real political clout, and by maintaining the tightest of controls over them, Melton roared out of the sixties with a string of election victories that was into its third decade by the time Franklin Justice won the Governor's chair.

Melton was old and reclusive now. He still held all the reins, but a person never heard from him unless there was a game going whose stakes were very high, high enough to hold potential for damaging the party apparatus or party control of the government.

Justice had known the call was coming. He just didn't know when.

But how to respond to Melton? Besides the President of the United States, this was the only man on earth that the Governor felt compelled to answer to. In order to survive politically, Justice had to have this old man's support— during and especially after this Minnis debacle.

If he survived it.

There could be no excuses, no explanations, no mercy. This was a fire that would be raging by noon and it simply had to be put out.

"You're right, Rex. This is a bad one."

"Worst I've seen, Frank."

Justice could feel his heart race as he looked nervously around the wall and the ceiling, searching for what to say and how to say it.

"What did you think you were doing seeing this woman?"

"It's not like that, Rex. Annie and I—"

"Frank!" The name was spoken with authority, clearly to cut the statement short. "I'm not your Sunday school teacher. Cut the bull. I thought you had more brains than this."

"Look, Rex—"

"I've seen this over and over." Melton spoke slowly, deliberately. "Some well-intentioned guy scores politically and it goes to his head. He thinks he's got a right to build a little empire, harem and all. Frankly, you've been playing with fire for too long now. This one's gonna burn you bad." The old man swallowed the last word and let out a long, slow, tired, frustrated breath to punctuate his prediction.

"Look, Rex, I've got Barnett, Brown and Frizzell on this. We're going to control the damage and see if we can't turn the tide on this one before it gets too bad."

"Let me see if I can get a message through to your ivory tower, Frank. You've been sleeping with this woman for a long time. I know it. You know it. Now the world knows it. Here's what else I know: You get cozy with a designing woman and she'll suck your blood. This woman's bled you, Frank. I don't know where. I don't know how, but she's bled you. If you were so naive that you don't know where, God help you. You can be sure you'll find out, and so will the rest of the world."

Justice's stomach churned bitterly as Melton spoke. He hated the old man and his power, but he respected him and knew deep inside that he was right. He had given

Annie too much latitude and now it might all come back to haunt him. "What's your advice, Rex?"

"Huh!" Melton coughed up a frustrated laugh. "Now's a great time to include me among your advisors. I bet you've started praying recently, too."

"I just want your advice on how to proceed. I don't need any insults."

The old man sucked in another deep breath, quickly this time so the sound of it was sure to carry across the phone. The breath was for a pronouncement, and Justice knew it.

"Cut your losses and step down."

"Step down? Are you crazy? That would be admitting that I was involved with Minnis. It'd ruin me! I've worked too long and too hard to just lay down and die!" He was breathing heavily now, like he had walked too fast up an incline.

"You asked for my advice. I gave it to you. You step down now, you can get back into your law practice with a minimum of fuss. You keep going, the press is gonna crucify you." He paused, then added, "This one's bad, Frank. I know and you know this is the tip of an iceberg. The press have their hooks in it and they will pull up the rest."

"All right!" Justice said angrily. "You've had your say. Are you going to support me or not?"

"You play it my way, I support you. You walk further out on this limb, and the whole tree's yours."

▼ ▼ ▼ ▼

Evelyn rose early with Maria. She had slept like a baby.

When she had first laid down on the bed in the darkened guest room, the worries and fear and confusion of the day had started crowding in on her. But she closed her eyes and forced herself to relax and to think of Maria's warmth and her triumph over pain and loss much greater than her own. And she thought about the words Maria read to her from the Bible. The destructive emotions dissipated and she fell into a wonderful, restful sleep.

When she rose, she showered and dressed in the outfit Maria had brought to her the evening before. It felt good to have on a set of clean clothes and some of her own makeup.

Maria already was preparing a light breakfast when Evelyn entered the kitchen. "Hey, that's my job!" she called out in a playful tone.

"No, no. You are my guest, Mrs. Justice."

Evelyn walked to the coffeemaker and poured two cups. "I had such a restful sleep," she said as she doctored the first cup of coffee. "Three months ago—no! two days ago—I'd never even have hoped for such a quiet night. Listen," she said as she began to work on the second cup, "I have to meet Franklin at home for lunch, and I have to make a call to an attorney. I'm going to ride the bus in with you this morning."

She picked up the coffee and carried it to Maria, who was slicing fruit and arranging it neatly on a plate. "A little cream and no sugar, if I remember correctly."

"For me?"

Evelyn loved Maria's sense of grateful surprise when she waited on her. It seemed to Evelyn that Maria's stripe of true humility must have come from her pain. For a woman in big-time politics, sincere humility was as rare as the proverbial hen's tooth, and Evelyn was sure she'd never seen any one hen's tooth.

▼ ▼ ▼ ▼

"Is this great, or what?" Dan slapped at the paper as he bounced into Lindy's cubicle shortly past eight-thirty. The night before, the two had called Paul Tomass, their managing editor, shortly after their conversation with the anonymous caller and persuaded him to change the front page with a hold for a photo. Tomass was thrilled to hear of the possible scoop, but warned the two that they had better deliver on this one.

Tomass had come straight back to the office while Dan made a beeline for the post office where the drop was supposed to occur and Lindy began work on the new piece. It had all worked the way it was supposed to.

"The Pulitzer's ours, Lind. This will blow the competition right out of the water. Why, when we have this series finished, it'll be world-class recognition for us!"

As usual, Lindy didn't turn her swivel chair away from her desk to greet Dan. She didn't raise her hand or even grunt a hello. Instead, she took another sip of coffee from the waxy paper cup with the useless wings that were supposed to pass as handles and continued staring at the picture that embellished the front page of the morning *News*. She hated the coffee from the machine in the break room, but if she'd had a smooth, rich cup she would have had difficulty concentrating. The break-room coffee made her think about something else.

Dan grabbed the back of her chair and spun her around. "Whoa!" he shouted when he caught a glimpse of the coffee cup Lindy was trying to keep level against the force of the turning chair. "A deadly weapon!" He laughed heartily.

It was infectious. Lindy first scowled as she checked her blouse for coffee stains, then she smiled, then began to giggle at Dan's overacted entrance. "Dan, you are—"

"Go ahead! Say it! Dan Li-pong, you are a brilliant journalist, a cunning reporter, a dashing partner, and one sexy piece of male flesh! Go ahead! I can take it!"

She was laughing now. She never could stand up under his irrepressible cheerfulness.

"Enough of this baloney," he announced as he dropped his paper onto her pristine desktop. "Oops!" He picked it up again and dropped it onto the messy floor. "I forgot. That's yesterday. We've got work to do—today!" He put his foot on the fallen paper and stepped over to sit on the edge of her desk.

"This is the way I see it. We've lit up the sky with the drug and politics connections on this thing." He motioned upwards with one hand. "I say we pursue that with everything we've got. I think the hot issue is how prevalent drug use is among state employees. We can do a series of interviews—hidden-voices type thing. I'm sure the statehouse will be crawling with sinners eager to confess if it will embarrass the big kahuna further.

"Then, the next article we pick up on the love connection between Justice and the dead woman. That's iffy to me. The other, though—man! That will be easy to write. Can you believe the timing on this? Not even twenty-four hours after his big announcement!"

Dan was so full of himself that he hadn't even noticed Lindy's almost complete lack of excitement over his strategy. The giggles had faded and she had picked the paper up off the floor and had turned back to contemplating the picture of an angry Annie Minnis and the Governor in an obvious confrontation of some kind.

Finally, Dan realized she wasn't paying attention. "Lind, whadda you think? Got another winner here?"

She didn't answer. She just made a face and shook her head like she was confused or doubtful—or pessimistic.

"Uh-oh," Dan said. "I smell the distinct aroma of woman's intuition again."

"I don't know, Dan," she said, still not looking up from the photo.

"Well, I do! Trust me on this one. A feature on drug use by public employees is just crying to be written." He was talking faster now, obviously scrambling to head her off whatever detour she was contemplating. "It'll be so easy I'll be ashamed to take my next paycheck."

Lindy looked up at him, the smile returning to her face. He seized on the contact and spoke right into her eyes. "You said it yourself. These guys aren't gonna go along with some edict that invades their privacy. They'll be ready to talk." He added, slowly and distinctly for emphasis, "It'll be a piece of cake!"

The smile dissolved back into the perplexed look and Lindy looked past Dan to the posters on her wall.

"Lindy, I'm not saying that we shouldn't follow up on whatever you're thinking. Let's do it! But first things first. The next logical piece in a series will write itself!"

"Dan, you don't even know what I'm thinking. How can you say we'll follow up on it?"

Dan pulled one of his long legs up and across the other one, like the bow of a violin coming to rest at a right angle to the strings. His shoulders slumped and he reached out to finger the tassel on the loafer that adorned the near foot. "I know it. I'm not trying to ignore you or railroad you." He stopped and looked at her. "Okay, I am trying to railroad you. It's just so clear to me what we need to do—before anyone else does it!"

Lindy leaned back in the swivel chair and thrust her feet under her desk, then pulled her hands together across her stomach and looked again at her posters. "I'm no expert, but I think that all philosophy is about one of two things: life or death."

She was looking at each of the posters, one at a time, talking almost as if she had one phrase addressed to each. "I didn't realize it until I sat alone in that room yesterday with a dead woman, but all my interest in philosophy has been in what bits of wisdom I could find to help me be more alive." Her tone became acerbic. "More successful!" She was mocking herself and the values that had driven her in life.

"Dan," she still was looking at her posters, "Annie Minnis taught me something that no philosopher ever

could, and I owe her for it." Now she looked up at her
partner. "You do the series piece. I have a debt to pay."
She looked back at the picture on her desk.

Dan had stopped fiddling with his tassel and had
crossed his arms, concentrating on Lindy. How can I
resist her? he thought as she spoke. How can I resist a
woman who is this thoughtful, this honest? This beautiful!

When she finished, he drank in the soft lines of her face
for a few seconds more, then picked up the paper she was
staring at and laid it across his lap. "We're a team," he
said affirmingly. "What's next?"

▼ ▼ ▼ 15 ▼ ▼ ▼

Chief Brown stood waiting in the hall outside the Governor's office in the Capitol building as Rosemary Kleindorf arrived for work. "Morning, Chief," she said as she walked up, flipping through the keys on her key ring to get to the right one.

"Morning," he said with a grunt. He was in no mood to talk, especially to the Governor's secretary. He'd been on the Minnis case most of the night, riding the county coroner not to put off the autopsy until morning, and using his clout with the city police to put a night team on processing evidence. Then he'd been back and forth between homicide and the morgue till past 1 a.m. What he finally walked away with had taken most of the rest of the sleep from his eyes.

He was in no mood to talk to Rosemary.

He was in even less of a mood to talk to his boss.

"I guess you saw the papers this morning?" Rosemary's words sounded like a visitor at a funeral asking the deceased's spouse what disease did the job.

"No. I've been at it most of the night."

"Umh," she grunted. She opened her mouth to continue as Brown dropped into one of the chairs lined up for visitors along the north wall, but she evidently thought better of it and just closed her mouth instead.

Brown was glad. The fact that she asked about him reading the paper was a clear sign that the paper presented a problem this morning. And he hated problems. He hated messes. He especially hated problems and

messes that had to do with his boss when he was responsible to help fix them.

This morning was one of those times he wished he was
still sitting on the shoulder of an interstate highway
shooting speeders with a radar gun.

Rosemary set her purse and the mail on her desk,
slipped her light coat off and went straight for the intercom, even before she put away her things.

"Governor?" Rosemary's voice sounded tentative. She
normally came in later than her boss and didn't interrupt
him until he called for her, usually sometime between
eight-fifteen and eight-thirty. But this morning she
buzzed him.

"Yes?" The Governor's voice was clearly brusque, even
through the tinny sound of the intercom. The amplifica-
tion was weak, a sure sign that Franklin Justice was
pacing behind his desk, his face not turned toward the
phone.

Rosemary looked at Chief Brown, then picked up the
receiver for more privacy.

"Sir, Chief Brown is waiting to see you. Mr. Barnett and
Mr. Frizzell both stopped me in the hall, and both said
they would be here in a matter of minutes. They said you
were expecting them."

Rosemary listened to the Governor's response, then
added, "Yes, sir. One other question."

She paused.

"I saw the paper this morning, sir." Obviously she was
treading softly, choosing her words carefully. "I assume
you'll be meeting with Mr. Barnett and Mr. Frizzell over
the issue. Should I cancel any of your morning appointments?"

Brown couldn't hear what the Governor said, but he
could see the effect of his words on Rosemary Kleindorf.
She was shaken. Visibly shaken. She lowered the phone

to its cradle, then said to Brown, feebly, "The Governor is ready for you, Chief."

Brown felt a burst of fire in his ulcer as he leaned forward till his head was in front of his belly so he could stand up. His wife continually complained about the size of his stomach—"a beer gut!" she'd chide. Her griping did nothing to reduce his girth but it did help keep his ulcer healthy.

Franklin Justice was pacing behind his huge, polished desk when Brown entered the room. Brown closed the door gingerly, then made his way toward the leftmost of the two leather wingback chairs that stood at the ready in front of the desk. He felt less vulnerable in that one.

"Chief," the Governor barked in greeting. "What news?" He turned and saw that the chief of the state highway patrol was standing next to the chair, waiting for some signal to be seated. "Sit. Please."

"Thank you, sir." Brown stepped in front of the chair and settled himself slowly into it. "Not good news, I'm afraid."

"Give it to me."

"First, I spoke to the trooper who made contact with your wife last night. She was pretty bent out of shape by the time he left. He's a rookie, and he did make a dumb remark about your wife not trying to escape."

"I'm not worried about Evelyn. What do you have from the Minnis investigation?"

"Before I tell you that, sir, one other note about your wife. She did spend the night with the Arvizu woman. I presume that's where she's been all the time. Unless—"

"Unless she left long enough to kill Annie Minnis out of jealousy? You can say it. I'm a big boy now."

Brown adjusted his wide behind in the seat to ease the uncomfortable glare of his boss's bloodshot eyes.

"Get on with it, Chief. What do the city police have?"

"The first positive lead concerns the murder weapon. They are sure that the knife used to kill the victim was carried into the apartment."

"How could they know that?"

"You shoulda seen this woman's kitchen. Matching everything. The knife that was found in her neck wasn't like anything else in the kitchen. Not proof positive, but solid enough to go on."

"Does that matter?"

"You better believe it matters. This new hybrid drug gang that they suspected has a well-ordered system for this kind of public-service-announcement murder. In that system their weapon of choice is a knife from the victim's own kitchen. CPD thinks it comes from some sort of twisted sense of humor. Anyway, that caused them to question last night's assumption that this was a gang job."

"Just because the knife wasn't from Annie's kitchen?"

"That and the coroner's report."

Justice stopped his pacing and stared long enough to prompt the chief to continue.

"In addition to the stab wound, the victim was badly beaten. The autopsy made them change their minds about this case matching the M.O. of these gangs."

"Why?"

"The coroner says the beating took place *before* the stabbing. The blood in the bruises had circulated for a while and aged the wounds. Had the stabbing and the beating been committed at the same time, those bruises and cuts would have had a very different appearance."

"Why would that change their opinion?"

"Doesn't fit. The woman wasn't raped, but the coroner thinks there was a period of time, probably an hour or slightly more, between the time she was beaten and the time she was killed." Brown lifted one leg and grabbed his ankle, pulling foot and leg back toward him. His paunch made it difficult to cross his legs without manual assistance.

Justice paced a few more steps, head raised thoughtfully, waiting for the rest of the explanation. When it wasn't forthcoming, he stopped and leaned over his desktop on his knuckles. "And?"

Brown shrugged. "That's it."

"Why would that change their minds?" Justice repeated, clearly frustrated.

"That's simple, sir," Brown said, releasing his leg and sitting up again. He'd relaxed too soon. "These guys wouldn't—"

"What guys?"

"The gang. They wouldn't have hung around for an hour between the time they beat on Minnis till the time they killed her, at least not unless they were raping her. They're too bright to hang around and we know she wasn't raped."

"Maybe they came back later to finish the job."

"No, sir. That's not how they operate. These guys have a system, and with as much money at stake as they're playing with, they don't veer from their system."

Justice looked at Brown intently, then without speaking, turned and resumed his pacing.

Brown kept his mouth shut. So far, his ulcer was behaving and he didn't want to tempt fate.

Justice made about three circuits behind his desk when Rosemary buzzed on the intercom. "Governor, Mr. Frizzell is here."

"Send him in," Justice said, still moving. "And Rosemary, send Barney in as soon as he arrives. No need to announce him."

"What's their theory?" Justice asked Brown as the door opened and Dave Frizzell entered. He motioned for Frizzell to take the other wingback and he kept pacing.

"Three possibilities. One: Whoever beat her stayed around, then put her out of her misery after about an hour. Could have been a lover—"

Brown caught what he'd said but it was too late. It was already out.

Justice's eyes met his and flared with anger.

Without hesitating, Brown added, "They don't like that one at this point." He wanted to fix his mistake, badly. "At least the last I talked to them about three-thirty this morning."

"Have you seen the morning paper, Chief?" the Governor asked.

"No, sir."

"Go on!" Justice ordered, clearly angered by the report.

"Yes, sir. As I was saying, the second possibility is that the guy—or possibly the woman—beats Minnis, leaves the scene, later realizes Minnis could identify her assailant, then returns to the apartment to put her away for good."

Brown paused. He didn't like the third one any better than the first two. They all seemed to hold his boss or his boss's wife in suspicion at some level.

"And three?" Governor Justice prompted, sounding anxious to hear.

"Three, someone else did it, someone other than the one who pounded on her. Came along an hour later and did her."

There was stunned silence in the room as the three men contemplated Chief Brown's theories. Finally the Governor broke the stillness with an exasperated sigh.

"This whole situation keeps deteriorating. It's not just that Annie got fouled up with druggies and we didn't know it. Now the police think that someone other than a druggie killed her." He stopped pacing, pulled out his chair and slumped into it. "Now we've got drugs *and* a murder, and they may not even be related."

"This is like a bad dream, Frank," Frizzell said.

"Tell me about it. I've been awake through it all."

The door to the reception area opened and Barnett stepped in. He looked haggard and worried.

"Barney, you look like something the cat dragged in."

Barnett walked to Justice's desk, shoulders stooped like he'd been badly beaten in a fight. He opened a worn leather valise that must have made him stylish in the sixties and pulled out a single piece of paper with a few neatly typed sentences. "Frank," he said as he extended the page to the Governor.

Justice took the paper and read it. He'd scanned only a couple of lines when he lifted his head and snarled, "Barney, what is this garbage?"

"Exactly what it appears to be, Frank. I'm resigning."

▼ ▼ ▼ ▼

"Thanks, partner," Lindy said to Dan in response to his remark about working as a team. She liked Dan's willingness to cooperate with her, to follow her instincts as enthusiastically as he would follow his. She knew that he respected her, and she felt profoundly comfortable with the fit.

She straightened up in her chair and looked at him with a grateful smile, one that was meant to repeat what she just had said in words. As she looked at him, relaxed on the corner of her desk, something deep down tugged at her heart.

It was a feeling of appreciation.

But it was more.

It seemed to flare up from beneath her heart and suddenly fill her insides. She involuntarily sucked in air, as if fighting back its invasion of her upper body. She swallowed, trying to quell the feeling, then cleared her throat.

"You okay?" Dan said as he leaned in her direction.

Her ears tingled from mild embarrassment, as if when he leaned toward her he had looked inside and seen what she was feeling. She didn't want to admit what it was, and she certainly didn't want him to be able to see it.

"Yup," she said as she took the paper from Dan and pointed to the photo. Lindy pushed the strong feeling back down inside and began to talk excitedly about what she saw in the incident at 1277 North Capitol. "I don't think this is about drugs. I don't think Annie Minnis died because she was using." She pointed to the photo as she spoke, first tapping the image of Annie, then of the Governor. "Look at it, Dan. This is a crime of passion, not revenge."

"Come on, Lind. Get real. Are you saying that the Governor is involved in Annie Minnis's death? The Governor?"

"No, I am not," she said matter-of-factly as she leaned forward onto her elbows and looked away from Dan. "But my instincts tell me—"

"My instincts tell me that the story that's shouting to be written is the one on drug use among state employees. I think that's a lot more credible."

"I didn't say I think the Governor did it. I said I think it was a crime of passion."

"Convince me, Lindy."

She swung around to face him again. "Think about it, Dan. What do we know about this whole thing?" She brushed at Dan's leg to get to a drawer. "Move!" He leaned back on the desk like a rocking chair, his whole body rigid, so that his legs rose without being lifted. Lindy opened the drawer and lifted a yellow legal pad from its place among the other fastidiously organized materials she kept on hand.

She dropped the pad on top of the morning edition, being careful not to cover the photo, then poised a pen above its surface and said, "Talk to me. Tell me what we know."

"Okay. Fine," Dan said. "Let me think. We know that a state employee was murdered yesterday," he elongated the final syllables of "yesterday" to give him time to line up his next remark, "and that drugs were found on the premises, and that the Governor was present sometime before the murder, and that a wicked-looking unknown showed up soon after the Governor."

Lindy wrote the first two comments down, then shrouded the pencil in her hands and began twisting it in her fingers.

"What? Is this not what you asked for?" Dan said.

"No, that's not it," she said. "That's not what I'm trying to get at."

Dan picked up the pad and lifted the twisting pencil from her hands. "Fine. I'll write, you talk."

She thought for a minute, then began, "We know that the Governor was in Annie's condo for a reason yesterday."

"Do I write that down?"

She gave him a frown, then continued. "Our informant thinks it was for a lunch-time quickie. I agree."

"Where do you get that?"

She began to speak a little more excitedly again. "While we were looking for a phone, it also dawned on me that whoever had done this might still be in the apartment, so I checked it out."

"You what?" Dan stood up in alarm from his perch on the desk. "Lindy, that was the stupidest move you've ever made."

"I realize that now, Dan. But I was really shaken then, and angry. I kind of hoped someone would be hiding so I could see some justice done."

Somewhat mollified, Dan settled back to the desktop. "What'd you intend to do, hit him with your purse?"

She looked at him with a curt little nodding gesture and said, very properly, "I didn't have my purse, thank you." She looked away again and continued in her normal voice. "I know it was stupid, but I searched the place anyway. The apartment was a mess. Somebody tore it up really well. But there were a couple of things out of place."

"How could you tell anything was out of place if the rooms were all trashed?"

"I could just tell. In what was obviously her bedroom, stuff was out of the drawers and dumped all over the place. But at the foot of the bed, there was a sexy little negligee in a pile—garter belt, silk stockings and all—like she had taken it all off and dropped it there."

"Pardon me, miss. But wouldn't you expect something like that to be in a pile by the bed? After all, the whole purpose of putting on one of those things is to get it taken off again anyway."

"Dan, this was in a pile. The pieces weren't strung out all over the bed and the room the way you'd expect if she'd been in the heat of passion. They were in a pile! And the bed was made! Silk sheets, like she was expecting action. It was messy because of the trashing, but it was still spread—unused.

"And look at this photo." They both leaned over the paper. "Remember the geek telling us that she was decked out with black stockings and a robe? If you'll notice, she's wearing a robe here. And look at her legs. Stockings! Net stockings!"

Dan looked up from the paper with a question mark across his face. "So?"

"The negligee she's wearing under the robe in this picture is the kind all decked out with stockings, G-string and garter belts. The kind I saw in a pile on the bedroom floor."

"So?" he repeated, the question mark still present.

"Dan," she said as if her patience were wearing thin, "think about what you saw when you came for me. What was she wearing?"

"Uhhmmm, a sweatsuit. Yeah. A white sweatsuit."

"Don't you get it?"

"Lindy, obviously I don't get it yet, so why don't you just spell it out for me in a way my simple mind can comprehend."

"Listen. In this picture, Annie Minnis still has on her sexy little outfit. It's under the robe, but it's still on. We know from our informant that this was during lunch-time."

"Okay," Dan said, making sure he was following her.

"Annie died in a sweatsuit. After the Governor left, apparently after an argument of some kind, she went into her bedroom, took off the negligee, dumped it in a pile, and changed into her sweats."

"I'm following, but I still don't know where you're leading."

"Our informant told us that he shot the picture, went down to the main floor men's room, laid low for about ten minutes, then went back up to find the black guy standing in the hall in front of Annie's door."

"Yep."

"Well, let's assume for a moment that the black guy was her drug connection. Let's also assume that she really was murdered by the guy, or the gang, who was running the drugs she was using."

"Okay."

"Do you think a dealer who had come to murder Annie was going to pass up an opportunity to rape her too, if she's all dolled up like a sex kitten?"

"Maybe he did. I can check around for what they found in the autopsy."

"That doesn't matter. Maybe he did rape her. But he *didn't* rape her, then dress her up in a warm sweatsuit, then kill her."

"I see your point. But what would have prevented her from changing clothes after Justice left?"

"Nothing, of course. But I have to put myself in her position. If I'd just had what obviously was a bitter fight with my lover, the last thing I'd do would be to go in, change into my sweats and curl up with a good book."

"What would you do?"

"I'd want to get out of there and blow off some steam, but first I'd have to put my face back on and then I'd want to dress like a queen, just to show him that I didn't need him anyway."

Dan's face showed that he was confused. "Lindy," he said, frustrated. "If Justice didn't kill her and the black guy didn't kill her, then who killed her?"

"I'm getting there," she said in the prim tone she'd used earlier. She patted him on the knee. "Patience."

"I'm being patient," he said in mock revulsion. "Don't patronize me or I'll slap you with sexual harassment charges."

"Back to my line of thought. I think when Justice left, Annie came back into the condo and changed in a hurry. I think she wanted to get out of her place on the double."

"Why?"

"That leads us to what you found out from your friend in the state police dispatch, and what you found out from the gardener about Evelyn Justice. Dan, Evelyn Justice was a nutcase. The gardener said she'd tried to commit suicide *with a knife, an ordinary kitchen knife*. She left the Governor's mansion sometime Tuesday evening, and someone higher up the pecking order had reason to stake out 1277 North Capitol at the same time they put out an APB on the First Lady. Coincidence?"

"That was the question I was going to ask."

"No way. Even your dispatcher friend wondered what was going on. Try this on for size. Wednesday morning, when they weren't able to find the loony wife, Justice calls Annie to warn her. He's afraid to say too much over a phone line, so he arranges to see her at noon.

"Evidently, they had some history of these little noontime liaisons, because when Justice shows up, she's dressed and ready for action. But instead of romance, Justice gives her the lowdown on his wife and the threat the wife's posing for Annie—*and* for him! I think he warned her to get out of her condo until his wife was found. That, no doubt, led to a battle royale and the scene our informant captured."

"But—"

"Let me finish. Annie goes back into the apartment, steaming, but the idea of a flipped-out, angry wife with a death wish gives her second thoughts. She hurries to the bedroom, pulls off the negligee, jumps into her sweats, grabs her wallet and heads for the door."

"And meets Mr. Universe in the hall." Dan was with her all the way now.

"Exactly. She wasn't expecting him. Let's say he's the one who beat on her and trashed the place, some sort of a lesson for users who don't pay their debts or something. He leaves Annie Minnis in her apartment, too hurt and afraid to worry about a phantom threat from a loony wife.

"Sometime later, Evelyn Justice shows up, having trailed her husband but slowed down by the security in the lobby. She knocks on the door. Annie, probably groggy from the beating and not thinking straight, opens the door and lets her in. Evelyn Justice picks something up or uses something she's carried in to knock her down again. Then she goes to the kitchen, pulls a knife out of the drawer, walks over to the semi-conscious Minnis and plunges it into the back of her neck."

"Does she know that's an M.O. for the drug gang murders?"

"Who knows? Maybe so, maybe not. Maybe she just stuck the knife in the nearest piece of exposed flesh. Who knows?"

Dan grabbed one knee with both hands and leaned back on the desk to reflect. Lindy slumped in her chair and let her arms drop over the armrests.

They stewed on the ideas in silence for a while, then Dan spoke up. "I don't know, Lind. It makes a pretty good story, but I think it's full of holes."

"Yeah. So was my hunch about the new drug policy."

Dan took a deep breath and exhaled it long and slow. "You're right. I'm with you on this on two conditions: First, we find proof, or at least a lot more evidence to bear out your theory."

"Agreed," she said. "What's the second condition?"

"The instant one of the holes leaks, we drop this like a hot potato and pick up the line on drug use among state employees."

Lindy grabbed Dan's hand and shook it. "Deal!"

"How do you wanna proceed, partner?"

"Simple. Your first condition. We prove the theory. You track down an autopsy report and anything related to the police activity surrounding both the APB on Evelyn Justice and the Minnis case."

"And you?"

"I'm going to find Evelyn Justice."

▼ ▼ ▼ ▼

"This is the most outrageous piece of nonsense you've ever uttered!" Franklin Justice boomed in response to Barnett's announcement of his resignation. "What'd you do, read the paper this morning and decide it was time to abandon a sinking ship? Even rats stay on board till water fills the hold!"

George Barnett slowly closed the valise and looked straight at Franklin Justice, unmoved. "Frank, I'm going to add that remark to the hundreds of other demeaning comments you've made about me over the years. And I'm going to forget it, just like I've forgotten all the others." His voice was calm and deliberate. "I've seen the paper and I'm sure you'll weather this storm like you have all the others. That's not why I'm resigning."

Justice had one arm on his desk and one arm on the armrest of his chair, leaning toward the letter and Barnett. His eyes fell from Barnett to the empty space between the two wingbacks. He took two deep breaths, then without looking at Barnett, said in a low, frustrated rumble that seemed to come from deep in his chest, "Okay, Barney." He exhaled loudly. "That was uncalled for. I apologize."

He looked away for another few seconds, then slowly raised his head back to Barnett. "What's this all about?"

The intercom clicked to life. "Governor?" It was Rosemary again.

"What is it?" Justice barked angrily.

"There's a call for Chief Brown. They said it was urgent."

Justice looked at Brown and said, "Take that at her desk, Jim." Then he turned back to the phone. "Rosemary, don't interrupt me again. For any reason."

"Yes, sir."

Brown rolled forward in the wingback and stood up. He appeared glad to get out of the room.

"Now, Barney," Justice continued, "tell me what this is all about."

Barnett laid the valise flat on the desk, rested the tips of his fingers on it as he squared his shoulders, and quietly announced, "I'm going to spend as much time with my family as I possibly can before I go to jail."

"Jail?" Justice shouted as he jumped up from the chair. Frizzell sat up in his chair and Brown paused to look back before he exited the room. "First drugs, then murder. Now what have *you* done?"

"Nothing," Barnett said. "Absolutely nothing. And that's what I'm going to jail for."

"Would you stop with the stupid riddles?" Justice was leaning over his desk toward Barnett, his head bobbing to emphasize every word he shouted.

"Annie Minnis screwed us, Frank."

Justice said nothing, but he stood motionless, the color draining from his face.

"I spent all evening on the campaign committee's financial files. I still could find no record of actual delivery of champagne or perfume or any of the other pricey items Annie was buying. So I called around to some of the staff and the volunteers."

"And?"

"Nobody, I repeat, nobody, has seen the first bottle of champagne or the first ounce of perfume. Nobody has ever seen Bruhof personnel and nobody has ever had dealings with the Bruhof company. She used us, Frank."

Justice was speechless. He slowly sank back into his chair as Barnett continued.

"The drugs the police found?" George Barnett lifted the valise again and pulled out a file. "She must have been buying them from someone at Bruhof under some bogus invoicing scheme." He dropped the file on the desk. "Look for yourself. Lots of money out and nothing to show for it!"

Justice didn't even glance in the direction of the file.

Brown quietly reentered the room and took his seat as Barnett vented his feelings.

"Sooner or later the Federal Election Commission is going to find out that your mistress was financing her drug habit with funds donated by the public to your campaign treasury. And then, you and I are going to go to jail." He lifted his valise from the desk and tucked it under his arm. "Now I am going home to my family and pray to God that some miracle occurs to keep me out. You'll survive the morning headlines, Frank. But the FEC is going to make you and me both sorry that Annie Minnis was ever born."

George Barnett turned and, like his unusual departure of the previous day, walked out of the room through the door to the reception area instead of the private entrance.

A deadly silence hung in the air.

▼ ▼ ▼ ▼

Chief James Brown's ample belly was burning now. The phone call he had received had been like swallowing lava, and what he heard of Barnett's calm statement had only thrown gasoline on it. Now the silence fanned it.

Several long, painful minutes passed before anyone spoke. Frizzell finally broke the silence. "Can it get worse, Frank?" he said in a stone-serious voice.

"God only knows, Dave. First it was Evelyn. You don't know about that and you don't need to. Then it was Annie. Then the paper this morning. Now this bombshell." He shook his head. "God only knows."

More silence. Brown squirmed in the wingback. He would have given anything at that moment to be anywhere else on earth. He didn't want to have to say what he had to say. He squirmed again, then leaned forward in the chair, rested his elbows on his knees and nervously rubbed his hands together. "Sir," he said, looking at the floor.

Justice looked at him.

Frizzell looked at him.

Brown's eyes were still on the floor. "Sir. I'm afraid it can get worse."

Both other men stared and waited.

"The call I got?" Brown said, still rubbing his hands. "It was Gonzalez. He's been in on this since the beginning. I've had him over at City Police since before dawn to keep watch on their progress."

Brown stopped rubbing his hands and squeezed them together in an oversized fist as he raised his head to the Governor. "Following the morning news story, the chief of detectives has ordered a full investigation of your relationship to Annie Minnis with an eye on the possibility of your involvement in her murder."

▼ ▼ ▼ 16 ▼ ▼ ▼

Lindy Blakely was determined to scare up enough information to either confirm or disprove her theory about a crazy First Lady. She and Dan had agreed that he would follow the official trail and she would follow the one her instinct was blazing.

That instinct told her that the place to start in trying to locate Evelyn Justice was at the Governor's mansion. Lindy didn't really expect to find her there, but if Dan had scored with one of the staff, so might she.

She pulled into the long, gracefully curved drive at the mansion and thought again how remarkable it was that the Governor's mansion seemed as accessible as any other house in this old northside neighborhood. There were no high brick or stone walls, no security fences, no guard posts—nothing that one might expect at the home of the state's chief executive. Just a beautiful old home with a manicured lawn which sprawled lazily down the gentle slope till it was interrupted by a ribbon of a concrete sidewalk.

Lindy stopped the car at the side of the house where the driveway widened either to accommodate parking for several vehicles or for dropping off guests. Hers was the only car parked in that wide area this morning. In fact, hers was the only car parked anywhere around the house. She could see a small parking lot on the extreme northwest corner of the property and assumed it was for staff, but she saw no signs of any other vehicles around. This is either good luck or bad luck, her philosopher self said to her professional self as she stepped out of the car.

What must it be like to live in a place like this and not be happy?

▼ ▼ ▼ ▼

Maria and Evelyn had stepped onto a bus (the first of two they had to ride that morning to get to the mansion) exactly fifty-nine minutes before they stepped off at the mouth of the driveway. For Maria, it was just another ride to work made lighter with Evelyn's presence this morning.

But for Evelyn it had been a roller coaster ride. First she was up with the excitement of going home, feeling in control. Then came the bus ride and the down of feeling like a cow being herded into a stock truck—it had been a long time since she had ridden a city bus. She was feeling very self-conscious anyway. With dark glasses, a scarf tied under her chin so that its edges covered much of her face, and a wide-brimmed hat she'd borrowed from Maria, she felt like a movie star trying to hide from her fans. "This is ridiculous," she had said in frustration to her reflection in the dressing mirror that morning. But after talking it over with herself, she decided that ridiculous or not, it was probably wise to do all she could to disguise her identity that morning. She didn't know if it would fool the young officer who had intruded on them the night before, but she did know that she was uncomfortable with the idea that troopers may be following her, even if she only was going home.

The welcome catharsis of spending the ride time chatting with Maria lessened her uneasiness. They talked about the weather and grocery shopping and spring flowers and all the mundane things normal people talked about.

That led to a downer of empathy for the people who had to depend on a bus to get around town and do some of those mundane things. Then another plunge of self-doubt as the bus hit Meridian and neared the mansion.

Evelyn's roller coaster leveled out as she pulled the cord to signal the driver to stop. Watching the huge lumbering coach veer to the right and grind to a stop because of her gentle tug on the stop cord made her feel in control again. To Maria's assurances that she'd do fine, they moved down the aisle. "Your Mr. Justice is a good man," Maria said as she stepped off the bus. "I see it. He will understand and all will be well."

Evelyn was behind Maria, who by now was on the pavement. Evelyn grasped a handrail from her perch on the bottom step of the bus and leaned out the door to whisper in Maria's ear: "*My* Mr. Justice is a political animal. If all turns out well, it will be okay for him, not necessarily for me." She took the final step to the pavement, then turned and watched the bus pull away with a grinding roar and its trademark belch of gray-black smoke.

How out of touch with real life I am, Evelyn thought as she tilted her head to catch one more glimpse of the backs of the bored passengers' heads. Maria was already walking up the long drive as Evelyn turned from the retreating bus and faced her home.

"Maria," Evelyn said from her spot on the concrete curb.

Maria stopped and turned.

"One more time, tell me that I'm going to do all right and that I'm going to get through this."

Maria walked back to her friend. "Mrs. Justice," she said as she leaned forward and took hold of Evelyn's left hand. "You will do fine. It will not be easy, but you will do fine and all will come to be well."

Evelyn looked with appreciation into Maria's eyes. "Thank you." She put her right hand over Maria's and squeezed her friend's hand with both of hers. "I wish you could be with me when I speak to Franklin."

"I will be." She smiled.

Evelyn looked askance at her, a question in her expression.

"I will be with you in my praying."

The thought of Maria praying for her made Evelyn laugh. Her face lit up with a smile and she giggled like a schoolgirl.

"Is it not right for me to do?" Maria asked.

"Oh, no," Evelyn said, then realized she had responded negatively and giggled some more. "I mean, of course it's right," she hastened. "It's just that while there have been a lot of times in my life that I've tried to pray my way out of trouble, no one ever told me that *they* would pray me out of trouble. In fact, the thought never even crossed my mind."

Evelyn and Maria began walking up the drive with a deliberate step. "With both of us trying, maybe we can get through to somebody up there." She laughed again, more heartily than before.

At that moment Evelyn felt, for the first time, a glimmer of hope.

▼ ▼ ▼ ▼

Lindy had no better luck with the security guard stationed just inside the front door than had Dan. He curtly informed her that Mrs. Justice was not available and if she wanted to schedule an appointment, she should call Mrs. Justice's secretary. He also warned her that because of Mrs. Justice's recent illness, she was receiving almost no visitors.

Back on the stately front porch, surrounded by the erupting colors of green and white and yellow in the neatly trimmed beds of spring flowers, Lindy went directly to Plan B: find a go-fer and pump him or her for gossip. Dan had lucked out with a male, but Lindy knew that what she wanted was more likely to come from the more observant sex.

That's when she turned and saw the two women approaching from the street, a Hispanic dressed in a maid's uniform and a caucasian dressed in hat, scarf, sunglasses and a casual-but-stylish outfit that might be appropriate for one of the administrative staff who did not meet the public.

Lindy smiled. Lady Luck was looking after her. She stepped quickly down the steps of the grand porch and across the rich green lawn to intercept the two women. "Excuse me!" she called as she accelerated into a jog.

The women looked up at Lindy and slowed their pace, finally stopping as Lindy planted herself squarely between them and the house.

"Do you work here?" Lindy asked, huffing slightly from her mild exercise.

The maid spoke up. "Yes."

"I'm Lindy Blakely from the *News.* I wonder if I could ask you a few questions."

The two looked at each other, then the maid said, "No. I do not think it would be good." They began to walk again.

Lindy stepped sideways to block their advance, but they continued moving up the drive. Undeterred, Lindy took a couple of quick steps to catch up. "Please," she said gently, "I'm not digging for dirt. I'm just trying to do my job." She decided the better approach would be the direct one, so she added, "I'm just trying to locate Evelyn Justice to do an interview for an upcoming article on how the Governor's mansion has been decorated for spring. I'm getting the runaround from official channels. No one's answering my calls or letters. Just tell me one thing: Is something screwy going on here or is everybody truly playing bodyguard for a sick First Lady like they say they are?"

She looked back and forth at both women as she spoke. It was clear that her plea wasn't scoring with the Hispanic woman. The other woman looked familiar, but she couldn't place her. And she didn't appear as resolute as the maid in her unwillingness to talk, so Lindy concluded her question looking directly at her.

The Hispanic woman had been shaking her head *No* through Lindy's pitch. "No!" She finally verbalized her obvious intent. "I do not think that—"

"Just a minute, Maria," the other woman said graciously to the maid as she interrupted. "It won't hurt to help out for a minute." She glanced at Lindy as they walked, then turned her face away and spoke. "It is true that the First Lady has been ill lately, but I can't imagine the staff treating you discourteously."

"I don't mean that they weren't courteous. They're just not cooperative. Usually, politicians' staffs are falling all over themselves to get positive press coverage."

"I'll ask around to see if there's a problem," said the woman. "Why don't you try calling back this afternoon. Ask for Jane Elander. She's the one who takes care of most of those things."

Something about the cooperative woman tugged at Lindy. Something didn't fit. She certainly didn't act like a go-fer. She was too confident. The woman's bearing was far more poised than that of a typical staffer. Maybe she was a volunteer, or a friend of Evelyn Justice. But she certainly didn't act or look like the kind of woman that rode the bus to get around.

Lindy decided to probe a little deeper to see if she could find out more. "Do you work for Mrs. Justice?"

The maid leaned to walk away, pulling on the woman's arm, quickening their pace slightly. "We will be late."

"No," the caucasian said to Lindy as she stopped walking. "I do not."

▼ ▼ ▼ ▼

Evelyn and Maria walked away from the reporter with a show of calm determination, but inside, Evelyn could feel her hopefulness ebbing and her emotions slipping back onto their downward track. And more so with each step.

She hated the depressive condition she'd battled so long. She hated the awful, flat emotions of her drugged state in which she felt like no more than a functional zombie, and she hated the awful ride she took when she wasn't taking the drugs.

But in the last two days, she'd had a taste of feeling good again—good about life and about herself—and she wanted to regain that feeling.

Permanently.

The sensation of slipping downward again scared her. She wasn't sure she could face Franklin if the slide continued. She clung to the only hope she had—Maria Arvizu. She leaned on Maria as they walked the last twenty yards to the corner of the house. Involuntarily, she tightened her grip on Maria the way she gripped the comforter on her bed when she felt herself falling into the pit.

Evelyn whispered, "Something's wrong."

Maria looked at her and kept walking, hurrying their pace just a little.

They walked to the side of the house and toward the door that opened onto the kitchen. Again Evelyn said, a bit louder this time, "Maria. Something's wrong. I'm feeling it and it's causing me to lose control inside." She stopped just short of the wide, chicly decorated kitchen stoop. She looked back to make sure the reporter was still a distance away and saw her walking up the drive somewhat behind them, headed for her car.

Evelyn turned back to Maria and squeezed her arm even harder. "I cannot stop to talk to the staff. I haven't had a chance to tell you everything, but yesterday afternoon the chief of the state patrol intimated that he wanted to question me in the death of that Minnis woman. Then the trooper showed up looking for me. Now a reporter is snooping around my house asking my staff questions that are clearly colored by the same suspicion.

"Please, help me walk through the kitchen without being stopped. Then let's go directly to Franklin's study." She looked deeply into Maria's eyes for the extra boost of strength she needed to run the gauntlet of well-wishing and inevitably curious employees whom she would have to face after a disappearance and a two-day absence.

"I will do what you need," Maria said.

Maria Arvizu, because of her own struggles, did for Evelyn what Evelyn couldn't do for herself—she gave her an anchor to hold on to.

The two opened the kitchen door and entered the gauntlet.

▼ ▼ ▼ ▼

Lindy had walked back to the car with an eye on the two women, especially the white woman with the uncommon bearing. She just could not resolve where she had seen this woman before or why she might know her.

She glanced around the house again. Still no other cars and no sign of anyone else around. If there were other staff here, they must be at work in the house.

She watched the two women approach the house, look back at her, then engage in some rather intense exchange.

For a brief few seconds, Lindy felt an acute twinge of jealousy at the closeness of the conversation. The display was a painful reminder of something that had been troubling her conscience since yesterday—her sacrifice of meaningful relationships on the altar of professional advancement and recognition. Since moving to town three years earlier for a job at the *News*, a double step up the career ladder, she had made scores of acquaintances, but only one real friend. And she wasn't letting him anywhere close to the real Lindy Blakely.

As the two women disappeared into the house, Lindy let linger the poignancy of the scene and her response to it. She sighed, then reached for the keys she had left in the ignition of her Miata.

But before the engine fired, she raised her head abruptly. "The kitchen!"

Lindy levered the door, jumped out of the bright blue sports car, and walked briskly to the door the two employees had entered only moments before. She paused to knock, thought better of that, and in more typical form grabbed the doorknob and let herself in.

There were several women in the cavernous kitchen, all in uniforms. One was making a comment as she busily assembled items from a cabinet onto the countertop while the others stood nearby enjoying what was clearly a spirited tête-à-tête. They all stopped their talking when Lindy entered.

"Can we hep you?" asked one of the ladies in a thick Southern drawl.

"Yes, you can!" Lindy said brightly as she stepped toward the gaggle of women. "I was just speaking to the two ladies who came in and they were very helpful in answering some questions for me. I wonder if you ladies might help, too?"

"And just who might you be, comin' in here askin' questions?"

"My name is Lindy," she said, using her most charming voice to win over the women's confidence. "I work for the *News*. I'm researching a story on the spring decorations in the Governor's mansion. The other two were so helpful." She had made intentional eye contact with each of the women to strengthen the thin ice onto which she'd skated.

The women were looking at each other with smirks on their faces, the sort of knowing looks that carry inside jokes. She decided she'd thickened the ice enough to slide out a little further.

"Between us," she said with a coy, girlish giggle in her voice and a little lift of one shoulder, "I'm not nearly as interested in the decorations as I am in some of the more interesting stuff." She had been stepping closer to the women as she talked, and now she was almost as close to them as they were to each other. She decided this was just the right distance.

"Like what stuff?" the Southerner asked, having clearly established herself as the spokeswoman of the group.

"Oh, you know," Lindy said, trying to be included immediately as one of the girls. "Like what's going on with the First Lady. I'd never write about it, but I'd rather discuss it than her furniture any day."

This time they looked deliberately at each other with those knowing looks, almost as if to mock her.

The Southerner spoke up again, "I guess you would, reporter. I guess you'd like to know 'bout the Governor, too."

"And maybe some of the real slimy stuff that goes on in this house," another of the women taunted.

"Well, I'm not interested in dirt," Lindy said. The ice was cracking beneath her feet. "I *am* curious about the First Lady's health, though. People say she suffered from exhaustion recently, but *I've* heard," she said in a way to indicate that she was offering a juicy tidbit, "that she's really been depressed." She paused for effect. "*And* that she's disappeared. Maybe run away."

With that, all five exploded in laughter.

Lindy faked a laugh along with them, hoping to be let in on the joke.

One of the two ladies suppressed her laughter just enough to blurt, "Honey, if you wanted to know so bad about a disappearing woman, you shoulda asked her while you had her!"

That set them all to laughing again.

Lindy forced a chuckle or two. "What do you mean?" She beamed a wide, innocent smile meant to elicit response.

The woman spoke up again, "You just said you talked to her outside, girl!"

Then the Southerner added, "You walked through that door not sixty seconds after her, and now she's disappeared on you again!"

▼ ▼ ▼ ▼

Chief Brown's announcement of CPD's intention to investigate the link between Justice and Annie Minnis fell like a bomb in the already rarefied atmosphere of the Governor's office.

The Governor then slowly leaned backward until his chair relinquished its upright position to the backward pressure he put against it. It stopped at about a sixty-degree tilt, leaving him staring deeply into the wide, solid walnut crown molding that graced the perimeter of the ceiling.

Frizzell had watched Brown as he spoke, then he too sat in stunned amazement as the meaning of the announcement made its way into different scenarios his mind was painting at a furious pace. And he too leaned as if the weight of the words was bending him. He leaned forward till his elbows rested on his knees and his chin landed in the cups of his waiting hands.

Brown didn't move. He was the messenger bearing bad tidings. He was afraid that if he moved and called attention to himself, he'd be professionally and politically dead. If this ulcer doesn't kill me first, he thought.

Silence . . . broken at last by Justice's red leather executive chair squeaking to let the Governor lean slowly forward toward his desk. Slowly. Painfully.

His shoulders were stooped. His normally taut middle-aged abdomen was pushing on his pants and partway up his suspenders. His hands dangled loose, one at rest on the patch of leather seat between his leg and the chair's arm and the other suspended over the opposite side of the chair.

He looked to Brown like an aging man just now.

"Dave, I gave you a litany of woes a minute ago," Justice said to his trusted political advisor. "The chief just added one more." He paused, as if he were rolling something around in his mind, not sure how it should come out. "But there's one you don't know about yet."

Dave Frizzell, still bent over his knees, raised his head to look at the Governor's eyes but didn't lift his chin from its cradle in the palms of his hands. His eyebrows were leveled almost flat in concern.

After another long pause, Justice continued, heavily, as if he were being exhausted by an awful load. "Rex Melton called me this morning. Early."

Frizzell's eyebrows perked up slightly, but still he didn't lift head from hands.

Brown still didn't move. He was straining to become or stay invisible.

"He thinks I should step down. Immediately."

Very slowly, thoughtfully, Frizzell began to sit upright.

"Today," Justice added.

Once spoken, the words enveloped the hearers and seeped in.

Brown fought against the Governor's words inside. He didn't want to hear any more. He didn't want to be privy to any more political machinations. He didn't want to think about his job being threatened.

Justice took a deep breath, raising his chest as he breathed in. Then he continued, this time with a touch of the theatric in his voice, as if he were beginning closing arguments in a courtroom: "I've never been a quitter! In twenty years I've fought every fight myself. I've rolled up my sleeves and seen every problem to its resolution. I can't even imagine turning and running now."

He slowly sagged back to his exhausted position like an old tire losing air.

"What does Rex intend to do?" Frizzell asked.

"Nothing," Justice snarled bitterly from his stooped position. "Absolutely nothing unless I play it his way."

Silence. Silence so thorough this time that the ticking of the old, immaculately restored Regulator clock on the wall behind the Governor's desk resounded in the oak office.

"Frank," Frizzell finally said with an upward inflection in his voice. "I think you should take Melton's advice."

"You *what?*" exploded Justice. "You think I should quit? You think I should announce to the whole world that I am a lying, cheating, philandering, thieving, murdering politician?" Justice stood to his feet, snapped his legs straight in a way that shoved against his chair and sent it scooting away from his desk, and resumed his pacing. "That's just what it would be, you know. And every two-bit gas station attendant in the state would be judge and jury on me, pronouncing how they knew all along that I was a crook."

He pulled his gyrating hands behind his back and locked them, then turned and began to pace his regular path on the lush carpet. After a few circuits, he slowed. At one corner of the desk he stopped and looked Frizzell directly in the eyes. "I suppose this is your way of resigning. Persuade me to step aside and that leaves you with the patina of faithful supporter—*and* an effective out."

He let the words sink in as he held Frizzell's eyes. Then he added, "At least Barney had the guts to jump ship like a man." He stared at Frizzell for a lingering moment, then resumed his pacing.

Brown was sucking in his beer gut, quite unconsciously, to make himself somehow less conspicuous.

Dave Frizzell slowly rose to his feet and stepped around the desk, planting himself directly in the path of the Governor's pacing.

Justice turned at the far end of his route, saw Frizzell standing at the opposite end of the desk, and belligerently walked straight up to him. He stopped only inches away, in Frizzell's face.

The men stared at each other, like two boys in two cars with wheels half over the railroad track, staring at the headlight of an oncoming train and waiting to see which one would be the first to break off.

"Frank," Frizzell finally said in a low, firm voice. "You're angry at being caught in a hellishly compromising situation. You're angry because you don't like any of the options that you've got right now. And no doubt you're angry because a woman took you to the cleaners."

Justice didn't flinch.

Neither did Frizzell.

"But instead of dealing with the situation, you're taking your anger out on the people you need most. Barney's gone. If you make one more remark about me or my loyalty to you through your prima donna stupidity, I'm outa here. I don't know what you meant about a problem with Evelyn, but after your unfaithfulness, she's probably ready to leave you. Brown here hasn't said a word. He may be ready to walk too."

Justice turned a sullen face to the blotter on his desk as Frizzell continued.

"Melton is not your enemy. If he told you to resign, he said it because it would be best for you and for the party. As it stands now, Fitzwalter can step up from Lieutenant Governor to your chair with a minimum of damage done. But if you persist, the press will crucify you publicly, we'll lose credibility as a party, and probably lose the Governor's office and who knows how many legislative seats in the next round of elections.

"You may have some personal battles with the FEC, but they'll be a lot easier to fight if you're a private citizen again than if you're still the chief executive. And this CPD investigation won't mean diddly in a week. They're just covering their rear ends."

Justice, eyes still fastened to the blotter, backed up till his hands and legs found his chair, then again he slowly lowered himself back into it.

He remained quiet a minute, apparently mustering his energy and focusing himself for what lay ahead. Then he took a deep breath and stood again. He stepped toward Frizzell, hand outstretched.

Frizzell took his hand and grasped it firmly, barely shaking it.

"Dave, thank you," Justice said. "As usual, you're exactly right in your assessment. It's why I've kept you around so long." He raised the corners of his mouth in a sickly attempt at a smile, then added, "If I make the announcement, will you be at my side?"

"I'll be with you even if you decide to stick it out."

Now the two men shook their clasped hands, Justice drawing his left hand up to add an extra squeeze of appreciation. They looked at each other again, this time with the knowing looks of battle-experienced soldiers preparing to enter their toughest fight together.

Then Justice turned to Brown, who was feeling mightily relieved that Justice's anger hadn't turned on him. "Chief, will you give me a ride to my house? I have an important matter to discuss with my wife, and I'm in no condition to drive."

▼ ▼ ▼ 17 ▼ ▼ ▼

In the kitchen Evelyn smiled a greeting to the somewhat surprised female workers, women whose last expectation had been for their mistress to suddenly show up at the kitchen door after a two-day hiatus. It wasn't like her.

She had gone directly to her room. Evelyn wanted to spend a few minutes in the calming sanctuary of her bedroom, among the pretty things populating her private world, free to think her private thoughts in that world for a few minutes.

Normally, she would have clicked on the radio or the mini-TV on the vanity, or spread a newspaper before her as she groomed herself. But she'd intentionally avoided all that this morning, instead yearning for her sanctuary.

At the vanity in her private bathroom, she had removed the hat and the scarf, then sat on the soft stool and looked at the image of her private world in the mirror as she brushed out her hair with slow strokes.

As ready as she'd ever be, Evelyn faced the gauntlet as she walked back down the stairs to meet Maria in Franklin's study. All the women of the house were gathered at the foot of the grand staircase, abuzz with excitement.

At first they chattered to Evelyn about the reporter who had followed her into the kitchen and how they "shut her down, honey!" in the words of the Southerner. Then they gushed statements of concern for her absence and pleasure at seeing her again.

None of them dared ask where she had been.

Since she wasn't forthcoming with any explanations that would satisfy their curiosity and concern, they turned their noisy welcome into questions about the house and specifics regarding this duty or that preference in completing some project. They seemed genuinely glad to see her.

At first Evelyn felt somewhat cheered and encouraged by the attention. However, it rapidly changed into a suffocating pressure that she didn't want to deal with, one from which she wasn't able to extract herself. She knew they'd be discussing her problems all day. She just wanted to get away.

Maria stepped forward from the back of the group.

"Silencio!" she called as she moved to Evelyn. *"Silencio!"* The group quieted.

"Mrs. Justice needs quiet." She turned to Evelyn as she took her arm. "Come. Rest yourself. We will let you have some peace." And she led the First Lady through the gaggle of employees into the study at the end of the hall. Once inside, Maria said, "You sit. I will move them back to work, and then I will return to you."

Obediently, Evelyn found her way to one end of a long leather couch, a part of a very expensive suite of furniture Franklin had the state purchase for this room in the first month of his administration. He had a passion for leather furnishings.

She didn't like leather furniture that well. Too hard. She preferred soft-but-firm chairs and sofas, especially those with bold, flowered prints. The softness was inviting and the prints reminded her of the garden and the sunshine she seemed starved for.

The room smelled of Franklin. Leather. Books. Cigar. It felt masculine. The hard, linear edges of the bookcases. The stiff resistance of the leather to her soft presence. The dark walls. It was comforting, almost reassuring, and at the same time almost intimidating.

She felt the threat of Franklin's presence. She knew that her noon meeting with him was going to be a case of the protective lion roaring at his lioness. So she closed her eyes and breathed in the smell of leather and cigar as a meditating Hindu priest inhales the ubiquitous smoke of burning incense. She focused on the strength it brought and thought about the courage she had borrowed from Maria.

Evelyn Justice passed several minutes this way, focusing, calming herself. Preparing for her hurdle.

"God, give me strength," she whispered.

A gentle knock at the door interrupted her reverie. She opened her eyes to see Maria, half in the room, leaning on the doorknob, not wanting to intrude on her thoughts.

"Come in," she called. "Please."

Maria crossed to the leather sofa and patted Evelyn's relaxed arm. "How do you feel?"

"Okay. Fine, really. Thank you for rescuing me."

"No problem, Mrs. Justice," Maria said with a tender smile. She turned, walked around behind an ottoman that matched the opulent leather furniture, and pushed it forward till it came to rest in front of Evelyn's legs. Maria sat on the ottoman and leaned toward her, as if announcing that she was ready to give what Evelyn needed.

Evelyn began, "I must impose once more and ask for your advice on how to deal with the issue at hand. Before Franklin arrives, I still must call an attorney about that atrocious invasion of your privacy by the State Patrol, and I need to ask him what to do about possibly being under suspicion myself. But first there's something more pressing."

"Very well," Maria said. "I am not fit to be an advisor to you, but I listen, and we may find guidance from God."

"I need it. Believe me, I need it."

Evelyn rearranged herself on the sofa, pulling her legs up underneath her and leaning forward as if to say the serious work was about to begin. "Maria, as you know, I gave Franklin an ultimatum last evening. Either he comes here today at noon to speak to me or I go to the press and give them information that would be harmful to him."

"Will he come?"

"Oh, yes. He'll be here. The fact that I made the threat got his attention and let him know that I really needed him. That's been his way—so consumed by his own life that I've had to resort to drastic measures to get his attention when I needed it."

"Like trying to kill yourself?"

Evelyn blinked as if caustic smoke had blown into her eyes, then looked quickly away. "Yes, I suppose that could have been a reason." She closed her eyes and breathed deeply, looking for a handle on her feelings.

"And the terrible thing is that once I had his attention I couldn't keep it. That's what I'm afraid of now. I want desperately for the two of us to come together and confront the problems we're both facing, but I don't know how to tell him that. I don't know how to get past his strength to the part of him that needs me, and I don't know how to make him want to use his strength to support my weakness." She sighed heavily. "I don't even know what to say to keep us from instant argument."

She looked away, shaking her head at the futility of her situation.

Evelyn felt Maria take her hand and hold it. She didn't look at her.

"Mrs. Justice," Maria said, softly. "I cannot tell you what to do. I can only ask why you do not say with Mr. Justice what you just say with me?"

"He'd never listen."

"But if you try again to threaten him, will he hear better than if you share with him how you feel?"

Still Evelyn looked away. "No, he won't," she replied deliberately, this time with tears back in her eyes and her voice. "But neither will he hear me if I tell him how I feel from my heart. I'm just afraid that no matter what I say or how I say it, our relationship is so far gone that we'll never find each other again."

"Why don't you try taking this lady's advice?" said a male voice from the other side of the room.

Maria swung around on the ottoman, and Evelyn jerked her head in the direction of the door to the voice she knew better than any other.

▼ ▼ ▼ ▼

Paul Tomass and Dan Li-pong were engaged in a spirited conversation in the hall outside the two reporters' cubicles as Lindy rounded the corner from the wide open spaces of the main room of the City Desk. She stopped dead when she saw them, then began to step backwards toward the main hallway.

Tomass's eyes caught hers and held them as she made it back around the corner.

She didn't want to talk to him now. She was frustrated and embarrassed because she had appeared so foolish at the Governor's mansion. Appeared? She *had* been foolish.

And she was in no mood for a boss. She wanted to get back into her sanely ordered little world and think. She wanted to push through the embarrassment and sort through her options. She was sure she was right about the whole Minnis affair, but she was at a loss as to how to prove it. She just wanted to get into her cubbyhole and push down this formidable barrier to logical thinking.

And she wanted to be near Dan. In addition to feeling her embarrassment, she also was feeling, really feeling, the need to begin connecting with other human beings on something like a meaningful level—whatever that meant.

She didn't want to face Paul Tomass now or deal with an assignment in which she simply wasn't interested— another European community story, no doubt. But he'd locked onto her eyes, just as if she were a hooked fish, and his presence was reeling her in.

Back around the corner she came, sheepishly, till she landed where the two men were standing.

"You came at just the right time," the editor said. "You two did great work on that Minnis story yesterday. I've got Malichi and Goldman making their contacts with the state and city police. Hamilton is doing the political rounds on it. And I want you following up, too. Dan here says that you've been looking into another angle. Any luck?"

She just shook her head *no*. She wasn't ready to try to recast her story in an unembarrassing format.

"No problem. I'm glad you're thinking." Tomass became more animated. "I agree with Dan that there's a natural follow-up in the interview-state-employees line. It *is* likely that where's there's smoke there's fire. He's gonna get on that this morning."

Lindy looked at Dan, surprised.

"I didn't have any luck at police headquarters," he said, raising his hands and acting out an *I'm innocent* look. "That place was as tight as a jug."

"What about that informant?" Tomass asked Lindy. "Can you get back in touch with him?"

"I don't know who he is," she said. "He called me. We got the film in a blind drop."

Tomass frowned and shook his head disapprovingly.

Dan chimed in. "We told him to call us back today."

Tomass grimaced as he thought through the situation. "Well, one thing's for sure—there's no story to be had with you hanging around here. I'll leave word with the receptionist to handle any of your callers with kid gloves. We'll get them to call back, say at noon. In the meantime, you," Tomass said to Lindy, "go back to that drop site and hang around for a while. Or go talk to your security guard friend at the Minnis condo. You might get lucky."

"And if I don't?"

"Then check in before noon, and get over to the state-house after lunch and help Li-pong with the interviews. You're pretty good at squeezing blood out of turnips."

"Do you mind if I spend a few minutes in my office?" she said sarcastically, her head shaking sideways as she spoke. It was one of her little acts of defiance, to show that she'd prefer following her own leads.

"No, I don't mind," Tomass responded in a high mono-tone, head shaking to mimic her. "Just be sure to get out there before the morning's over." He huffed a single laughing *Humph* with a big smile and added, "You guys are good. I'm proud of you. Get out there and do it again."

▼ ▼ ▼ ▼

"Franklin," Evelyn acknowledged as she stood to her feet. Maria stood too, remembering her place. She backed away from the two, well out of the line of sight estab-lished between them.

"It's not noon yet. What are you doing home?" Inside, Evelyn was alarmed at the appearance of the roaring lion, yet strangely warmed by his invitation.

He stepped forward, enough to clear the doorway, then walked toward Maria. With an outstretched hand and a practiced grace born of a thousand political appear-ances, he said, "How kind of you to take in Mrs. Justice when she was distraught."

With both his hands he took Maria's right hand. He looked down at her with a cordial smile. It had always seemed to Evelyn when he approached someone like this, as tall as he was, that his arms formed a chute through which his graciousness flowed, washing over the one being greeted. She knew that it was an irresistible force.

"You know, it's entirely my fault that Evelyn was in that condition in the first place. Please accept my deepest thanks for the service you've rendered us."

"It is nothing, sir," said Maria, meekly.

He pulled her toward him with his right hand, then stepped beside her and laid his left hand on her back as he propelled her toward the door. "I will see to it that you are rewarded for your kindness," he said as he escorted her into the hallway. "Thank you again."

Evelyn squared her shoulders and lifted her chin, preparing to take the offensive. "Franklin," she began, careful to load her voice with resolve, "I'm glad you're here. We have a great deal to talk about."

"Evelyn, darling. I've been worried sick about you."

"I'm sure you've been worried sick, but I doubt that it's been on my behalf."

Franklin crossed the room and stopped in front of her. "I can understand how you would feel that way. I've been grossly unfair to you for a long time. I've been unfaithful as a husband and undependable as a friend. I don't expect you to feel any differently about me now. I only hope that in the future, I can demonstrate my regret in a manner sincere enough to warrant your forgiveness, and ultimately, a restoration of your love and trust."

Evelyn wasn't prepared for this. She was ready for the lion to roar, not to return to his den with his tail between his legs. She had prepared to roar back, to rail on him for his infidelity and lack of support. She was ready to lay down an ultimatum to get his attention, to coerce him into a repentant attitude.

But she wasn't ready for this. She didn't know how to respond, so she kept quiet.

"Please dear, sit down." He took her elbow and guided her backward till her calves met the leather of the sofa, and she sat. "There is so much I have to tell you," he said as he backed up to the leather wingback which matched the two he had in his office. "And a decision I must make with you."

Until that point, Evelyn had just been a bit disoriented. When her husband added the part about a decision to be made, a twinge of fear rose up in her stomach. He must be ready to end it, she thought. And that option really hadn't entered her mind yet.

"I won't go into great detail. I think you know the situation I'm facing."

Her resolve arose again. She didn't really care what problems he was facing. It probably was some political fire burning because of the death of a staff member. She didn't really care. "And perhaps you know the one I'm facing. I left here the other night in desperation. I didn't know what to do. But since then, I've found a little piece of myself and I want you to know that I don't want things to be the same."

He opened his mouth to respond.

She continued, "What you've done is the coldest, most heartless act a man can commit against his wife. I want our marriage to work, but it will be at your expense this time, not mine." Evelyn was both surprised and pleased at the firmness of her voice.

"Evelyn!" Franklin exclaimed as he leaned forward, his elbows coming to rest on his knees. "I love you." He said, punctuating his sentence with his fist. "I've always loved you!" He stood up from the chair, still bent over, and dropped to his knees in front of her. "I need your help. Power got to my head. It warped my thinking. It made me lose perspective on who I really am and what life is really about." He drew closer to her, burying his chest in her knees and gripping her forearms.

With this surprising confession, Evelyn felt a surprising conflict of emotions. His words brought a rush of memories of earlier, simpler days. She hadn't felt needed for years.

But was it just a show? A manipulative trick by a master politician?

Her insides surely couldn't tell.

Then he turned his head away from her. "It took a very cruel circumstance to teach me what is valuable in life." He turned back to her, pulled her down so she was even closer, and held her eyes as he pleaded, "Evelyn, will you help me? Will you put aside your anger with me just long enough to weather this political storm and allow us to resume the life we love so much?"

Evelyn's heart sank. *The life we love!* She wanted to scream, "I love you, but I don't love the life of forgotten wife of a self-intoxicated politician!"

She pulled back from his grip and sat up, raising her chin up and away from his face. But her feelings were less definite than her actions. "I don't forgive you for what you've done," she said, shaking her head. "There's too much damage right now. But if you promise me two things, I'll help you."

"Anything, darling, to show you that I am sincerely sorry for what I've done."

She turned back to him and tried to find in his eyes whether he was lying or telling the truth. She couldn't see anything but him.

"You must see that this pall of suspicion of your mistress's murder is removed from me. You know I would never do such a thing."

He took her forearms again and pulled her attention toward him. "I'll put the best attorney in the state on it," Frank said. "I'm sure he'll find a way to dissociate your state of mind from the events of yesterday."

"What do you mean, 'find a way'?" Evelyn responded with sarcasm to what he made to sound like a major task.

"I'm innocent and I have a witness as to my whereabouts. Why would some lawyer need to 'find a way'?"

"Is that maid your witness?"

"Yes, of course. I've been at her house."

"Was she at her home with you or here at work during the middle of yesterday afternoon?"

A twinge of fear washed through her with the understanding of what he meant. She didn't answer him.

"Did you disappear from this house in a rage two days ago, distraught over what your private investigator told you?"

"Yes, I mean no, but—"

"Did you take with you a knife from our kitchen?"

"Yes, but it's still in my purse. I swear I didn't—"

"Have you suffered from reality impairment lately, bringing on hallucinations and even a suicide attempt? Have you been stable enough to say for sure that it is not possible for you to have left that house yesterday and allow your subconscious to act out what you never would have the courage to do consciously?"

Evelyn just shook her head, unable to answer his charges.

"Are you? Are you able to do that?"

"No!" she snapped. "I'm not. I'm not able. I've only just begun to sort out the pieces of my life and my thoughts. But I did not murder anyone, not even your mistress."

"You *think* you didn't, but are you sure?"

Evelyn looked away, choking down the thought that maybe she hadn't begun to get a handle on her life, that maybe she did need the drugs after all.

Still on his knees in front of her, Franklin said, "I assure you, dear, we'll see to it that all suspicion is deterred. And if you did it, I can find doctors to help you put things back together.

"Now, what is that second request you have of me?"

Evelyn was dazed. She was going to insist that they begin counseling when this storm blew over, but she didn't have the strength to insist now. Feebly, she responded, "I just want for us to get counseling when this is all over and try to get our lives back together."

Franklin raised up and put his arms around her. "Oh, Evelyn. Leave it to me. I'll call the attorney today, and as soon as this whole affair is cleared up, I'll have John Bates arrange for that counseling—whatever type we'll be needing."

He hugged her, then drew his mouth to her ear. "I knew I could count on you," he whispered.

▼ ▼ ▼ 18 ▼ ▼ ▼

Franklin rose from his knees, embraced her once more, then backed up to his chair. He bent over and pulled on it to bring the two closer, then sat down. "Evelyn, darling. I need your help. I must make a decision. Now. This morning. And you must help me make it."

"Is this about us or about you?" Evelyn said, not sure she wanted to hear what this big decision might be. She was reeling from Franklin's warmth—and the cold reality that she still could be considered a suspect in the Minnis murder.

"It certainly will affect us, but it's primarily about me."

Evelyn breathed a *humph*. She had guessed that. "Tell me."

Franklin sat back in his chair and looked down, clearly focusing his thoughts for what he was about to say. "I trust you've seen the morning paper."

"No," she said, "I haven't."

Franklin rolled his eyes ceilingward and let his head follow. "I suppose that's even better." He looked back at her, "Yes, that's even better. This way you'll hear it from me." He screwed up his face in thought in a familiar way, characteristic of the times he had talked to her about important matters.

"This morning's *News* ran a photo of me taken yesterday in the hall outside Annie Minnis' apartment. She was in the doorway."

Evelyn leaned her head forward in disbelief, squinting at her husband to try to see if he really was saying what she thought he was saying.

"I can explain being there. Really. It was yesterday afternoon. I'd gone there to cut off our relationship, just as you wanted. I felt that I had to see her to tell her. I owed her that much."

Evelyn didn't speak. She felt the same knot of anger that had helped her focus herself and rise out of Tuesday's fog. It was hard and real and she took hold of it to get oriented. When she did speak, it was slow and as hard as the knot she held to. "You *owed* her? You owed consideration to a two-bit whore when for years you abused my trust and our relationship in the worst possible way?" She couldn't believe her ears.

"I know what you're feeling," he said in a pleading, almost distraught tone, "and you're perfectly justified. But believe me, I went there to cut it off."

Evelyn's anger mixed with relief. Maybe he did care about their marriage.

Franklin continued more matter-of-factly. "The problem is, the picture was taken sometime shortly before Annie was killed. It's bad enough that we already had a public relations nightmare on our hands because of the affair, and the drug links to the murder, but I found out only an hour ago that the police have included me as a suspect in the murder investigation."

That was a hammer-blow to Evelyn, one that drove her anger down like a nail in soft pine. She'd been reluctantly ready to deal with the possibility of her own guilt. She was used to feeling responsible for the bad things that happened around her. But she was entirely unprepared to believe that Franklin—habitually successful and in-control Franklin—would be considered a suspect.

"That's not all." He rested his elbow on the arm of the chair and lowered his chin to his hand. He stroked it with thumb and forefinger, almost like he was trying to coax the right words or even a solution from it. "This morning Rex Melton called me."

"And? What did he want?"

"He advised me to step down."

"To resign?" She felt the dizziness again.

"Yes. Rex thought it would be best for the party and felt that I'd have an easier time fighting any legal battles as a has-been than as the chief executive of the state.

"Dave Frizzell advised the same. Barney resigned this morning because he believes Annie may have embezzled money to fund a drug habit. If that's true, then I will be in serious trouble, even if the police investigation clears me entirely of suspicion in the murder.

"One way or another," he added, "I'm dead politically."

Evelyn sank back into the leather of the sofa as far as her weight would take her. She wished at that moment that she had been in an overstuffed chair that just swallowed her and took her away from the scene.

Instead, she looked at Franklin and spoke, a glimmer of suspicion beginning to glow in her eyes. "*Did* you kill her while you were there?"

"Evelyn!" Franklin shouted as he jumped out of the chair. "How could you? What possible reason would I have for killing this woman? *I* wasn't jealous! *I* wasn't depressive and unstable. How could you imagine for one moment that I would risk my future—our future—on so ridiculous an act?" He ended his outburst and turned to pace the oriental rug.

Evelyn didn't know how she felt. The fog was blurring her mind again. Then a thought of Maria flashed across her mind and she realized that she and Franklin didn't have to face this alone. As poor as their relationship was, they had each other. Franklin wasn't lying dead at the hands of a death squad like Maria's poor husband. Plus she now had Maria—and Maria's faith in a good God. Maybe they'd make it.

She was sure that they wouldn't if they continued to doubt each other. Neither she nor he needed to be living with an enemy.

"Franklin," she said, straining to be deliberate and purposeful, "you must do what you think best. Your instincts have never failed you politically and I'll be behind you 100 percent no matter which course you choose. My own opinion is that you should remain in office and see this through. Any other action would be an admission of guilt in one or many of the problems that have surfaced.

"I think I can help you. You know that I hired a private investigator to follow you when I finally decided to face the truth about your infidelity."

"Yes, an action I think was very unwise. Most of those men are either thugs or ex-policemen who didn't make it on the force. Whether you know it or not, you took risks. How would you come in contact with such people?"

"The yellow pages," she said proudly. "I looked in the yellow pages and found an address that seemed to be in the right part of town."

"Evelyn!" he chided. "Do you know how foolish that was? I'm the Governor!"

"He did the job!"

That let the air out of Franklin's balloon. "And we may live to see him do another," he said to the floor. "On us." He looked back to his wife. "Why are you telling me this now? It's not that I don't have enough to worry about."

"Don't you see? This man might be able to help us now! Annie Minnis was black and so is he. He'll know what's going on in the black community and he'll be able to help us. He'll find out more about Annie Minnis's drug connections in one day than your State Patrol or the City

Police could in a month. The only thing they know how to do is write speeding tickets."

Franklin sat quietly, shaking his head. Clearly he didn't like the idea. "I don't see how that can help me now," he finally said.

"I think you should try it."

Franklin stood and crossed his arms on his chest. "And my future as Governor? Should I resign or stay and fight?"

She stood and stepped up to him, laying her hands on his crossed arms and looking into his eyes. "I told you. I know you'll make the right decision about whether to resign. But in either case, you must fight!"

He looked at her. She wanted to lean close to his eyes and blow away the anguish from them as she would blow the dust off a treasured possession. During a conversation about his dead mistress, she still wanted to comfort him. God help me, she thought. You are one bundle of fouled up emotions, Evelyn Justice.

She was brave enough only to give him the most heartening smile she could muster. "I'll be beside you no matter what course you choose."

He smiled a grateful, distracted smile, then bent and kissed her forehead. "Thank you, Evelyn. I'll call you and let you know what I decide."

And with that, he turned and walked purposefully out of the room.

Evelyn followed him to the door and watched as he walked down the hall and through the front door onto the wide porch. She then hurried in the opposite direction, up the grand staircase and down the hall toward her room. Maria was at the far end. Evelyn motioned to her to come as she dipped into her bedroom and plopped down on her bed next to her nightstand.

She opened the drawer and rummaged around until she found the slip of paper she was looking for. She dialed the number as Maria walked into the room.

The phone rang on the other end. And it rang. And rang.

"Oh, please be in," she said, as if by mind power she could will the private investigator to be in.

The click of a raised receiver cut the ringing tone off in mid-ring.

"Yo?" a deep voice croaked on the other end.

"Mr. Frog? That is the name you asked me to call you, isn't it? This is Evelyn Justice. I need your services again."

▼ ▼ ▼ ▼

Dan Li-pong trusted his own instincts as much as he did his partner's. He knew that when the leader of the pack showed signs of weakness or was bleeding from a wound, the pack would turn on him. He knew that if he fished around the statehouse among people with whom he'd had previous contact, he would find a wolf or two ready to bare fangs.

And he had.

Three people had been ready to talk. Two of them stepped out of their offices and into the hall for a short turn around the capitol rotunda with Dan. The other promised to meet him after work at a bar out of the vicinity of the capitol, someplace the government groupies didn't hang out, to reduce the chance of being seen with a reporter.

Dan respected Lindy and her abilities. As a partner, he was ready to drop his line to pick up hers whenever she felt strongly about something. But he often felt that she was reluctant to do the same. Not that she didn't listen or show interest in his reasoning. They worked well together. But she never seemed willing to extend the same trust in his direction.

He had thought about it a lot and had come to the conclusion that many women today were having the same difficulties dealing with power and control in the workplace as their fathers' generation had twenty years ago. She was a woman, but she seemed awfully busy proving that didn't matter on the job.

Dan headed back to the office to write up his material. He was walking down a long, typically government hallway in a new wing of the old state office building when a guy dressed in a technician's smock stopped in front of him.

"How ya doing?" Dan said to the unexpected company.

"I see from this morning's paper that you got my film."

Dan was stunned. He looked at the guy in utter surprise. "Are you . . . ?" he asked, so incredulous that he wasn't even sure how to finish the sentence.

"Yeah. I talked to you and the girl reporter last night. I seen you when you picked up my package."

Dan got a mental flash of Lindy hanging around the post office drop site. Why had she been so stubborn and not listened to him for once? "We asked you to call today."

"Like you'da been there to answer?" he said nonchalantly, shrugging his shoulders. "I was gonna get around to it, but then you show up on my doorstep. Why should I waste a quarter? Anyway, I see you used my picture today."

Dan was very excited. At first he could hardly believe his luck, then he realized that there was far less luck in this encounter than it seemed. It was luck that he had come there this morning after scouting out the central police offices. It would have been luck to get something from the police this morning, and if he had, he'd probably not have come to the state offices.

But it made sense. The guy said he knew Minnis. Like any informant, he wanted his ego stroked on how brilliant his information was, and like in most other cases, that desire for strokes took precedence over the desire for anonymity, at least vis-à-vis the press.

Now that he had him, how would Dan use the contact?

The guy solved the problem. "You like that one, you'll like some of the others I got."

"Other pictures?"

The guy looked up and down the hall, then added, "Of course, other pictures. Whadda ya think?"

"Any more of the, uh . . . subject of today's photo?"

"Nah. That's the only one of him you'd be interested in. But I got other good ones that you reporters might like."

Dan looked at him, wondering how to handle the situation and trying not to look as bumbling as he felt.

"But it'll cost you the next time."

Money! Dan thought. That's the way in. "Look. I'm trying to scare up something interesting today. Something to help tie all the loose strings together. Any chance you can show me what you've got?" Maybe he and Lindy could meet this guy tonight.

"You ready to pay?"

"If the shots are as good as you say they are *and* if the price is right."

"Then whadda we waitin' for?" The man peeled off his tech smock and started moving down the hall in the direction of the parking garage. "You drivin' or am I?"

"You mean now? What about your job?"

"Huh!" the man huffed, not looking back. "This place'll never miss me. I got independent assignments to fix terminals." This time he did turn. He gave Dan a smug look, like he was really pulling a fast one. "I'm just gonna have to spend longer than I expected on one of this morning's assignments, if you know what I mean."

Dan almost had to shake off his disbelief. He hurried to catch up. "We need to go pick up my partner."

"No problem. Where's she at?"

"The post office you named as a drop site last night."

"What's she doin' there?"

"Hoping to make contact with you."

The guy laughed out loud. "Reporters! It's a wonder you guys can find your way to work every morning."

▼ ▼ ▼ ▼

"Word to yo mutha," the low, croaking voice greeted Evelyn. "I figgered you'd call back, after I saw the morning paper. You ready to nail his hide to the wall?"

"No!" said Evelyn. "I need you to help me find whatever it is that we need to be sure my husband's name is cleared."

"Honkies!" the man laughed, derisively. "Uppity honkies." The voice was full of derision. "Well, I don't care why you want what you want, but this time it'll cost you."

"And why would that be?" Evelyn asked properly.

" 'Cause the publication of that picture this morning has made the whole mess a lot nastier, and more dangerous for someone like me to be involved."

"How can it possibly be more dangerous?"

"Lady, you're either dense or you're wantin' to lie. Big boys like to step on little frogs like me."

"Very well," she said, acceding the point. "What is your new fee?"

"You can't pay what I'm gonna charge."

"What do you mean?" she said, alarmed. "I need your services and I'm willing to pay."

"It's no problem, mama. You'll pay. But I need to talk over my fee with your husband. He's the only one who can pay me what I want, and I knew sooner or later we'd get to negotiate."

"Would you please explain?"

"It's like this. I knew you'd be callin', like I said. I saw this picture this mornin' and I saw somethin' you'd never be able to see. I saw who took it. Right there as plain as the nose on yer face."

"I'm sorry, but I haven't seen the picture."

"Well, that's real nice. Anyway, I know who took it and I figger that piece of information is worth a little more, so I been out already. Earnin' my fee."

"And what do you intend to do now? Can you help me clear my husband of any connection to this dreadful murder?"

"Maybe I can and maybe I can't." He paused. "But I can have a little chat with the guy who took that picture. I know where he lives."

"How will that help?"

"You one dense mutha! Maybe it helps, maybe it don't."

"All right. When will you do this?"

"Not now. Later. This afternoon. Late. I have company right now, more important than business. Ain't that right, mama?"

Evelyn heard a female voice respond. She felt disgust toward this man. She had felt it before and she felt it now.

But he was effective.

"Will you call me when you know something?"

"Believe it!" the voice said, then the line went dead.

Evelyn pulled the phone away from her ear and looked at it with repugnance. She replaced the phone to its cradle, then motioned for Maria to sit down next to her on the bed.

"Did it go all right with Mr. Justice?"

"Oh, Maria, I don't know. For the first time in years I felt the old Franklin. He's in a terrible situation, one that will almost certainly ruin his career. But at the same time I was absolutely furious with him and what he's done to me over the years. Oh, Maria," she said with anguish in her voice, "one minute I feel that my life is coming together, the next I feel like I'm drowning in my own instability."

"What will you do?"

"I know of two things I must do, but I don't know if they'll help him any. What I'm sure of is that I have to do something. I'll fall back into craziness if I don't." What she didn't say was that she also had to do something to warrant being needed again. She was afraid of being left alone.

"What two things?" Maria asked.

"I told you that I called a private investigator to follow him before?"

Maria shook her head.

"Well, I did. That's who was on the phone just now. He says he knows who took the picture in this morning's paper. You don't know about that, but evidently it's part of what's precipitated this crisis for Franklin."

"I do know," Maria said. "The women in the kitchen, they have the picture."

"And I'm sure I know what the conversation in the kitchen was all about."

"They are mad. They think you are hurt in this. They like you and don't want you hurting."

"I appreciate that," Evelyn gave her friend a warm glance, then looked away as she thought out loud. "This man is going to find out what he can about who took that picture. I don't even want to see it!" She paused. "And there's at least one other thing I can do right now to help Franklin."

"What is that?"

"I can try to get the press on our side. If there's one thing I've learned in politics, it's that you want to be on the good side of the man who buys ink by the barrel and paper by the ton."

Maria looked confused.

"Never mind. Just help me. Do you remember the name of the reporter who stopped us in the driveway this morning?"

▼ ▼ ▼ ▼

Lindy was flabbergasted when Dan drove into the crowded parking lot of the post office at Edgewood and Meter Road and announced that the man in the car with him was the gentleman with whom they'd spoken the previous evening regarding Annie Minnis and Governor Justice.

She still felt the astonishment as she sped toward 2223a South College in her blue Miata, the address Dan had given her as the man's apartment. "Duplex to be exact," the geek had added. He was more insufferable in person than on the phone, but she was glad to see him.

She would have gotten in the back seat of Dan's car in a heartbeat if it hadn't meant leaving her Miata in an unsecured parking lot. And she would have insisted that Dan leave his car and the two of them ride with her if she'd had more than two seats.

But how had he found the man? One thing was for sure. Dan was one up on her now.

When she pulled up to 2223a and stopped in the road beside Dan's already parked ancient Malibu, Dan and the informant were standing on the right-hand porch of a duplex which was in sad need of a facelift. In fact, the whole neighborhood could have used reconstructive surgery. There were rundown cars parked up and down the street, and Dan had taken the only parking space within several car lengths from the front of the house—well outside her comfort zone.

She motioned for Dan to come to the car.

He jogged to the curb and around the front of his Malibu and to the passenger door on the Miata. "Yeah?" he said, the door open and only his head stuck in.

"Can you move your car down the street and let me park here?"

"What?" Dan said in mock surprise, a grin spreading across his face.

"You know how I feel about my car. I don't like this neighborhood."

"Lind, I was here first," he smiled, then added, "Besides, it's broad daylight."

She gave him a stern look, almost like that of a schoolmarm using her deadly looks to bring an errant pre-teen into submission.

"Touchy, touchy!" he said with a chuckle. "You can't take much of a joke."

"Not about my baby."

"Pull back," he said as he slammed the door. He pulled out of the slot and up the street as she slid the little blue ball of fire into the gap he'd left.

"Nice car," the geek called out as she closed the door and locked it. Dan was just making the final approach to a slot up the street. He wasn't a very good parallel parker. He always had to make several runs at it.

"You and me are gonna have to take that machine for a real workout some evening," the geek said, trying to unleash what he obviously believed to be his animal attractiveness. "Then maybe you and me could work out too? If you know what I mean."

Lindy felt sickened, but she was a professional. She wasn't about to blow the chance at getting a lot further on a feature story. She slowed her pace up the walkway, deciding exactly how she'd play this hand, until by the time she reached the steps to the porch, she was moving like a cat closing in on its prey.

Good guy, bad guy, she thought, remembering the way Dan had handled the guy the night before. I get to be the bad guy today.

The man saw anger in her eyes and made another off-color remark.

She advanced up the steps deliberately.

"Whatsa matter? You got no sense of humor?" He was backing up.

"Listen, filth. I had all of you I could stomach on the phone. You got your satisfaction from me when that photo ran this morning. You'll not get another ounce at my expense."

"You come here wantin' more, though."

"You're right. But not more of your revolting presence." She stepped closer and jabbed at his chest with her finger, her left forefinger, to punctuate her words. She wasn't lefthanded, but the nail on her right forefinger had broken and she'd filed it down. She wanted him to feel her words.

"Let me tell you this, you worm. I know that you got that picture by accident. You happened to be in the right place at the right time. But it was no accident that you chose to go there in the first place. You were there to take advantage of that poor woman. You probably had dogged her and even taken your stupid pictures of her until she couldn't stand it.

"Well, you've had all the satisfaction you're going to get from me or my partner. And if there's any connection to be made between you and Annie Minnis's death, I'll do my best to see that it's made—publicly, where everyone will see."

She turned and stormed off the porch.

"You! Hey, you!" He stepped off the porch after her. "You swore you'd keep me outa this."

On the main sidewalk, Dan neared the walkway to the duplex and slowed to try to see what the commotion was.

Lindy winked at Dan as she brushed past him on her way to her car. "He's yours now," she said, satisfied that she'd killed two birds with one stone. "I softened him up for you."

"What?" he asked, a puzzled look reiterating his question. He turned to the duplex and saw the man hurrying down the sidewalk after Lindy. Dan stepped in his way.

The geek stopped, looked around him toward Lindy, and then got right up in his face. "Look, reporter. You said you'd keep me anonymous. You guaranteed. You let this woman go and do something like talk to the cops about me and you'll pay." He grabbed Dan's shirt. "Get it?"

"What'd you say to her?" Dan asked as he brushed the man's hands off his shirt.

"I didn't say nothin'!" the man shouted. Then he looked up at Lindy and yelled even louder, "That girl's crazy!"

Lindy stood looking at the two for a moment, one leg in her Miata and one leg on the street. She felt like a big game hunter with her foot resting in victory on a downed trophy.

"You go on," Dan called. "I'll meet you at the office in a while."

Lindy squinted out one last dirty look to both men, then dropped into her seat, slammed the door, and brought the engine to life. She backed up enough to clear the bumper of the heap parked in front of her, then floored the accelerator.

Her tires squealed all the way down the street past where Dan had parked.

▼ ▼ ▼ 19 ▼ ▼ ▼

Lindy decided to reward herself for what she considered to be a cheeky move—slimebusting. She decided to drive north, just out of town, to her favorite restaurant, a quaint little country boutique with a lace-and-frills luncheon terrace.

She relished the satisfaction of blowing the geek off.

Lindy thought about Annie, the life she must have lived and the death she died. She was convinced that Annie's murder was not at the hands of the drug lords. The murder scene, the photos, the unstable wife—to her they all pointed to passion, not profit.

As she finished her pasta primavera, Lindy resolved that getting to Evelyn Justice was the key to further progress. Through her aides, her friends or her front door, Lindy had to get in to see the First Lady!

On the drive back downtown, she thought about Dan. That just confused her. It seemed almost embarrassingly evident that he'd been trying to come closer to her, especially in the last few weeks.

But she wasn't sure. Maybe he was just wanting to give her the support she needed.

But she knew she wanted to get closer to him. There was no doubt about how warm it felt to be near him, but maybe that was just the pleasure one feels with closeness during an emotionally vulnerable moment.

She wasn't sure. It would be fun finding out, though.

By the time she had driven back to the city, stopped to cap off her reward with frozen yogurt in the deli around the corner from her parking lot, and walked back to her office, it was almost two o'clock.

She walked into her cubicle and stood, looking at the neatness of the desk sandwiched between the mess on the floor and the walls. This is exactly who you are, Blakely, she thought. One little slice of clarity and everything else a mess. She kicked at the piles of paper, first on one side of the mushroom-shaped path, then on the other.

"Lindy?" a voice called over the carpeted wall dividers.

She sat down in her chair and looked at the papers she'd kicked. "I'm gonna clean this mess up someday," she said as she made her way to her desk.

"Lind! Where you been?" It was Dan, looking over the top of the wall divider. "Stay there."

She swung her chair around so that she could see him coming through the opening of her cubicle.

"Lindy, where have you been?" Dan repeated urgently as he clopped into her room.

She didn't answer. She just sat regally in her chair and responded with a blank, teasingly innocent look, like *oh-my-I-didn't-realize-there-was-a-problem.*

"Did you hear about the press conference at noon?"

She perked up. "No. What?"

"Franklin Justice made a statement!"

Her mouth dropped open. She could have kicked herself for wasting time on a dish of pasta when there was action going on.

"He called a press conference for noon and showed up in the State House briefing room at twelve o'clock on the button."

"What did he say?" Lindy's juices were beginning to flow.

"Just a minute." Dan ran out of the cubicle.

Lindy could hear him next door rummaging around in some papers. In thirty seconds he was back.

"Listen." Dan held up the statement which had been issued to the press on official letterhead and read, *"'I've called this press conference to answer recent negative publicity regarding both my Administration and my personal life. First of all, one of my top aides was murdered yesterday, an incident which police believe to be linked to the drug underworld. It is this very plague and this kind of concomitant tragedy which I will address by redoubling my efforts toward a thoroughgoing drug policy for this state. I pledge to the people of this state that their public employees will be at the front of the line in being drug-free.'"*

Dan looked up from the press release and added, "Here's the part you'll like!

" 'Second, I bitterly resent the tabloid journalism practiced by the News in their publication of the photo of me in this morning's issue. That was an actual photo of me in the hall of my aide's apartment building in what appeared to be an emotional exchange. Indeed, it was an emotional exchange, but not of the kind that the dirty minds in editorial offices had in mind.

" 'I had learned of Ms. Minnis's drug use fewer than twenty-four hours after the Tuesday press conference at which I announced my Administration's drug initiative. I was so furious at this breach of my trust that I went personally to this employee's apartment and dismissed her. It was noontime on Wednesday and she had called in sick that morning. My action led to an angry response from her, a response captured by the photo which the irresponsible editors at the News chose to print.'"

Dan began reading straightfaced, but by the time he'd finished this paragraph, he was dramatizing the lines. "Now get this line.

" 'It is a sad day when community leaders such as the editors at the News sacrifice their principles and compromise the integrity of others for their personal or corporate gain.'"

Lindy said nothing. Her mental wheels were racing as she processed the statement. "Is that all?" she asked.

"Almost." He lifted the paper and finished reading, "'*I categorically deny any involvement in this woman's private life, any previous knowledge of her drug use, or any involvement whatsoever in her demise.*

"'*That is the end of my statement and I will accept no questions.*'

"And that was it!" Dan exclaimed. "He just turned around and walked away—like all we poor misguided slaves of a corrupt press were going to just take our comeuppance and get down to our real business of writing obituaries and the sports page!"

Lindy's engine was running like her Miata's now. "I know why he did it," she declared.

"What?" Dan laughed. "You been with some gazer and her crystal ball?"

"I don't need superstitious nonsense to see through such a transparent ploy."

"Lind, you're either crazy or you know something that no other reporter in town knows. No other person as far as I know. What are you thinking?"

"I'm not thinking, Dan. I know. This proves what I've suspected all along. Franklin Justice is not covering his political backside. He's blowing a thick, dark smoke screen to protect his wife."

"From suspicion of murder!" Dan said in a flash of revelation. "Lindy, that's it. That's the only thing it could be. No politician as savvy as Justice would gamble his political future by publicly tackling the editors of the state's leading newspaper—"

"—unless," Lindy interrupted, "there's more at stake in the gamble than what's on the surface. And as far as I know, you and I are the only ones who know enough about what's going on to have put two and two together."

"Lind, you're brilliant." He grabbed her head and gave her a huge, noisy, euphoric smack of a kiss on her forehead.

He headed for the door. "I'm going to police headquarters to see if I can trade this for a little more cooperation. I'll be back by five. Leave me a note if you get any brainstorms."

He disappeared into the hallway, then a moment later, stuck his head back around the opening and added, "Hey, two things I almost forgot. Great move you pulled on our informant. He was like butter after you left. The guy had been trailing Minnis and a bunch of other women in responsible positions, and had pictures to prove it. Some of them were very interesting. I left him hanging with a threat of exposure. We'll get some good material from that guy in the future.

"But," Dan said, his face and tone of voice turning pedantic, "from now on, give me a warning or a count-down or something to clue me in on what you're going to pull."

She sat up straight in her chair, regally again, like a queen accepting the obeisance of a loyal subject.

He added, "I could have wrung your neck at first, but you really yanked that guy's chain."

She smiled broadly.

"Another thing," he added. "A Jane Elander called. Number's stuck on your phone. Said she wanted to schedule an appointment with you and that you'd know what it was about. See you later."

▼ ▼ ▼ ▼

Evelyn Justice heard about her husband's news conference from Maria Arvizu. Neither had been near radio or TV at the time, but the news spread through the staff as if the whole building were one giant receiver.

"I'm glad he stood up to the public eye," Evelyn confided to her friend. "He's a fighter and he'll come through this, but truthfully, Maria, a part of me wishes he'd just resign. I think his political career has been his real wife and mistress for the past decade."

She knew him. She knew that he would be home soon after the announcement. He would stay long enough to bark a few orders and set a few wheels in motion, but then he'd be home to get her reaction. Evelyn Justice never had figured out why her strong husband needed her approval when he stuck his neck out. It had baffled her and finally she'd just accepted it as one of the quirks of his personality.

True to her expectations, he returned to the mansion shortly after two o'clock, looking like he'd been beaten by a gang of thugs.

She met him at the front door, the only one he'd ever use, and simply said, "I heard." She took his arm and steered him into his study, guiding him toward the burgundy leather wingback.

After arranging him in the chair, she walked around to the back of his desk and opened a panel in the wood-covered wall. From the bottles she selected a single malt scotch which she knew to be his favorite. She took two ice cubes from the refrigerator/freezer built into the wall beneath the hideaway bar and dropped them into a glass. Then she poured the scotch over the ice cubes. She knew better than to pour the scotch, then add the ice cubes. He knew the difference and he hated the former.

She took the glass to her battered husband and handed it to him. "Scotch and water, sir. Just the way you like it." Then she sat on the arm of the couch a couple of feet away.

"I'm done, Evelyn," he said after a couple of pulls on the whiskey. "It would have been better for both of us if I'd never heard of politics."

She crossed her legs and folded her hands on her knee.

He took another long sip. "I'm really worried about this murder investigation. If there's a public outcry, they'll come after me. They'll do it. Even though the D.A. is one of us, he won't be able to resist the temptation."

"I thought you worked well with Tischfield. Would he really be that base?"

He looked up at her with a mixture of pity for her naïveté and burden for having to endure it himself. "He's a good man, but this is a public gold mine. He'd salivate over the thought of the press he'd get if he can convict me." Franklin looked away from her and back to his glass as it rose to his lips. "No matter about someone's innocence."

That brought Evelyn to life. She knew that if she was going to get her life back, she'd have to take it back. "Franklin, I think you must be active in clearing yourself of any suspicion in this whole affair. You're an attorney, you're a capable and experienced man, and you know who's who and what's what in this town. You made a great start at the press conference. Now finish the job!"

He didn't share her enthusiasm. He just took another drink.

She lifted the glass from his hand and set it down on one of the tables that matched the leather sofa and chair. "That's enough to drink. Right now you need to act to protect our dignity and our lives. If you don't do it, who will?"

It was one of those surreal moments that had occurred a few times over the last who-knows-how-many years. Tough Franklin turned soft and weak; Evelyn turned leader and prodder. She'd never understood it but she was up to the part today.

Franklin didn't stir. He just brought his hands together on his lap and brought a scowl to his face. "I can't right now. I'm so numb and exhausted I wouldn't even know where to start."

"Well, I do!" she snapped. Evelyn walked around to the front of the chair and stood before him, ready to pump him up for action. "I told you I was going to hire that private investigator to help us. I spoke to him this morning to engage him. He said that he'd expected my call after seeing the morning paper and that he's already done some checking of his own."

"And?" Franklin said, fingers still intertwined on his lap but his eyes lifting to meet hers.

"He said that he knew who took the picture that ran in this morning's paper." Franklin sat up straight.

"How did he know?"

"He didn't say. Just something about seeing what I couldn't see."

"When was he going to see the man?"

"Late this afternoon he said. He had a woman there and was clearly preoccupied with her."

Franklin stood up, stepped behind the chair he'd been slouched in, and began to pace. "Evelyn, don't you see?"

"See what?" she asked.

"I've been so stressed out for the last few days that the issue of who took that picture never even crossed my mind. I guess I just wrote it off as the press pulling another magic trick. God knows they come up with enough of them."

His look became intent. He was focusing on the possibilities at hand. "This could be the very thing that saves me. If this can lift suspicion from me, I'll end up a public hero and the press will end up eating crow! And the positive PR would be a big boost for reelection, and even better if I decide to tackle the Senate seat next fall."

He was clearly excited now, but Evelyn was feeling mixed emotions. She was thrilled that she had apparently done right by calling the investigator. But the talk of more politics frustrated her.

I'll cross that bridge when I come to it, she thought. Right now, first things first.

"Franklin, I don't understand why this is so important."

He continued to pace as he spoke. "Whoever took that picture was at Annie Minnis's condo for a reason. Nobody but Annie knew I was coming and she didn't know why I was coming." He looked at Evelyn and added, "Had she known that I wanted to break off our relationship, she might have set me up. But she didn't." He looked away again. "This guy could be the killer."

"What if he's not?"

"That's still all right. If he was around that day, he had to have seen the killer. The best guess the police have is that the whole thing was drug-related. She was using drugs," he said, counting that as point number one with his fingers. "She was beaten, like they wanted to send some message," he pointed to finger number two, "and the murder was committed the way those low-lifes do it." Point number three.

"If the man who took the picture was around to see me break off our relationship, then he quite possibly was around to see who murdered Annie, if he himself didn't.

"Evelyn, I've been in politics long enough to know that when there's a potentially damaging situation, you seize it and turn it to your advantage. I have to get to this guy—either way—when he thinks I'm the most vulnerable, when he thinks he can get the most out of me. Then he's mine!"

He made another two circuits behind the chair. "Did the investigator say where the man lived?"

"No," Evelyn replied thoughtfully, wanting to be sure she recalled the conversation correctly. "He just said he was going to see him this afternoon and that he'd get back to me."

"Do you have his number?"

"Yes, upstairs."

"Get it."

Flustered, Evelyn looked at Franklin as he resumed pacing, then hurried off to her bedroom to find the telephone number of the man who, only days earlier, had confirmed her worst fears. But she was troubled. When she had come home that morning, it was with the intention of getting her old Franklin and her old life back.

But now she wasn't sure.

He wasn't the old Franklin.

We all change, she thought. *She* had changed. She hoped God knew she had changed, and that He could do something about it.

About them.

She retrieved the phone number and rushed back to the study.

He met her halfway into the room, snatched the sheet of notepaper out of her hand, and turned to the desk and his phone.

"What's his name?" Franklin barked after dialing the numbers.

"I believe it was Jackson Greene. He told me to call him Frog, of all things. So I did."

Franklin turned away to address the voice on the phone. "Greene? This is Franklin Justice. I . . . yeah, yeah. Cut it. You do business with me, you watch your mouth."

Evelyn couldn't hear both sides of the conversation, but she knew what a rough man Mr. Greene seemed to be. She wasn't used to seeing Franklin handle such people, and with such directness.

"My wife tells me you have a line on the man who took that picture in the morning's paper."

Long pause.

"I want to be there with you. What's the address? Twenty-two-twenty-three-A College Avenue? . . . Fifteen minutes! . . . All right, four o'clock. Be there on time."

Franklin hung up the phone.

He turned to his wife. "Thank you, darling. I'm very glad you did what you thought was right. It may be our salvation."

Oh, she thought. Shades of the old Franklin.

"I have several things I must do before I meet this man." He looked at his watch. "Gotta go." He pecked her on the cheek.

She grabbed his arms when he leaned to kiss her, and when he pulled back hurriedly, she wouldn't let him go.

He smiled. "Thank you," he repeated, then bolted for the door.

Evelyn hugged herself and looked out the window, trying to sort out the conflicting emotions churning inside her. She squeezed herself and allowed a smile to come, a small one. There was no sign of the monster.

"Mrs. Justice."

Evelyn turned. Jane Elander, her personal secretary, stood in the doorway, the light from the hall framing the beautiful figure in her business-like suit. "Yes."

"Linda Blakely, the reporter you asked me to call? She's here to see you."

Evelyn's eyebrows raised in mock surprise. Press piranhas, she thought.

"I'm sorry, but she insisted on coming immediately."

"Thank you, Jane. Please show her into the Hall of First Ladies."

"Yes, ma'am," the secretary said, and withdrew into the hall.

Evelyn turned back to the windows and the welcome sunlight. She gave herself one more hug, congratulations for a good decision in the pursuit of her new life.

Then she turned and moved for the door.

I'm coming, Ms. Blakely.

▼ ▼ ▼ 20 ▼ ▼ ▼

Lindy sat in the Hall of the First Ladies, legs crossed, microcassette recorder in hand. This woman's good, she thought as she looked around at the unique memorabilia from a century and a half of statehood. She's put me in this room for a reason. She foxed me once today, and she wants to emphasize the fact by appearing in the presence of her predecessors.

She raised the recorder to her lips, pressed the red button, and spoke to the machine, "And Evelyn Justice, after your husband's announcement today and this interview, you are as much history as all the old lace in this room."

With an exaggerated motion, she shut off the machine, laid her hands across her lap, and pumped her crossed leg excitedly.

"I believe we met earlier this morning," Evelyn Justice said as she stepped into the room and closed the door.

"But we weren't properly introduced." Lindy didn't rise to greet her. Two can play this game, she thought.

The Governor's wife crossed the room and, as she approached Lindy, extended her hand in greeting. "I do hope that after our talk you'll understand about that. I'm Evelyn Justice," the woman said with what struck Lindy as a humble, genuine welcome.

Lindy took her offered hand and returned the greeting.

The Governor's wife released Lindy's hand and gestured to the impressive collection of dresses and framed letters and everyday knickknacks that were meant to show how human First Ladies really were. "I wanted to meet you in this room," she said. "Sometimes I love it—the history and the drama, the pomp and circumstance. And sometimes the reality of it weighs me down. It always helps me focus my thoughts on a task at hand, like these women know and understand and are somehow on my side."

Unlike the press, Lindy thought, then said, "Mrs. Justice, may I ask why you called me for an interview?"

"Oh, certainly, Ms. Blakely," she said as she glided to the seat nearest Lindy and sat down. "I need your help." She settled into the chair as if she expected to be there for a while.

"And just what help do you think I can give you?"

"I need you to help me exonerate my husband."

Lindy was startled. She didn't know quite how to respond. "I think you will want to see an attorney or a minister about that. I'm strictly press."

"That's exactly why I called you. It was the press who precipitated this travesty. I can only reason that it must be the press who will be able to make it right. You seemed an enterprising young woman when we met this morning, and I thought you might recognize an exclusive opportunity when you see one."

Lindy had no interest in being Franklin Justice's private spin doctor, especially with the suspicions she harbored toward the First Lady in the case of the murdered mistress.

She felt a need to get on the record, early. "I have a couple of things I think I need to say. First, my loyalty is to my employer and to the public we serve. If what you have to say will serve those two, then I'm interested. If it is for your benefit, forget it. Even if I wanted to help you, my editors would never print parochial pieces or articles as clearly biased as you seem to be suggesting."

Evelyn Justice smiled. "My dear, I think that your idealism may have the best of you. Newspaper editors grind out their own agenda and call it 'objective.' That which does not meet with their agenda, be it philosophical or economic, they deem subjective or parochial. It is a very convenient arrangement."

"Mrs. Justice, if you called me here to seek my help, you certainly have a strange way of asking for it."

"I believe that if I tell you the truth—about myself as well as about how I feel about your newspaper—you will help me by plying your trade."

"And what truth do you have in mind?" Lindy said *truth* with a cynical twist. "The kind you doled out to me this morning?" Lindy was sure now that she was being played. Fat chance, First Lady.

"I understand perfectly how you feel. You were just trying to do your job."

Lindy didn't respond. She thought she'd leave the ball in the other court for a while.

"Please allow me to explain."

Lindy nodded her approval and lifted the tape recorder, making a show of pressing the record button and pointing its built-in microphone toward Evelyn Justice.

"This morning, your newspaper ran a photo of my husband and his mistress—"

"Mistress?" Lindy blurted. "Annie Minnis was your husband's mistress?" The thought of it made her head swim with new possibilities.

"*Was* is correct. I did not see the picture, nor do I wish to see it, but it has brought a great deal of personal stress to the boiling point. Franklin went to that woman's apartment to dismiss her from our lives.

"While I understand that you people have a responsibility to share with the public that which affects the public, I also believe you have a responsibility to be fair and equitable to the subjects of your reports inasmuch as what you print has profound effects on those people's lives."

"Mrs. Justice, you sit there and lecture me on my paper's irresponsibility, then verify for me that what that photo implies is in essence the reality of the situation. You ask me to help you clear your husband's name, like the story that picture told was some sort of gross lie, then you tell me he's guilty! Are you playing me for a fool?"

"No. Not at all," the First Lady said, quite calmly. "That photo did accurately tell a story, but it was only *part* of the story. Its publication out of the context of the whole story will lead without question to a public lynching of my husband. His enemies will use it to bring *him* under suspicion of the woman's murder, and in this business, the public's perception *is* reality!"

"If the man's mistress is murdered shortly after he sees her at an odd time, don't you think the public has a right to suspect him?"

"Certainly they have a right!" Evelyn Justice insisted. "But when the press's attention shifts to the juicy follow-up and the details of the scrutiny he is likely to be under, the rest of this story will be considered old news, and you people will move on to the next piece of sensationalism—" Evelyn was very serious now—"leaving behind a ruined life and career, even if all suspicion of guilt is wiped away."

"Mrs. Justice," Lindy replied, hardly before the First Lady had finished her sentence. "Your husband made his own choices about being in the presence of a woman shortly before that woman was murdered. Not me. Not my paper. He burned his own blister and now he's the one who has to sit on it."

"Oh, I see. Hail gallant reporter, brave and true. Go forth to do thy righteous duty."

The mocking tone of Mrs. Justice's voice irritated Lindy. It was the second time that day that she had been taunted in this house. She wanted to fight back, but she still wasn't sure where this conversation was heading or what she'd get from it, so she swallowed her pride. Stay on it, Blakely, she said to herself. Do the right thing.

"You're right. My husband's choices are his own, and we live with the results of those, good and bad. But the press makes choices, too, and—" Mrs. Justice had been glancing irritably at the tape recorder in Lindy's hand as they were speaking, but now she stopped and said, "Turn that thing off. Can't we talk like two women instead of two public adversaries?"

Lindy looked at her, not sure how to respond. She still had the distinct suspicion that a savvy, experienced political hand was toying with her. But at the same time she sensed something real coming through. She lingered a moment over the quandary, then snapped the recorder off. "Okay. Woman to woman. But you have to be straight with me." She laid the palm-sized machine in her lap.

"I can give you nothing else right now. I'm not able."

That struck Lindy almost like a brazen, barefaced lie, calculated to draw her in.

Or a remarkable piece of candidness.

"Is this little chat to be on or off the record?" Lindy asked.

"What I'm going to tell you is off the record."

I figured, Lindy thought to herself.

"I'm willing to give you the context you'd need to properly interpret our situation. You may ask me any questions you wish. After I'm finished, I will go on the record and you may ask any further questions you might have."

"Fair enough," Lindy answered. But she leaned back in her chair and crossed her arms across her chest—a little message via body language to let the First Lady know just where she stood.

With that, Evelyn Justice told Lindy her story. She started from the beginning of their political career and told everything, every high and every low, including the lurid details of her "recent illness"—the suicide attempt that had been kept super-secret.

To Lindy's utter amazement, the woman gave a frank response to every question Lindy put to her.

Mrs. Justice finished her tale recounting the very recent call to the *News* to schedule this appointment.

Lindy sat back in her chair and tried to let go of the emotional tension that had built up during the story. She needed to process what she had heard.

The two sat in silence for a few moments, then Lindy slowly began to frame her big question. "Mrs. Justice, you've been remarkably open with me. In fact, I've never had an experience like this one in my entire professional life. I owe it to you to be equally candid."

"I sincerely hope that you will be."

"I came here today with a gnawing suspicion, and while the moving story you've just told me is one I can believe, it has not dispelled the heart of that main idea. If anything, what you've said has strengthened it."

"What idea is that?"

"From what I have been able to discover about the situation that's unfolded in the last two days, especially in light of the details you've just given me, I am led to believe that the murder of Annie Minnis was a crime of passion, not a gang killing."

"And you think that Franklin committed that crime of passion?"

"No," she said calmly. "I believe you did."

Mrs. Justice paused a moment, studying Lindy's eyes. "I knew that this morning. You weren't very subtle about it. And you're in good company. The chief of the state patrol had the same suspicions yesterday afternoon, and as far as I know he still has them today. Even Franklin has parroted the suspicion . . . ."

"Then I ask you, off the record, to be as honest about this central question as you have been with the peripherals."

"The story I shared with you may be peripheral to your concern, but I assure you that it is anything but peripheral to me. It is the truth about my life." She seemed a little agitated, but she continued. "And to answer your question—and this can be on the record—I have neither seen nor spoken to Annie Minnis in quite some time, and then only inasmuch as I related to her in her duties for Franklin's administration or his campaign."

"Mrs. Justice, I was there in Annie Minnis's apartment before the police arrived. I found her body. I saw the condition of her apartment. I know by our investigation that you indeed attempted suicide and that you used an ordinary kitchen knife in your attempt."

"How did you know that?"

"Sources."

Mrs. Justice looked away in disgust.

"The night you disappeared, the city police and the State Patrol transmitted an all-points bulletin to locate you, and at the same time sent a team of men to Annie Minnis's building with special instructions to watch for the woman identified in the APB."

Lindy uncrossed her legs and abandoned her detachment, leaning into her argument. "I think you followed your husband to her building the next day and made your way to her apartment, whether to kill her or not, I have no way of knowing. Maybe you were just going there to tell her off.

"In any case, I think that when you arrived, you found a woman who'd been beaten by some thug and made vulnerable in a way you didn't expect. I was there. I saw that she'd been beaten and that her apartment had been torn up. And I know a man who can place such a thug at that apartment before the murder."

"Then why do you suspect me?" Evelyn said, coolly.

"Because a drug thug had no reason to cut off a paying customer in high places. Maybe you went there to tell her off. Maybe she was belligerent to you, maybe defiant. I don't know. But I think something snapped in you and you murdered Annie Minnis with the same kind of knife you had used on yourself. *You* had the motive, Mrs. Justice."

Evelyn Justice sat unmoving.

Lindy continued, "I had no idea where you were, but after your tale today, it makes even more sense. You leave the apartment and make your way back to your maid's house in plenty of time to beat her home, then cry this same tale onto her shoulder to make her feel guilty and cinch your alibi tight. You're a *very* bright lady."

Lindy leaned back in the chair.

At first, Mrs. Justice didn't respond. She just shook her head and looked between Lindy and the floor.

But then she spoke, ever so quietly, apparently exerting a great deal of energy to maintain control. "I feared this would happen if I talked to you." She sighed. "I feel violated." She looked up. "I was as honest with you as I could possibly be, but you heard only what you wanted to hear."

"Listen—" Lindy began, uncrossing her arms to join the discussion again.

"No!" Mrs. Justice said firmly, raising her hand, palm outward. "I heard you out."

Lindy settled back with a shrug to let Mrs. Justice know that she'd play along, but that her mind was made up.

"I have three things to say, and then I'm done. Two of them are for my sake, one is for yours. First, I went to my maid's house because of fear of the depression that's haunted me and fear that I'd have to endure another round of drugs and doctors. All I could think about was finding someone who would listen to me. I just wanted to unburden myself of the awful feelings in hope that it would make me feel better. I wanted to tell someone all that I've just told you.

"But I couldn't. For the first time since this battle with depression began, I found myself confronted with the reality of a person who had suffered much more than I, yet who was the kind of whole person I only dreamed of being.

"In fact, after the time I spent with Maria and the self-revelation I received, I thought I'd never tell this story again. I thought that doing so would only obsessively refocus me on myself. But then it occurred to me that by actually verbalizing these things for the sake of someone other than myself, something good might actually come of it."

Lindy was listening, not sure where the soliloquy was heading, but keen to hear the part meant for her.

"The second thing is that your suspicion is at least partly true. I *have* wanted to murder my husband's mistress." She intertwined her fingers and held them against her lips. Admitting this was both difficult and cathartic. "The hallucination I told you I had two nights ago, the one that prompted my running away . . . ."

She was growing more intense in her tone, emphasizing her words by thrusting her joined hands at the air in front of her face. "In it, I did take the knife I'd used to cut my own wrists and I did drive it into her neck. For hours after I heard of the woman's death I was so disoriented that I couldn't decide whether *it* was the dream or my being at Maria's was the dream! I honestly wasn't sure. But I *did* sort it out and it *was* only in my mind!"

"And how can you be sure that you weren't in some semi-conscious state after you fled and that you didn't act out that desire?" Lindy asked. "Did you see a doctor or remain on any stabilizing medication?"

"No, I didn't!" She stood to her feet and her voice grew louder and louder. "But I know that I could not have acted out the hallucination because of how it ended. In it, I murdered her, then slit my own wrists again. I died and in the most horrible moment of my life, I fell into hell itself."

Mrs. Justice's eyes filled with tears. She appeared distraught, almost pleading as she continued. "Can't you see that that night I came to an absolute end to myself? I realized that inside me is the kind of evil that *would* enable me to commit such an act. You're right to suspect that I am capable of it, but you're wrong to believe that I did it.

"I was running away from *me* that night. I understand it now. It's me that's the monster. It's me that invites the shrinks and the drugs. It's me that's capable of murdering a human being.

"But when I got to Maria's house, at the end of myself, ready to spew this all out and then end it all, I found something that I didn't expect. Something that kept me from going any lower."

Lindy was leaning forward again by now, deeply interested.

Mrs. Justice dropped back into her chair and mustered her energy to continue. "After catching that awful vision of my true self and the horrid reality of where it must lead me, I then saw in Maria the exact opposite. I saw a woman who had been through worse than I, but who obviously had found a source outside herself to secure her sanity."

"What source?"

"She says it's God," Mrs. Justice said calmly.

Lindy didn't like the way this conversation was turning. "What's the third thing?" she asked, anxious to get off this and hoping that wasn't the item Mrs. Justice had meant for her.

"Please wait here for a moment," the First Lady said as she rose to her feet. She left the room, but returned less than a minute later carrying a purse. She resumed her seat across from Lindy and opened the handbag.

Evelyn Justice drew a knife, an ordinary kitchen knife, out of her purse and held it up in front of her face. "This is the third thing." She turned the knife and offered it to Lindy, handle first.

"Why are you showing me this?" Lindy asked, examining the blade in her hand.

"Because when I left the house that night, I did leave with a kitchen knife." Mrs. Justice reached back into her purse and pulled out the pistol. "And a gun. When I left the house, I didn't know where I was going. Part of me wanted the knife. Part of me wanted to find someone on whom I could spill my depression, then go and end my life in some out-of-the-way place. That's why I put the knife in my purse. But the other part of me rose up for a sort of self-preservation. I didn't know where I was going or what I'd encounter, and I wanted this gun precisely because Franklin had given it to me for my protection." She shook her head and looked at Lindy. "Schizophrenic, isn't it?" She looked at the gun as if it were the symbol of her folly, then dropped it back into the purse.

"You see, Ms. Blakely, I carried that knife with an intention of using it on *me*. You must understand that I saw the truth in my hallucination. Between me and Annie Minnis, *I* was the one who'd committed the greater wrong." She lifted the knife from Lindy's hand, dropped it into her purse and snapped it shut.

Lindy couldn't speak for a long moment. She didn't quite know what to say.

Then it came.

From her heart.

"I believe you."

Evelyn Justice again raised her hands to her face, the tips of her fingers meeting just below her nose. This time tears welled up in her eyes.

"I *do* believe you. But I'm still convinced that Annie Minnis's murder was not a simple drug killing. I know it in my heart." Lindy gritted her teeth in thought. The answer had to be buried somewhere in what she knew already.

"You said that you rehired the private investigator who had tailed your husband before?"

"Yes."

"And that he expected your call because he had seen the morning paper."

"That's right."

"Why would that picture make him expect your call?"

"I'm not sure. He just said he saw something in it that I couldn't and that he knew who took it."

Lindy grabbed Evelyn's hand. "What do you mean, he knew who took it?"

Evelyn looked concerned as she answered. "That's all he said." Then she remembered, "No, he said he'd done a little checking around, that he knew who took it, and that he was going to the man's house this afternoon. Franklin has gone to meet him there."

"This investigator. What's his name?"

"His name is Jackson Greene, but I think he goes by the nickname Frog. At least that's what he told me to call him."

"Oh, no." Lindy released Evelyn's hand and raised her own till it covered her face. Through the muffling of her hand over her mouth, Lindy asked, "Governor Justice is *not* meeting that man right now!" Her words formed a kind of question/exclamation whose answer is known but dreaded.

Evelyn was clearly disturbed. She scooted forward in the chair. "Why? Is there something wrong? Tell me what's wrong."

Lindy dropped her hands decisively, grabbed Evelyn's, and said sharply, "Your husband may be in great danger. Jackson Greene is known on the street as the Black Frog. He's a kingpin in a new drug ring that's brought together the black and Jamaican gangs in town. There's rumor that it's really controlled by the owners of a legitimate international distributing firm in town."

"That can't be the same man," Evelyn pleaded. "I got this man's name from the yellow pages."

"All of the principals have a legitimate cover. Greene's is a one-man investigation firm. He'd have had you for lunch before this was all over."

"It just can't be!" Evelyn was shaking her head, trying to banish the realization that she might have doomed her own husband.

"That's what's been missing!" Lindy stood to her feet, the thoughts flowing. "It *was* a drug murder after all. And without knowing it, you hired a drug lord to tail your husband. The Governor! He must have gotten his fangs into Annie, and she must have resisted him in some way, especially after the rejection by your husband. Who knows what he'll do now that he's got his fangs in Mr. Justice? That explains it all!"

She turned to Evelyn and spit out her words rapid-fire, "I've got to get to that house to see if I can prevent any more trouble. You call the police and tell them to send cars to 2223a South College. That is the address your husband wrote down, isn't it?"

Evelyn jumped to her feet. "I'm going with you. This is all my fault and I will not leave Franklin exposed to danger by himself."

"Suit yourself," Lindy said as she turned and ran for the door.

Evelyn grabbed her purse and followed. She stopped in the hall and called, "Maria! Hurry!"

The maid appeared at the top of the stairs.

"Call the police and tell them to send a car to 2223a South College," she said. "Franklin's in danger."

Lindy let her catch up at the door, then bolted for her Miata.

▼ ▼ ▼ 21 ▼ ▼ ▼

Lindy jammed the brake pedal on her Miata and brought it to a screeching halt on the *b* side of the duplex at 2223 South College. The street in front of the house was still littered with cars, so she hit the gas again and whipped the tiny blue streak into an open slot, half a block away from the address.

"That's Franklin's car," Evelyn said as she pointed to a silver Cadillac parked further down the block and across the street.

"So he's here," Lindy said as she tried to process the circumstances, "but we don't know who else is." She turned to Mrs. Justice, "I'm going to go check out that duplex. You stay here and watch for the police. Be sure that when they come, you direct them immediately to the correct house. It's the ramshackle gray one back there."

She levered the door and leaned on it to pop it open when Evelyn's hand halted her.

"Don't even think about coming along."

"I'm not going to argue with you, Lindy. Just be careful."

Lindy stood up and found that she had a terrible lump of fear in her throat. She slammed the car door and started walking toward 2223a and tried to swallow the lump or at least drive it down where it wasn't choking her.

But with every step, the lump got larger. It spread fingers of fear down into her chest and she could feel it squeezing on her heart.

She tried to talk to herself, but kept coming to the conclusion that what she was doing was insane.

The fear gripped her tighter.

A drug dealer, an experienced killer no doubt filled with mortal intent, was in the house she was walking toward. And she had nothing, no weapon of any kind, to carry with her.

It was harder to breathe.

But at least one innocent man was in danger and possibly one innocent bag of slime.

It was insane.

But she had to do it. She had to find out what, if anything, was happening, and if there was anything she could do to prevent further loss of life.

She ducked onto the sidewalk of the house two doors down from the duplex. Crouching, she sneaked under the living-room window on the side of the house.

Cautiously, hoping she hadn't been seen, Lindy raised her head until she could look through the grimy window and the open, unkempt curtain into the main room of the tiny duplex.

Nobody.

At least nobody she could see.

She put her ear to the glass in hopes of hearing commotion or conversation or something.

Nothing.

Lindy squatted and looked back toward the Miata. Evelyn Justice was standing beside it.

When she got Lindy's attention, she made a motion like "I'm coming to join you." Lindy waved her off vigorously and turned back to the house, trying to decide what to do.

"Move, Blakely," she said to herself aloud.

She closed her eyes long enough to take a deep breath and focus her resolve, then stood up tall and looked full into the window.

It was hard to see through the grime, but it looked like there was a body draped across a stuffed chair under the window on the front wall.

Again she dropped to the ground. The fear welled up. *What should I do?*

She didn't look back at Evelyn. She didn't want to encourage her to come any closer.

"Move."

Lindy raised up to a stooping position, then scurried around to the front of the house and stopped again under the front window. This one wasn't any less dirty, but it was a double-wide window with shades drawn.

She raised up to look inside, but couldn't get any view that would let her see inside.

She dropped back to the ground.

The fear returned, but so did the overpowering feeling that she had to make a conscious effort to do something to help in this situation. Her ghosts were too present to allow her to walk back to the Miata and wait for the police.

She shook her head in the affirmative to give herself permission to move, then stood up tall and once more pressed her ear to the glass. Hearing nothing from the duplex and seeing again in her mind's eye what looked like a body slumped in a chair, she moved toward the porch. The police were nowhere to be seen or heard. She had to help if she could.

The wooden slats on the porch clearly hadn't been painted for years, and when Lindy stepped on them to get to the door, they groaned.

She froze. Listening.

No stirring in response, so Lindy tiptoed ahead, ignoring the porch boards, until she reached the door.

One hand on the handle, she paused for one last listen and leaned toward the glass in the old entry door. Light was coming through the window on the opposite wall, the window under which she'd first squatted.

She squeezed the doorknob and squinted.

In the light she could see that it was Franklin Justice slumped in the chair under the window.

That sight galvanized her. She twisted the knob and pushed her way into the room, her momentum propelling her to the motionless body of the Governor.

But before she could slow herself, Lindy felt her feet contact a large, soft mass and she tripped, falling face first into the shins of the slumped body of the Governor.

A sharp pain shot through her face and down the back of her neck as her nose struck the bony hardness of his shin and she bounced away.

The fall dazed Lindy. She mustered enough energy to push herself up, then collapsed onto her own arms and lay still, trying to clear her head.

She had to breathe through her mouth. A metallic tang filled her taste buds and between breaths she worked her tongue around the inside of her mouth to find the source and get rid of it.

She found it when her tongue touched the outside of her front upper teeth and followed the bitterness to a warm stream flowing from her upper lip into her mouth. Lindy raised her fingers to the stream and realized her nose was bleeding, maybe her lip too.

She had to get up, get control.

She pulled her hands under her shoulders and pushed backwards, enough to rise up onto all fours. She was still dizzy with the pain of the fall, so she dipped her head to try to clear the haze.

Head down, she saw another body, that of a black man, lying face up on the floor. When she realized that she'd tripped over the man, her fear seized her again, clearing the fog away and bringing the reality of the situation slamming against her consciousness.

"You all right?" a voice said, clearly broken by the speaker's pain.

She jerked her head up in a start.

Franklin Justice stood over her, his right hand clutching at a bleeding abdomen and his left reaching out to her.

She pushed up further and stood to her feet. "Oh, Governor," she said weakly, "thank God you're alive. I saw you in the chair and was afraid I was too late. Oh, thank God!"

"I had fallen . . . into that chair," he looked back over his shoulder to a ratty chair stained with blood, "and was in and out of consciousness." He spoke only a phrase at a time between breaths. "You must have fallen on me, because a shot of pain snapped me back to." He put his free hand on her shoulder for support.

"Oh, but you're alive."

"How did you know I was here?" he whispered.

"Your wife," she said, feeling the swelling in her mouth and trying to talk around it. "What she told me put the pieces together and we thought you'd be in danger. I'd been here once today and knew where it was. The man who lived here gave us the picture we ran in the paper."

Suddenly recognition focused his eyes. "Lindy? From the *News*?"

"Yes. My partner and I broke this morning's story."

She thought she saw a flash of anger dance across his eyes.

"But that's not important now. You're alive." She took his free arm and directed him back toward the chair he'd apparently risen out of. "You sit. I'll call an ambulance. The police will be here any minute."

Now she actually looked for the first time at the room. Her eyes first met the body of the man she'd tripped over, an ugly black man with pitted face and deformed cheeks, dressed in a very expensive suit and lying on the floor so

close to her that she'd have to step over his arms to find
a phone.

She looked away quickly, not wanting to see violence
again this soon after her terrible vigil with a dead Annie
Minnis.

There must be a phone, she thought as she glanced
around the room. But another gruesome sight grabbed
her attention and turned her stomach.

The geek informant whom she'd blown off only hours
before lay, arms and legs akimbo, over the top of an old
gas room furnace on the far side of the room. A kitchen
knife protruded from the back of his neck—exactly the
way she remembered Annie Minnis.

She pulled her eyes from the awful sight and back to
the Governor's eyes. "Are they . . . " she stopped to swallow the turmoil in her stomach.

"Dead?" He finished her sentence.

She shook her head in the affirmative.

"I'm afraid so," he exhaled. "I was to meet . . . this
man," he nodded toward the man on the floor, "so we
could question the other . . . When I arrived . . . that one
was dead," he motioned his head toward the body
sprawled across the heater. "This one came at me . . . ."
He stopped moving, apparently in too much pain to walk
and talk at the same time. "I had a gun . . . tried to get to
a phone . . . finally shot him . . . he shot me . . . ."

"Uuuuh." A long moan seeped up out of the depths of
the black man's gullet.

The Governor froze.

Lindy turned around to look toward the sound without
letting go of the Governor. "He's alive," she said as she
lifted his hand off her shoulder.

She dropped to her knees and bent over till her face was
near his. She shook him and yelled, "You're alive. You're
alive. Just hold on. There's an ambulance coming."

She flexed her leg muscles to stand but was arrested by his two eyes opening. His hand latched onto the sleeve of her blouse.

He pulled on her, pulled her down close to his mouth.

She could smell a putrid mixture of expensive cologne and horrid breath. She choked down a column of bile that had been trying to rise out of her churning stomach and leaned into the stinking aura.

"Jus . . . tice," he croaked in two distinct syllables.

"Yes, Justice. He's alive, too." She started to turn to look up at the Governor whose feet she could see beside her, but the Frog pulled again on her blouse.

She saw the Frog's eyes look away from her and toward the Governor. They filled with fear and jerked back to meet her eyes again. Now they were wider, full of desperation.

This time Lindy froze.

One of the shoes she'd seen out of the corner of her eye came crashing into the temple of the dying man's head.

She saw the man's dread-filled eyes close a split instant before the shoe smashed into his head. The gut-wrenching sound of cracking bone emerged from his neck and then was muffled by the dirty carpet.

She was rooted to the floor.

The Governor's two feet shuffled closer to her until his legs were pressing against her arm.

"So you're the one who ruined my life?" he growled, this time his voice unbroken by pain, but clearly imbued with rage.

She didn't speak and she didn't move.

He pulled his knee back and struck her shoulder with it, knocking her over on top of the Frog.

She could feel the still-warm lifelessness of the black man's body inside the elegant fabric of his suit.

"Get up!" he ordered.

She swallowed her rising hysteria and gathered all the courage she had remaining as she pushed herself up and off the dead man.

She rose to her feet, stood erect to her full height, and looked defiantly at the Governor.

"You killed Annie Minnis!" she accused.

"Just like I'm going to kill you!" He lifted a knife between their faces.

"But why? Why would a man like you commit such awful violence?"

He lifted the bloody hand he'd used to clutch his side and grabbed the hair on the back of her head. He jerked her head sideways and shoved, forcing her to move her toward the room furnace and its attendant dead body.

"Because Annie Minnis betrayed me with drugs and threatened to blackmail me after I'd kept her like a queen for years," he snarled. "And because that piece of filth there betrayed me by following me and reporting to my wife, and because the worm in front of you took the picture that ruined my future."

He jerked sharply on her hair again, this time causing an abrupt cry of pain to jump from her lips.

"And you," he jerked again, "because you betrayed me by printing the picture and the story that ruined my future."

The pressure he exerted on her head coerced her forward until her legs came in contact with the room furnace.

She pushed backwards with her head and upper body, struggling against his weight and the compelling pressure he exerted. Her whole being fought in revulsion to keep away from the contorted frame draped over the metal box.

This time he didn't jerk on her hair. He just applied stronger, more unrelenting force on the back of her head.

It bent her closer and closer to the corpse.

She reached her hands around the back of her head and grabbed his arm, grappling with it and straining against it.

Then she felt a sharp, cold, hard point prick the skin on the back of her neck, just below her skull.

Fear, a deadly fear of dying that very moment, filled her and she ceased resistance, letting the pressure drive her face into the dead man's back until she felt the ridges of his spine bury themselves in her swollen nose and lips.

"I went to the house to meet a private investigator I'd never seen," he said in an eerily normal and pleasant voice, as if he was talking to someone else, "a man my wife hired to help clear my good name."

His voice grew louder, more deliberate. "Yes, your honor, I discovered that the man had killed a larcenous blackmailer . . . "

He's explaining his alibi to a judge, Lindy thought as hysteria rose closer to the surface.

" . . . and the reporter who'd used his vile photographs."

Her whole body began to writhe in a panicked attempt to free herself.

"I recognized the man as one of the key figures in a dangerous new drug ring." He pressed her face harder into the dead man's back and pushed the point of the knife in just until blood began to trickle from Lindy's smooth neck.

"I shot him to protect myself!" He concluded his litany in full voice.

"Franklin!" A female voice rang out.

"Franklin! Stop it. Now!" The voice was shrill, timid, shaking.

Lindy's face still was being driven into the spiny ridges of the geek's backbone by Justice's arm, but she felt the hot steel blade being pulled from her neck and sensed that he was slowly turning in the direction of the voice.

The pain swelled as the throbbing muscles rushed to fill the slit left by the blade. She was growing dizzy from the pain and pressure on her head.

"Evelyn!" Justice's voice was low, slow, angry and deliberate. "Go home."

"Franklin, I will not allow you to do this."

"Evelyn!" His voice was louder, more commanding. "Go home now!"

"Franklin, you've used people and then thrown them away all your life." Her voice was less shrill. "You used me and my background to climb the business and social ladder and then threw me away. You used countless people along the way to get yourself elected, then threw away the ones who couldn't help you get further. You used Annie Minnis to feed your bloated ego and your sick idea of power, and then threw her away too."

Lindy was crying now, breathing erratically and trying to keep her senses. She was afraid if she allowed herself to lose consciousness she'd never wake up again.

She felt Justice turn again, the pressure on her face and the pain in her scalp alerting her. Lindy felt his leg touch her again as he pivoted back toward her and away from Evelyn.

"Franklin. Listen to me." Evelyn's voice was shrill again, like she was losing control of the situation. "I will not let you do this. No more. Not again!"

Lindy's whole body jerked in shock as she felt the knife tip reenter the already burning wound, this time sinking deeper than before. She began to let out one long groan as she felt herself slipping into blackness.

But the blast of a gun roared through the room, reverberating off the dirty walls like a thousand bats beating their wings to escape the fire of hell.

Lindy's body reacted to the explosion with another spastic contortion of surprise.

Again the painful knife point was pulled from her neck. Her head was lifted off the back of the corpse by a dead weight that still clutched her hair. Her body followed, lifted up and turning over till she was looking upward as she dropped toward the floor. Her hips crashed into the cheap linoleum, then her upper body bounced to rest on another mass of flesh that must have been Franklin Justice.

The last thing she heard before the ceiling dissolved into darkness was a broken voice weeping, "No more, Franklin. No more."

▼ ▼ ▼ 22 ▼ ▼ ▼

"Yes, Ms. Blakely?" The voice coming out of the nurse call system speaker was clearly irritated.

"Look, if you don't get that doctor to let me out of here before the day's over, you're going to have a real emergency on your hands."

Lindy was frustrated. She'd been in the hospital for three days, fully awake and bored out of her gourd for one and a half of the three. Thirty-six long hours. She had an awful pain in the neck. Her face felt like a clown had taken three wiener balloons and tied them into the shape of a dog, then slid them under her skin. And she ached all over.

What's worse, nobody would tell her anything— about Evelyn, about Justice, about Dan, not even about the rankings in the NBA. "I'm sorry, Ms. Blakely," her doctor had chided, "but you've been through a traumatic experience. You were in shock when you were brought into the hospital and in a case like yours I order a minimum of forty-eight hours of observation after you regain consciousness. I don't want a lot of outside interference from TV or newspapers stirring you up, and I'm deeply concerned about possible neurological symptoms associated with that wound: respiratory depression, disorientation, loss of sensation in the extremities."

As far as Lindy was concerned, the only loss of sensation she'd experience would be in her brain when she lost her mind from boredom.

"Ms. Blakely," the voice from the speaker above her bed pleaded, "please reserve use of the nurse call button for matters related to your physical condition, not as a complaint line."

"I won't trouble you white-garbed gaggle of geese again if you'll just get me out of here."

Lindy turned back to the blank, sterile, yuck-white wall and crossed her arms so smartly that the whole bed shook.

A knock came at the door.

"I don't want any of what you've got," she snarled at the door. "Just get me out of here."

The door opened just wide enough for a hand, on the end of a male arm clothed with a regular, non-hospital sleeve, to slip through. It held a single red rose.

Lindy smiled. *Dan.* "Okay, I do want some of that!"

The hand snapped in her direction and flicked the rose across the room toward her. One of its thorns snagged on the curtain that had been pulled open and left at the ready at the end of her bed.

"Oh!" she said playfully, in mock pain. "It didn't reach me. I'm in terrible pain and I can't get out of this bed to get it. I think the doctor orders you to come and get it for me."

All but the first finger of the hand behind the door gathered together, leaving the first finger erect. The hand moved back and forth in a *No, no, no,* then disappeared.

She smiled again, this time wider. "I need more of what you've got," she called.

This time when the hand reappeared, it held two airline tickets, spread like a hand of cards so she could clearly count them. Again the hand flicked and the tickets came fluttering her way, landing on the floor well short of her bed.

"Oh!" She groaned a little more this time. "They didn't reach me and I'm still in terrible pain and I still can't get out of this bed to get them. I think the doctor orders you to come and get them for me."

Once again, the first finger rose above the others and the hand gestured *No*. Then it disappeared.

Now she was grinning ear to ear, smiling deep down for the first time since she had regained consciousness. "I *really* need more of that," she called to the mysterious hand, thinking to herself that what she wanted and needed more of was what was attached to that hand. She was so glad to see Dan.

She felt warm just to know that he was here, and that he cared enough about her to be here. And, she admitted with that grin, because she really wanted him to be near her and to care about her.

For a whole lot of the last thirty-six hours she'd thought about him and wanted, no, yearned, for him. Thought about how she felt about him, and about her, and about him and her.

But she had not let herself admit the *L* word.

She *was* glad to see him, though.

When the hand slid through the narrow opening in the doorway for the third time, it was holding a laptop computer with the cord dangling.

"Don't throw that!" she squealed, just as another hand appeared in the opening holding her leather notebook.

"Oh, Dan!" She was so excited she could hardly sit still. "Does that mean we've got an assignment?"

The door swung open and Dan jumped in. "Yes!" he yelled, then straightened his back, lifted his chin and raised the laptop and the notebook in front of him like a butler carrying a tray. He walked toward her like he was in the presence of royalty. He picked up the tickets, then the rose, and marched, chin held high, up to the edge of her bed. "A rose for m'lady's recovery."

"And?" she said expectantly, bouncing lightly on the mattress.

"Two tickets for m'lady's upcoming trip to Belgium, one for m'lady and one for her entourage."

"Oh, Dan," she said as she grabbed his arm. "You mean Tomass has given us an assignment in Europe?"

"A *working* assignment, he insists. Thus m'lady's laptop and notebook."

She snatched the tickets from his hand and smacked at his arm with them. "Okay. Enough's enough. Stop it and tell me what's happening."

He lost his rigid pose and dropped onto the side of the bed. "I think he felt sorry for you." Dan put his hand on Lindy's. "Said you'd been a pain in his neck long enough that he knew exactly how you felt. Said he needed a vacation from you so he's sending us to Brussels to do a series on the progress of the European community toward unity—trade and currency and problems and all that fascinating stuff."

"That's great!" she said as she bounced up and threw her arms around his neck.

A sharp, biting fire shot out of the wound on her neck. She grimaced in pain, coughed an *Uh!* and let go of Dan.

His arms slid around her before she'd finished the exclamation of pain. He held her up and then slowly lowered her back to the waiting mattress.

"Take it easy, Lind," he said as he raised up. "You aren't Superwoman, you know. You *have* been through a lot the past few days."

She breathed deeply and then let it out in a long, cleansing sigh. "I know." Then she raised her hand and grasped his arm just below the elbow. "Speaking of the last few days, nobody's told me anything about anything. Just cops pumping me to repeat what I remember— which is a powerfully little bit! What happened to Justice?"

"His wife shot him and saved your life, that's what happened!"

She strained, and a serious look took over her face as she tried to pull up details of the awful encounter. "I think I remember that," she said, tentatively. "Is he dead?" Evidently her trauma had driven the details deep inside.

"Nope. Not yet anyway."

"What do you mean?"

"I mean he's upstairs in this very hospital. Police are guarding him twenty-four hours a day. Intensive care. Critical condition. The docs won't say which way he's going. The bullet hit an artery in his shoulder and he'd have been dead on the scene if the police and EMTs hadn't shown up a couple of minutes after she pulled the trigger."

"That poor woman," she said, the details returning slowly. "What about Evelyn Justice?"

"Doing as well as anybody after shooting her husband."

"Where is she?"

"Home. At the Governor's mansion. I made time in my busy schedule to stop by on the way here to let her know I was coming and to promise I'd be by after I see you. Her family doc was there, and a Hispanic maid was watching over her like a mother hen."

"What do you mean, your busy schedule?"

"Gimme a break, Lind. This has been national news! The networks have been full of it; I've been going round-the-clock writing followups—I even did an NPR interview! In fact, I'm here today to get an exclusive with you."

Lindy gave him a look that would melt steel.

Dan's face burst into a smile as he leaned back and let out a loud laugh. "My, aren't we touchy when we're not feeling well?" And he laughed again. A smile still covering his face, he added, "Mrs. Justice wanted me to tell you something."

Lindy perked up but only raised her head. "What?"

"She said to tell you thanks. Said you helped save *her* life."

Lindy slowly lowered her head to the pillow, processing what the First Lady had said.

"What'd she mean? Your story to the police verifying hers?" Dan asked, casually.

"I'm not sure, but I have an idea." She grew quiet and fell back into thought.

Dan sat for a minute, then asked, "Well? Are you going to tell me?"

Lindy looked up at her partner and smiled. "I need to think about that for a while. And I need to think about how to thank her. Let me tell you later."

"Suit yourself," he said with a shrug of his tall shoulders, then stood up.

"Where you going?" she asked intently.

"I'm outta here. Promised I'd only stay a couple of minutes. Hate hospitals, anyway. Too many sick people."

"Didn't you come to get me?"

"Nope. Although a couple of the nurses down the hall told me they'd help arrange an unofficial dismissal down the back stairs if it would stop your harassing them."

"Very funny," she said sourly. "I want out of here."

"Patience, my dear partner, is not one of your virtues. My Chinese grandmother used to say, 'A patient man is better than a warrior.' "

"I'm neither a man nor a warrior. What in the world does that have to do with when I get out of here? And where in the world did your Chinese grandmother get all these dumb sayings?"

"Some from her ancestors, some from the Bible. The one about the patient man and the warrior is from the Bible. Proverbs, I think."

"Your Chinese grandmother quoted from the Bible?" That was a real surprise to Lindy. "Wasn't she Taoist or Confuscianist?"

"When she was young, yeah. Converted at the hands of American missionaries after the Boxer rebellion. Married one of the missionaries, returned to the States, proceeded on seeing that conditions were right for me to make my entrance into the world."

Lindy took Dan's hand. "I'm glad she did." She let the warmth of Dan's presence fill her again.

A self-conscious grin tugged at the corners of Dan's mouth and he bobbed his head like he was a little embarrassed.

That modesty is one of the reasons I . . . . Lindy caught the thought and stopped herself short of the *L* word. She shook the thought and circled back to the conversation, sternly declaring, "You're not leaving until you tell me when I get out of this place. What's the date on those tickets?"

"A week from tomorrow," Dan said, then added playfully, "and I'm sure the doctor will release you that morning."

She made a face.

"Okay, Lind. They're keeping you overnight and I'm going to pick you up first thing in the morning."

She relaxed into her pillow again. "Thank heavens!" As quickly as she'd relaxed, she tensed again and raised onto her elbow, raising a lecturing finger to punctuate the coming remarks. "First thing! Seven a.m. or sooner!"

"I'll be here with bells on." He started to back away to leave.

"Dan," she said, extending her hand.

He lifted his hand to meet hers and raised his eyebrows.

"I'm glad you're my partner."

He smiled and said, "See you in the morning," as he strolled out of the room with his characteristically long strides.

▼ ▼ ▼ ▼

Dan had made arrangements to meet his buddy from
State Patrol dispatch and buy him the beer he'd promised
after the trooper had given him the tip that helped start
the ball rolling on the Justice story. He'd stopped by their
favorite watering hole on his way home from the hospital
and met Corporal Smith in the parking lot.

"I'm buying dinner," Dan announced to him as he
slung his arm over his friend's shoulder.

Smitty looked up at Dan with a twinkle of surprise in
his eyes. "Dinner?"

Dan nodded his head in the affirmative, "Yep. Your tip
on the First Lady's car opened the whole story up for us.
I owe you."

The two joked around while they waited in the bar for
a table and Dan answered a couple of the big questions
Smitty had for him. But he begged off saying much more
until they were seated because the bar was jammed and
he didn't necessarily want the attention.

"Smitty," Dan said quietly as they leaned forward on
their elbows, waiting for the beers they'd ordered. "What
about women?"

"Can't live with 'em, and you can't shoot 'em," Smitty
said distractedly as he looked around the bar to see if any
more of his buddies were around.

"No, really. Any advice for a novice?"

"Nope. Except to tell you that it's great."

The bartender set the beers on the gleaming wood in
front of them.

"Whadda you do when you really like somebody but
you think maybe you screwed it up but maybe that
person really does care after all?"

"That's easy. You find out." With that, Smitty picked
up his glass and lifted it to his friend for a toast. "Here's

to finding out." The glasses touched. "It's half the fun," he added.

They both took a pull from their glasses.

Dan liked the idea. He thought he *would* enjoy finding out. "What's the other half?" he asked as he set his glass on the cork coaster.

Smitty smiled and leaned toward Dan, then whispered, "Knowing!"

ABOUT THE AUTHOR

Bob Massie is a marketing/fund-raising consultant whose not-for-profit clients include several political organizations and individual candidates. He is also an ordained minister and the head of Dynamics of the Biblical World, an organization that conducts Bible-learning events in churches across America.

Bob lives with his wife Dianna and children, Mary Katherine, Matthew, and Emily in Indianapolis, Indiana.